# JJ CARPENTER

# The Corner of Her Eye

*Book 1: The Keeper*

First edition

ISBN: 978-0-6486376-0-8

Cover art by Jackson Diosi
Editing by Angela Brown

This book was professionally typeset on Reedsy.
Find out more at reedsy.com

"Tell me not, in mournful numbers,

Life is but an empty dream!
For the soul is dead that slumbers,

And things are not what they seem."

– HENRY WADSWORTH LONGFELLOW

# Contents

# Acknowledgement

I acknowledge the traditional custodians of the land where this book is set, Australia's First Nations peoples. While the setting of this book — the cottage and town of Greenfields — are fictional, the land is not. I pay my respects to their Elders past, present and emerging, for they hold the memories, traditions, stories, and hopes of the First Nations people of Australia. We must always remember that under the roads, houses, towns, cities, ruins, and in the history of modern Australia is a much deeper and much longer history.

I must start my personal acknowledgments by thanking my twin sister, Sarah Graue, who has been my fiercest supporter and most honest critic since I started writing my books at age six, which I carefully stapled together and stored in a shoebox under my bed. She has read every one of my books, including the ones that will never see the light of day. She is the type of reader my books are written for.

Thank you also to my husband, Simon Carpenter, who is my rock and anchor. His unwavering support, no matter which way the wind blows, has kept me steady on this path. Thank you for always believing in me. Your love and support are reflected in our two beautiful children, Lori and George. I love you.

I want to give a loud shout out to the cover artist of my book, Jackson Diosi, a proud Malaitan man from Solomon Islands. Jackson has been an artist for as long as he has been able to hold a pencil. He is the definition of resilience, battling all his greatest trials through his art. A proud Solomon Islander, he represents his country, his culture, and the important issues of our time through his art. I'm so honoured to have his art grace the cover of my book. *Barava big tagio tumas barat blo me.*

To my editor — Angela Brown — thank you for polishing my rough edges. You always seemed to sense the days I needed a little pick-me-up. Those days, when you reached out just to let me know you liked the book, were exactly what I needed to keep on going. Thank you for always being ready with a kind word of encouragement.

Thank you to all of my Beta Readers! You are those I most trust in the world to give your honest feedback, while simultaneously keeping my confidence afloat. My mum, Cal Petrusma, my sister-in-law, Hailey Petrusma, and my adopted family Bella and Silvia Tchilinguirian. You were the first to fall in love with the world I created. My dear Maïté Petrement, *merci beaucoup*! A huge thank you from me, and from all the French speakers, for correcting my horrible French.

To my close friends, Laura Tchilinguirian, Jem D'Souza and Kath Bombell — thank you for supporting and fanning the flames of my ambition. And for encouraging others to do the same! I love you all.

Next, my amazing street team! You believed in me before you even knew me or my writing. Our book community is not just what dreams are made of, but where dreams are made. Readers, if you're on Instagram, please give these amazing folks a follow from me: @tifflovesthrillers @insanepixie75 @the_salty_islander @horror.books.and.chill @deathh_by_tbr @jemmsbookshelf @books_by_the_bottle @thrillreadz @karlas.literary.korner @greeneyedgirl0704 @spookybookylonnie

Finally, to my early reviewers — including the fabulous bestselling author Shani Struthers and award-winning author Kaaron Warren. I am so grateful for your time and uplifting words. My own words can't express what your support and encouragement have meant to me in this journey. A special thank you in particular to Shani, who added the final polish to my manuscript by picking up all my lingering literals.

# 1

# Va-et-Vient

The first time Charlie White nearly died, it wasn't anything like Hollywood had promised. There was no tunnel of light. Her life didn't flash before her eyes. Charlie's most prominent, logical thought as she felt everything dim around her was, *I didn't expect to die today.*

The second time she nearly died, something came alight inside her. A base, raw need to survive. With this survival instinct came panic, fear, and anger.

By now, Charlie had lost track of how many times she'd nearly died. She didn't know when the calm had replaced the panic — hiding the fear and anger deep within her.

A chill wind rustled her fine, white-streaked ginger hair, pulling her from her reverie. The dewy grass had started to soak through her jeans, numbing her bony bottom. The wind wound its way inside her oversize woolly jumper, making her shiver. Brushing the grass off her pants, Charlie stood, looking out over the rolling Australian grasslands. Slim, white-barked trees and grey mossy boulders dotted the landscape. She took a deep breath; the air was fresh, enlivening. Here, in the native grasslands of rural New South Wales, Charlie felt serene. And she felt alive.

"It's a good thing I've learnt to let go." She sighed, stretching her back, as she appreciated the beauty around her. She'd finally had to give up work — the thing on which she'd based most of her identity. Well, until this point in her life at least. Now forty-six years old, she'd essentially retired and was struggling to figure out who she was out of an office. She'd given everything to her work, never allowing time for anything else — no partner, no children. Commercial law may sound boring to most people, but to Charlie, it had been life. It had been everything.

Stubbornly, when her health had first deteriorated, she'd thought she could pursue a career unchanged. No matter what life (or near death) threw at her. And she'd been good at her job. Good enough, at least, for a comfortable early retirement despite not being eligible for any disability support — not unless she was willing to go through the torture of being declared a sufferer of chronic, crippling anxiety.

As Charlie started down the hill, she paused. There it was again, in the wind. A sound like deep, guttural, tonal chanting. The type of hum you felt in your chest rather than heard with your ears. Rationally, she knew it was the sound of wind forcing its way through the rocks and hills. But in her calm, she could almost believe it was music just for her.

Charlie's peace was pierced by a dark flash, glimpsed from the corner of her eye. A familiar rush of adrenaline sent tingles bursting down her limbs. The wind wasn't her only frequent visitor since she'd moved to the grasslands. Another dark, fleeting visitor always seemed to be right behind her, at the edge of her vision. Sometimes she thought another person must be strolling these forgotten hills, just out of sight. Sometimes she was certain it must be a crow or another dark-coloured bird swooping for mice in the grass. Every time, however, as soon as she turned to look straight on, the shadow slipped away. She spun towards the movement; this time, yet again, nothing was behind her.

Charlie physically and mentally shook herself. It was time to go home.

\* \* \*

Home was a three-bedroom cottage, a ten-minutes drive from the nearest neighbour and thirty minutes from Greenfields, the nearest town. Originally built in the 1920s, the house had since been lovingly renovated to a contemporary abode with white walls, polished hardwood floors, and modern plumbing. It was everything Charlie needed. The cottage's original California-bungalow-style facade with its perfect white windows had been maintained, as had the old veranda that wrapped around one side of the house. This cottage was Charlie's fresh start. Simple, peaceful, quiet, and most importantly, safe.

As she stamped her feet at the front door to loosen the dirt and any final blades of grass, her wall phone trilled. Charlie was one of the few modern Australians who still had a landline. This far from civilization, mobile phone reception was nonexistent, and a landline was her only connection to the outside world. At least until she could get her satellite set up.

"Hello!" she said, breathing slightly too heavily, ripping the handset from its receiver.

"Charlie, it's Tess. *Bonjour.*" The woman's accented voice crackled slightly on the other end. "Just checking in. How's life? Not 'smited' yet?"

Tess was the only friend who had bothered to keep in regular contact since Charlie had moved from Sydney. Originally from the French city of Sceaux, near Paris, Tess had been Charlie's instant and closest companion since their chance encounter ten-years earlier. Charlie's law firm had once represented Tess' employer — a big time department store. They'd caught each other sneaking cigarettes on company time behind the dumpster. As the legal case had dragged on, those daily cigarette breaks had been the highlight of Charlie's day. The "smiting" inside joke was their weekly *va-et-vient* (or back-and-forth for the English speakers like Charlie). Every conversation over the past six months had started the same way, ever since Charlie had joked that the big man upstairs must be trying to smite her but doing a half-arse job of it.

"Nope, no smiting here." Charlie laughed.

"*Bien.*" Charlie could picture Tess smiling into her mobile phone. "How's the new place? I keep forgetting to ask each time I call."

"Good," Charlie mimicked her friend, though in English. "You know, peaceful, cosy, quiet."

"And peanut free."

"Yes," Charlie chuckled. "Not a whiff of a peanut since I moved in."

The Oxford Language Dictionary entry recited itself in Charlie's head:

*"Peanut: The oval seed of a tropical South American plant, often roasted and salted and eaten as a snack."*

Small, common, and in Charlie's case, absolutely deadly. Now, even the smell of a roasted peanut would send her into anaphylactic shock. Adult-onset allergies — while relatively uncommon — were generally more of a nuisance than life-changing. That's what the medical professionals had frequently reminded her at least. Yet within five years, Charlie had gone from a regular, peanut-butter-loving middle-aged woman to a recluse. Now she couldn't even walk through a food court, grocery store, Sunday farmers market, or public park for fear of a small South American oval seed.

"Has the paint smell settled?"

"Weeks ago," Charlie replied, looking around her large living room. The kitchen to her right was on the small side, but modern, and gleamed cleanly. A fireplace took pride of place in the centre of the living room, with comfortable leather lounges and armchairs surrounding it. There were only two matching cushions on the couch, and no throws in sight. Charlie's style was classic and minimalist. The only artwork on the walls was a woman standing in the middle of an empty field, in the rain. Though she'd bought it years earlier, it somehow seemed to encapsulate how her life had turned out for her.

To her left was her desk. No TV, but what good was a TV that couldn't connect to anything anyway? Ahead of her was the door to the long hallway, from which her bedrooms and sewing room were reached. If you were to enter the hallway, only bright white walls would greet you. The only family photo Charlie owned was a silver-framed picture of her parents, sitting lonely on her bedside table. Over her shoulder, through the open front door, she saw the old gum trees waving slightly in the wind and the hills sloping upwards beyond.

"Good, well, maybe I'll finally visit you then," Tess said wistfully. "You're keeping well otherwise? Not bored? Not...mad yet?" She was never one to

4

mince her words.

"Not yet." Charlie smiled. "I'm still walking every day, which is easier now that spring is finally here. It's nice to be able to roam outside as long as I like. I'm still sewing too. I finally sold my first pair of culottes."

"Ha-ha, wonderful. I wish you didn't live so far, darling." It wasn't the first or last time Charlie would hear this. All of her former colleagues, family (what was left of them), and friends had tried to convince her not to move so far and so remote. *Allergies could be managed in suburbia. Hospitals were closer. Company was crucial.* But with Charlie's feeling of calm acceptance, she'd reasoned it was better this way. This way, with her own piece of Australia, she could have some freedom. She could walk as long as she pleased. Above all, she could expand her bubble of safety. In the city and towns, she never knew when the slightest whiff of someone's lunch would send her spiralling into anaphylaxis — and into the closest hospital bed. Here, there was just wide, open space and clean, fresh air. She didn't feel so confined – so claustrophobic.

"When I'm old and decrepit, I'll move in with you," Charlie said. "For now, keep calling me as often as you can. And get your arse down here and visit me. That guest bedroom has been empty since I moved in!"

Tess's laughter was momentarily interrupted by a loud bang. "Ah, *p'emmerdeux*."

"Leon is home I take it?" Charlie asked wryly.

"Yes, darling," Tess answered. Leon was Tess's twenty-seven-year-old son who still lived at home. He'd been the reason Tess had dropped out of university to follow her Australian lover halfway across the world. A torrid romance that had ended violently some ten years later when her 'lover' and his fists had finally pushed Tess too far. This was not long after Charlie and Tess had first met, and it had been Charlie's couch she'd slept on until she found her feet. "I promise I'll call again soon. *Salut, ma chérie*, Charlotte. *Je t'aimerai pour toujours*."

"Goodbye, Thérèse."

The phone clicked as Tess disconnected, and Charlie sighed as she put the handset back into the receiver with a dull clack. "I promise I'll love you forever too."

As the wind picked up outside, Charlie focused on its deep sound, feeling that familiar sense of calm wrapping around her. Once again, a dark shadow flicked at the corner of her eye. Charlie turned slowly this time, expecting to see her empty lounge, as she always did. She gasped as, instead of melting away this time, the shadow formed itself into the shimmering outline of a tall, distinctly human figure. Despite its near translucence and her difficulty focusing her eyes on this stranger, some details stood out clearly. The pointed white loafers on its feet. Its white pressed suit. The white top hat perched wonkily on its head.

"Fuck!"

# 2

# A Welcome Distraction

"Fuck!" Charlie screamed again, louder this time, despite feeling she was choking on the words. Without realising she'd even moved backwards, she thumped against the entry wall, the phone handset falling to the floor with a bang, the dial tone ringing out loudly. None of the noises startled the figure, which stared at her unphased. Charlie also couldn't tear her gaze away.

It was definitely human-like. At least six feet tall, age hard to distinguish, and so pale. All of it was as white as the clothes it wore. Without understanding how or why, she felt she knew what this person — if it were in fact human — was thinking. Indifference to start with, though its interest was starting to pique. Like it had been travelling a long road and suddenly spotted something amusing along the way.

Charlie continued staring at the spot where the white creature had been, long after it had shimmered and faded away, its feelings of surprised interest still floating in the air. It was the phone's dial tone that finally shook her loose. Quickly she bent down to retrieve the handset, fumbling as she thumped it back in place. "What the fuck?" She was panting as though she'd run a marathon — or was ready to run one now, away from this house. After striding to the kitchen, she poured herself a glass of water and downed it in one go.

"What the fuck?" she whispered again, rubbing her hands through her long red hair, trying to figure out what had just happened. She looked back to where she'd thought she'd seen the figure standing. *Thought I saw...? Yes,* Charlie rationalised. *I imagined it, letting my thoughts get carried away with that howling wind again.* The wind had picked up, and she jumped as something loose on the veranda banged loudly against the wall.

She grabbed her keys from the bowl by the front door, as well as her jacket and bag from the hook, and pushed her way back outside without even thinking. Charlie strode straight to her black Toyota RAV4, launched herself into the driver's seat, pulled her door closed, and punched the automatic lock. "What the fuck...?"

\* \* \*

As she bumped along the old country road, she began to rationalise again. In her little car — with the grassland passing by in a blur, dust kicking up, her acoustic rock playing softly under the general road noises — it was easy to dismiss her experience. She'd obviously been tired from the walk, emotions high from talking to Tess, and had startled at light coming through the window in a weird way. Maybe it had even been a painless migraine or a big eye floater. As she considered what she'd seen, she could almost picture the white creature's face staring curiously at her. Did it have a face? Did it even have eyes? Why could she clearly remember a top hat and loafers but no facial features?

Shuddering, she turned the volume up on her stereo and focused on drawing in deep calm breaths. "I was startled by the light," she muttered, a little breathless. Gritting her teeth, she said more steadily, "And I just needed to pop into town to grab some milk."

Only fifteen minutes away from Greenfields now, Charlie saw on her car dash that her phone had picked up enough signal for her to make a phone call. Pressing the favourites button for "Mum," she settled back into her car seat as the ring tone started. Just as she thought the call might ring out and was toying with the thought of calling her brother, Robert, instead, she heard the click as the phone connected.

"Hello?" her mum, Elsa, answered warily and confused.

"Hi, Ma." Charlie smiled as she responded, overly sweet. "It's Charlotte, your daughter."

"Where have you been?!" Elsa immediately threw at her. Charlie started to answer, but Elsa cut her off. "I haven't heard from you in weeks."

"It's been two days, Ma," Charlie replied, her twinge of irritation a welcome distraction. "I'm just calling to check in, see how you're travelling."

"Your brother hasn't seen me in months," Elsa whined, her voice taking on a dangerous edge. "You've all abandoned me in here." It was a bad day then, Charlie thought, feeling her stomach fall. Then feeling guilty for regretting making the call.

"Ma, you know Robert told me he was popping in to see you yesterday…"

"Don't you lie to me, you fucker!" Elsa spat, suddenly no longer the mother she'd grown up with but something else. Charlie took a deep, steadying breath. It was a very bad day. Until Elsa's dementia had taken hold, Charlie hadn't even known her mum knew swear words existed. In Elsa's current state, it wasn't worth arguing with her.

"You're right, Ma. I'll make sure Robert visits you tomorrow, okay? I'm sorry we haven't seen you." Whether Robert was free tomorrow or not didn't matter; Elsa wouldn't remember this conversation. Charlie heard Elsa grumble on the other end, but at least she seemed to be calming. "How's the weather? Can you see out your window?"

She pictured her mum turning in her large, patterned recliner in her room — at St Dymphna Nursing Home in South Sydney — to peer out her small window. The window was bordered by lace curtains, with Elsa's old ceramics collection on the windowsill. An array of pale, rosy-cheeked children for the most part. Her mum was in a garden view room, with a fountain close enough that she could hear it bubbling during the day. Charlie could almost smell the distinct nursing home smell as she pictured it — that fetid combination of antiseptic and urine.

There was a pause on the other end. "It's warm, Charlotte. Those bulbs have finally bloomed. I love daffodils." Her mum started humming 'Tutti Frutti' by Here's Little Richard — if she wasn't swearing and raging, she'd be singing at the flowers; Charlie much preferred the latter. "I wish you hadn't moved away," Elsa said in a rare moment of clarity.

Taken aback a little, Charlie said, "What was that?" This was the first time her mum had remembered Charlie no longer lived in Sydney.

"I just don't understand it. You had the loveliest apartment overlooking the harbour. Such a good job. I loved that apartment."

"I did too, Ma." Charlie smiled. "I have a lovely cottage now, though, surrounded by trees and grassland. It was just time for something different. Time to look after my —" She was about to say "my health" but thought better of it. "Myself."

There was another pause before Elsa started humming again. The Beatles this time. In the lull, Charlie found her mind wandering back to her living room. She wanted to talk to her mum about it; she always wanted to talk with her mum about everything. Before her dad had passed away four years ago, when things had really started to go downhill for Elsa, Charlie had talked to her about everything. There was never any judgment, no talking down to her about her mental stress, just a calm and understanding ear.

"Ma…" Charlie started. "Do you think —"

"They're stealing from me," Elsa suddenly said firmly. "They stole my shoes."

"They might have moved them to the cupb —"

"Don't you fucking lie to me, you cunt!"

\* \* \*

By the time Charlie reached Greenfields, she'd learnt two new swear words, which was impressive considering Tess swore frequently in English, French, and German. She should have hung up — it wasn't like her mother would remember — but she could never bring herself to do that. To leave the conversation on such a low note, and Elsa so distressed. At least Charlie had also been well and truly distracted from the excitement of earlier in the day. Exhausted from the conversation, she'd gone into automatic mode. She'd clipped her medical alert bracelet on, put a respirator mask over her face, pulled on her gloves, and done a decent but quick, grocery shop. Normally she'd preorder from the friendly grocer, so she'd enjoyed the brief jaunt through the aisles — a memory of normality — and absolutely dreaded every moment she'd turned a blind corner.

As her RAV4 made its way up her long, narrow driveway towards her cottage, Charlie felt the excitement of the day settle as weariness deep in her bones. On the drive back, the wind had picked up even further, bringing dark, low clouds and slanting icy rain. The unpredictability of spring: warmth and sunshine in the morning, followed by a surprise cold turn in the afternoon. As Charlie parked the car, a flash of lightning lit up the sky behind her. Thunder followed seconds later, an echoing rumble she felt deep in her sternum. "Damn it," she muttered, reaching behind her for her two shopping bags.

Just as she'd gotten her bags together, the rain started to fall again with gusto. "Argh," she grizzled as she got stuck behind the wheel of her car, overloaded with her things, the rain pelting her face as soon as she nudged the door open. By the time she fell against the front door, she was soaked, her hair matted to the side of her face. She didn't bother to bring the bags all the way to the kitchen, instead dropping them inside the entryway.

Even with her exhaustion, and the distractions the afternoon had brought, as soon as Charlie was inside her house, the memory of the white figure came flooding back. Her eyes were drawn to the spot where the creature had stood. Just as her eyes fell there, a flash of lightning lit up the dark room. This time, the lightning was immediately followed by a crash of thunder that crescendoed until the ceiling shook. In almost movie-like timing, the lightning illuminated a perfect set of loafered footprints on the living room floor.

# 3

# The Bogeyman

Charlie furiously tapped the "enter" key on her laptop as the coloured pinwheel mockingly spun. Her internet had worked perfectly all day, with three hours of Netflix binging (with only a few momentary glitches), two hours of YouTube music (ads and all), and an hour and a half of browsing fabrics online. Of course now, as she was trying to check out her shopping cart, her internet decided to drop to its lowest speed all day. Satellite had connected her back to the real world, which in and of itself was revolutionary. But her uplink was still a far cry from the saviour it touted itself to be. The outlay costs had been exorbitant (especially paying for it to be professionally mounted on her roof), the monthly fees took a sizeable chunk out of her living expenses budget, it had taken weeks for the dish to arrive, and customer service was near nonexistent. Still, since its installation a week back, she'd been able to receive WhatsApp messages from Tess for the first time in months. Video calls were still sometimes glitchy, but she absolutely took what she could get.

Sighing, Charlie leant back in her office chair, resisting the urge to keep tapping angrily at her keyboard. Perhaps it was a sign…her shopping cart had rapidly surged over her initial budget. And she still had fabrics sitting unused in her sewing room closet. As she was closing her laptop, she heard a slow, soft, yet deliberate rattle to her left; she knew what it was. Charlie turned quietly and deliberately, watching as the front door handle rattled before the lever was gradually pulled down. As the handle moved back to a neutral position, Charlie exhaled a long breath. The door handle rattled a few times more before stopping.

It had been two weeks since Charlie's shimmering white visitor, one week since internet had connected her to the outside world, and five days since her door handle had first started moving on its own. The first time it happened, she'd been making herself a cup of tea in the kitchen, the door only just in sight. As the handle had rattled, her heart had leapt into her throat and her mug had dropped from her hands, smashing spectacularly on the hardwood floor. All manner of scenarios had raced through her head. *A neighbour popping by because of some sort of emergency next door. A highway robber, come to take advantage of a woman living on her own. The satellite dish installer coming back to fix something he'd forgotten.* Every option, from benign to life ending, had swirled through her head in a split second. What happened next, though, she never would have imagined.

The door pushed open, letting in the cool twilight air, to reveal no one. There was enough light that she could see for hundreds of metres beyond the open door, away to the foot of the hills, and nothing but the breeze stirred. She paused for barely a moment before adrenaline took over and she leapt for the door. As she pushed it closed, she took a moment to look both left and right of the doorway in case someone was lying in wait. No one was there. She tried to dismiss the occurrence as the breeze, despite the obviously rattling handle and pulled lever. The second and third time it had happened made it increasingly difficult for her to blame the wind. Now she never left the door unlocked. Or the windows. At least whatever it was also seemed to need keys!

The door made one final rattle then stopped. Carefully, Charlie stood and tiptoed to the window, peeling the curtain back to look out onto the veranda. The sun was starting to set, and a blue glow had descended over the hills. To both her left and her right, she saw no one. The only signs of life were the little midgy bugs attracted to the warm glow of her porch light. Releasing another long, slow breath, Charlie made her way to the kitchen to boil the kettle. She wished the door was the only odd thing that had started up since her visitor's appearance. Things in the house had started moving too. Not much but enough to unnerve her. A mug she'd placed in the sink would be sitting on the bench the next morning. A chair she'd pushed under the table would be turned the wrong way when she next looked. All were small, almost unobservable occurrences, easily dismissed and forgotten as a once-off. Perhaps if she didn't live alone, she wouldn't have even noticed.

Settling herself on the couch with a steaming mug of Russian Caravan tea, Charlie opened her phone and scrolled through Facebook to distract herself. At least her phone still seemed to be connected. Amidst the myriad ads flooding her feed, there were snippets of her friends' and family's lives. A former colleague posting pictures of his trip to Prague (mostly photos of old buildings). The neighbour from her old apartment posting photos of her pregnant belly and complaining about swollen feet. And her brother, Robert, had posted a few days back with pictures of her two nieces, picnicking. She duly "liked" each post, leaving the obligatory "so jealous," "congratulations — it'll be worth it," and "miss you" comments.

Just as she finished scrolling, her Facebook messenger pinged with an incoming video call from Tess, who'd obviously seen she'd been online.

Her heart fluttered warmly, and she smiled as she answered, "Hello!"

"*Bonjour!*" Tess grinned brightly. The video glitched and stuck for a moment before quickly catching up. Tess's dark cropped hair was freshly washed, her tanned skin still gleaming from her recent shower. Her face was more well-rounded than Charlie's – though that wasn't hard, with Charlie's lithe frame. Where she was skinny, Tess was beautifully slim. "Success! We connect first try!"

"I know." Charlie laughed. "It's a miracle." She'd managed to call Tess a few times since her satellite had been installed, but it didn't seem to like video calls, often dropping out partway through a conversation if the video wasn't turned off. Charlie was hoping the connection would eventually improve as more satellites and uplinks were rolled out. Or whatever it was that made these things work. Even though Tess and Charlie had only spoken two days before, there were no awkward silences. They always seemed to have something to say to each other. Leon's girlfriend's latest judgy comments about Tess provided fodder for a good ten minutes.

"My new nickname for the girlfriend is *la pute*," Tess said. She tried to keep her face serious, but Charlie knew her well enough to see the humour. Charlie opened her mouth to chastise her friend but bit her tongue as Tess's expression changed. All humour had fallen from her face, replaced with a flash of confusion and then what Charlie could only assume was fear. She'd never seen Tess afraid before. "What's that?" Tess finally breathed.

Charlie swivelled to look behind her, the way her phone's camera was pointing. Nothing was behind her but her empty desk and entryway. "What is that?!" Tess practically shrieked, pointing once again behind Charlie, who stood quickly, knocking her chair, and pivoted around the room. Again, seeing nothing.

"What?! What is it?" Panic swelled inside Charlie. Tess didn't mind a practical joke every now and then, but this was next level. "Nothing's there."

"There..." Tess said breathily, but at least more quietly. "Right behind you, don't you see it?"

Instead of looking around the room, this time Charlie looked at her small thumbnail video image. A dark shape was flickering in the corner of her screen. She double tapped her picture to make it bigger. Her breath caught in her throat so spectacularly that she swallowed her own spit and started coughing. Standing in the corner of her living room, clear as day, was a dark, shadowy figure, its large piercing white eyes fixed onto her back. Just then, the call glitched and disconnected.

Charlie turned rapidly to look at the corner where she'd so clearly seen the figure. Though it was night, she had ensured plenty of lights were fitted during the renovation, and the space glowed warmly. There was no sign of any shadow figure. She jumped as her phone rang again, answering as fast as her clammy hands would let her.

"*C'est quoi ce bordel!*" Tess yelled, the connection suddenly perfect. So clear, in fact, that Charlie could see Tess's tanned skin had turned distinctly pale. "*Je suis folle...*"

"Tess..." Charlie said quietly, needing to get her friend's attention and reassurance. While Charlie may have learnt a few swear words and general

15

phrases from her friend, she was far from fluent; Tess often reverted to French when she was emotional.

"Tell me that was a filter or something," Tess finally said. "Why would you do that?! That was fucking terrifying."

"Is it still behind me?" Charlie blurted, swivelling so that Tess saw the full breadth of the room behind her.

"Wha—? *Non, non...* Keep spinning." Charlie spun slowly until she'd shown Tess the entirety of her living space, entry, and kitchen.

"Nothing?" Charlie said desperately.

"*Non*, no, nothing…" Tess's voice shook. "What was that?"

"Not a filter," Charlie said grimly. "God, I wish it was…" Her voice caught in her throat again. Now she was the one getting emotional — something that also didn't happen very often.

"*Oh, mon Dieu*, please tell me you haven't seen that thing before."

"No. No, nothing like that," Charlie clutched the phone tighter to stop it from shaking. "Can I please take you on a tour of the cottage? Just to make sure it's really gone?" Tess nodded in fervent agreement. Charlie took her time, walking slowly from living room to hallway to bedroom to bathroom, ensuring her friend could see every nook and cranny. The long hallways that originally had endeared her to the property now seemed foreboding. The large bedrooms she'd once marvelled at for sheer space now had too many corners to hide in. Eventually, with no more shadow figures detected, Charlie ended up back at the couch, which she promptly flopped herself into.

"Tell me what's going on," Tess demanded. "What did you mean by 'nothing like that'? What else has been happening?"

Charlie opened up about everything. The appearance of the white shimmering creature, the rattling door, objects moving around her house.

"I'm crazy…" Charlie sighed at the end, leaning back into the couch. "I mean, a top hat and loafers? How ridiculous!"

"If you're crazy, so am I," Tess said. "How do you even stay there?!"

"It doesn't all happen at once, I guess. I don't know… I didn't want to believe it was happening. I don't believe in ghosts. I'm rational."

"*ma chère*, it seems you don't have a choice now. My God, but it's a little exciting too, *non?*"

"Maybe for you!" Charlie finally laughed. "I swear I'm losing my mind."

"Did you research the cottage before you bought it? Did the real estate agent say anything? What about when you were renovating? Anything weird?"

"Why would I? I was interested in termites and whether it still had clay pipes. Not ghosts. No one mentioned anything weird."

"You need to do some research, darling," Tess said. "There must be records in Greenfields. Or talk to the real estate agent. Who knows what happened there or what the history of the place is? I'll be your research buddy. You'll have to let me know what you discover."

"I'm glad you're finding this entertaining at least." Charlie smiled, enjoying the warmth and brief normality.

"Well, it hasn't hurt you. I don't think ghosts even can hurt people, right?"

"I don't know. You do your research and let me know." Charlie yawned. The conversation had dragged well past dinner and into the night.

"I should let you go, *ma chère*."

"Sure…" Charlie said. "But…you wouldn't mind…one more time?"

"*Non, bien sûr.* Of course," Tess answered, not even needing to hear the question. Charlie took Tess around her cottage, once more checking every corner. Finally satisfied, she bade her friend goodnight.

"Good night, Thérèse. I promise I'll love you forever."

"*Bonne nuit*, Charlotte. *Je t'aimerai pour toujours.*"

# 4

# Life Is a Beautiful Dream

It was realer than reality. That's the only way Charlie could think to describe where she found herself in her dreams that night. She wanted to describe where she was as bright, but it was the intensity and variety of the colours all around her that felt bright. No matter where she looked, or how still she stood, there was a constant sense of movement. At times it felt mechanical, like she was stuck in a marble run. At other times, it felt more organic, more chaotic. Like she was being tumbled around inside a kaleidoscope. Despite the oddity of the dream, and how vivid everything was, she found it hard to hold on to memories of what had gone on just before. It was like, as the scenery flicked by so rapidly, her brain struggled to hold on to each fragment; they just slipped away.

All night she tossed and turned. At times almost waking, but rolling over, trying to shake the dream loose from her mind, and falling straight back to sleep. And straight back to the dream. As the first rays of dawn slipped between the cracks in her curtains, the dream finally slowed pace. She found herself standing on a platform. She wanted to describe the platform as grey, but that seemed too dull a word. All around her stood other platforms, connected by stairs and ramps and twisting loops. Most had doors on them or archways at least. There was no sky, no land — just space. Not empty but not earthly either. The feeling she wanted to associate with the platform was the same she would an actual train station, even though it in no way resembled one. It felt like she was waiting to be taken to a destination or for someone to arrive.

Although she knew she was dreaming, that didn't make it feel any less real. And despite knowing it was a dream, she had no control over her surroundings or anything happening to her. While the dream was odd, she also felt calm. Especially now that everything had stopped moving and spinning so quickly. There was a majesty to it. At the same time, there was an edge. Like at any moment it could turn, and she'd back in the chaos, or somewhere else. Somewhere less majestic...more threatening. It should scare her, but for some reason she felt safe.

Up until this moment, she had been the only person in her dream. As she stood admiring the arches, something rippled above her. A person stood there, her white nightgown blowing despite the lack of wind. Charlie could see her feet, her pale legs laced with varicose veins, and her off-white gown flapping in the absent breeze. Her torso and head, though, were hidden by a nearby column. Cautiously, lest the world start spinning again, Charlie took a curious step forward, arching her head to see better. As soon as she moved, the world she was in started to shift as well. She closed her eyes to stop the spinning. Taking a deep breath, as though to quiet a real dizzy spell, Charlie placed her foot back on the ground. When she opened her eyes, she found herself staring directly at the woman in the white nightgown.

"Hello, Charlie," her mother said. "Isn't it lovely here? The breeze in our hair, the sun on our back, the grass at our feet. This was my favourite place for our family picnics. Robert always had to rebuild his river dam every time we came. And you'd always get covered in a rash, swishing about in the long grass like it was your own special playground."

Charlie inherently knew where her mother was talking about — where she must think she was standing. A nature reserve near Sydney where she and Robert had played as children. She hadn't thought of that place for such a long time. Even though Elsa stood in the reserve, Charlie was still planted firmly in that strange grey landscape of archways and platforms. Somehow their dreams — their worlds — were colliding. "I remember," Charlie smiled.

"I often wonder if that's why you bought your cottage in the grasslands.

Because you always loved that tall grass so much." The clarity of Elsa's thought startled Charlie. Perhaps this dream was just Charlie's subconscious, but it was as if Elsa really had the thought independently. Elsa's theory made sense too.

"Mum, are you…?"

"Oh, yes, dear. I'm quite all right. Here at least." Charlie took another step forward, reaching out, desperate to touch this version of Elsa — this version of her mother. The same age as she'd last seen her. Just as skinny and wrinkled and frail, but different at the same time — more complete. As she stepped forward, though, Elsa slipped away, and the world started spinning again. As it spun, Charlie searched desperately for an anchor to lock on to. To stop and find Elsa again — this Elsa, who was whole of mind. Her eyes momentarily locked on to a figure. But it wasn't her mother. Rather, it was a completely white creature, with a white top hat, white suit, and white loafers. Instantly the anxiety of that day in her home hit her straight in the stomach, and the tumbling visions turned black around the edges.

Charlie blinked slowly as she woke up. Groggily she pulled herself onto her elbows, then fumbled for her phone on the bedside table. She had to blink repeatedly for her vision to clear. The surprise when she saw the time shocked her fully awake. It was almost 10:30 a.m.! She must have slept through her alarm, which never happened. And even if it did, she never slept this late. After throwing back the covers, she swung her legs out and to the floor, rubbing her temples to try to get rid of some of the sleep. Already much of the dream was fading.

As she padded to the kitchen, her mind was consumed with lists of everything she'd hoped to do that day. Wednesday was normally her day to make her way into town. To drop off clothes she'd sold at the post office, pick up groceries, visit the chemist if needed. She'd ordered her groceries for a midday pickup; she should still be able to get there in time.

As she reached the kitchen, all thoughts of lists evaporated. Every cupboard door was wide-open. Worse, each of her four dining chairs were precariously balanced on top of her small round dining table. It wasn't normal stacking either. Two chairs formed the base; the third was riskily balanced upside down; and the fourth perched on just two legs atop the third. It looked like it shouldn't stand. And perhaps if it had been off just a fraction, it wouldn't have.

"What…the…hell…" Charlie whispered. She felt rooted to the spot; it was an effort even to turn her head left and right to check the rest of her living space. That, at least, was just as she'd left it the night before. She was still clutching her mobile phone, and without thinking, she video called Tess. It only took a couple of rings for her friend to answer.

"Hello, darling. I've been thinking about you. How are you? Was last night okay?" Charlie answered Tess not with a response, but by flipping the camera and showing her friend the stacked chairs. "What the hell?" Tess said sharply on an intake of breath.

"That's what I said!" Charlie replied, the normality of the conversation instantly making her feel better.

"What the fuck is happening in your house?!"

"Oh, God, I wish I knew. It's like some cliché fucking horror movie."

"Cliché," Tess corrected Charlie's pronunciation, and they both started laughing awkwardly.

"Hang on," Charlie said, putting the phone on the table. "Give me a minute while I move these chairs." Despite how delicately they were all balanced, none fell as she removed them one by one. She then went about the kitchen, closing every cupboard door.

"Seriously," Tess said as Charlie picked up the phone again. "This is incredible. I've always been open-minded, but this is next level. To be honest, I thought people who told these kinds of stories were attention seekers."

"I guess that makes us attention seekers." Charlie sighed as she sank into one of the dining chairs. The laughter had momentarily made her feel better, but reality was starting to close in like a cold fist. "At least if you're seeing it too, I'm not losing my mind."

"*ma chère*, are you okay? Do you feel safe to stay there with all this going on?"

Charlie considered it. While the events were certainly frightening, the

21

cottage still didn't feel threatening. In fact, sitting at her dining chair with the sun pouring through the window, dust motes dancing in the air, she still felt calm. Safe enough. "You know, I think I'm okay; it's strange to say."

"I don't know how you can stay there. I would have been out of there like lightning last night! Never look back."

Charlie scoffed. "I guess I don't have a choice. I invested everything in the move. I have just enough saved, and just enough superannuation to see out my days in this cottage. And where would I go? You know how careful I have to be."

"You truly feel safe?"

Charlie paused before answering. "Yeah…it's strange, but I do. I'm okay." Saying it out loud made her feel better.

"*C'est bon*," Tess said. And it sounded like she really did think it was a good thing. "Last night, after our call, I lay awake thinking for hours. I was even scared of the shadows in my own house! I need to know what that was. I want to start researching right away, *ma chère*."

"That'd be great. Surely there are other accounts out there. Everything is on the internet."

"Well, not everything…" Tess said.

"What do you mean?"

"I tried to research your house last night. Aside from the real estate listing, there's nothing online. I tried several different searches. Nothing. But there must be records in Greenfields."

"I guess…" Charlie drummed her fingers on the table, looking around the cottage. With the chairs replaced and the cupboards closed, it looked completely ordinary. "I guess either way it'll be nice to know a little bit more about it."

"It's set then." Tess smiled, her face lighting up the phone screen. "*Allez!*"

# 5

# Let's Go

Charlie took a deep breath as she pulled the driver's door closed behind her and pressed the automatic lock. She pushed her back into the car seat, trying to force herself to breathe more regularly rather than in great gulping gasps. *I feel the car seat behind my back,* she thought. *I feel the warmth of the steering wheel from sitting in the sun... I hear people chattering near the post office... I hear the birds in the trees...* Opening her eyes, she took three more steadying breaths, already feeling better, and continued the mindfulness exercise. *I see the red post box... I see the sunlight hitting the leaves of the trees... I taste the tea I had this morning... I smell...* She paused, taking a breath. *I smell my car freshener... I don't smell peanuts.*

This hadn't been a full-blown panic attack. She'd managed to avoid those in public so far — at least in this town. It had felt close, though. It had happened as she'd paid for her postage satchels in the post office, mask securely fastened to her face, gloves on her hands. She'd turned to look at them automatically as she heard them enter the post office. A mother and her toddler, holding on to his mother's leg with one hand and chomping on a chocolate bar with the other. A peanut chocolate bar. Charlie had never had an allergic reaction just from being in the same room as a peanut — at least as long as that peanut wasn't cooking. But one flick of spittle at her face could be enough. And the fear was so ingrained in her now that she couldn't stop her heart from racing and her palms from sweating.

"Th-th-thank you…" she'd stammered at the cashier as he'd handed her satchels to her with a smile. "No receipt!" she'd practically yelled before snatching her bags and leaving the store with as wide a berth as possible from the chocolate-covered toddler.

"You're okay," Charlie told herself. "I'm okay!" Trying to shake off the adrenaline, she reached behind her seat to pick up the bag of clothes she was posting that day. Now that she had satellite internet and could check her socials more often, Charlie's sales had seen a massive lift. Apparently there was a growing niche for sustainably made, ethically sourced, natural-weave clothes in funky patterns. She'd sold five tops that week through her Facebook shop, plus two dresses and one camisole. Most of these clothes she'd made weeks ago and just never sold. She'd already received complaints about only stocking three sizes (small, medium, and large), despite their all being relaxed fit. If she were to keep up this turnover, her clothes hobby would become a clothes business. *I really should have held on to that receipt…*

As she stuck the last address label onto her package, Charlie checked her watch: 11.55 a.m. She'd made good time, considering how late she'd woken that morning. Her stomach growled impatiently, reminding her she'd skipped breakfast in her haste to leave the house. A quick stop at the library before picking up the groceries wouldn't hurt. Because the library doubled as the town hall, she was pretty certain the records for her cottage would be there. Her groceries — and her stomach — could wait a little. After replacing the mask on her face and making a dash for the red post box with her parcels, Charlie was ready for the short drive to the library. Before her life had changed, she would have walked the five minutes. Now the only place she walked was her own backyard.

Parking was always easier on a Wednesday (the quietest, and hence favoured, day of the week). As Charlie trotted up the library stairs she was pleased to see a large sign declaring, NO FOOD, NO DRINKS, NO SMOKING, NO PHONES. She smiled as she entered, pulling her mask a little looser. The librarian was a stubbled man, maybe in his thirties, not the typical old shrew or young nerd one pictured when imagining a librarian. He was, for lack of a better word, normal. Tall, slim, though with a small stomach poking over the top of his belted chino trousers. A tattoo peeked out of the collar of his navy polo shirt, which was pulled and fraying at the hems. Trust Charlie to notice that; she had sewing on the brain.

The librarian was incredibly helpful, settling Charlie into a desk while he hunted down the census records. "This will give you an idea of who has lived in your house over the years. Since 1961, the census has occurred every five years, so it should give you a pretty complete picture." It was a bigger pile than she expected. "Here," he showed her, pulling out the first record. "Everyone in Greenfields was required to list their address for census. You can start at the last census date, with the name of who you bought the house from, and work your way back through time. Thankfully the population's never been that big."

"Thanks so much," Charlie said. "I have to say census records aren't really my forte."

"Are they anyone's? Anyway, this is a good place to start. Greenfields' first *official* census was in 1881. I could go into the census history…" Charlie raised her eyebrows over her mask. "Ha-ha, but as you said, not your forte." She was starting to understand that this wasn't going to be a quick trip… or perhaps even a single trip. "Next time you can also try the newspaper records. I'm Trent, by the way. I'm usually here Monday to Friday, except public holidays."

"I'm Charlie," she said. "I usually pop into town on Wednesdays."

"Well, I guess I'll see you next Wednesday then, honey," Trent smiled. Charlie couldn't catch herself before she grimaced at his use of the word 'honey'. Her father had called her that, and it felt wrong coming from any other man. Especially one she didn't know. "You can leave the census records on the table when you're done. Photocopier is in the corner, coin or EFT operated." Trent gave her a friendly nod as he made his way back to the front counter. Charlie checked her watch again: 12:20 p.m. She'd give herself an hour then make her way to the grocer.

\* \* \*

Charlie heaved the last shopping bag onto her kitchen counter, chastising herself again for being so late to the store. It had been 3.45 p.m. before she'd made it, at which point the grocer was less than impressed, reminding her he had done this as a special favour and "wasn't a Woolworths." She'd promised to never be so late again, had said sorry another five times, then gone on her way.

Just as she'd put the last of the cold items in the fridge, her phone buzzed. Of course it was Tess. Charlie's brother never called her (Charlie always had to initiate), and her mother's phone could only receive calls, not make them. The nursing home had ensured that after a spate of midnight and early-morning phone calls from Elsa to cuss at Charlie. The nursing home's director had told Charlie it was brought on by the confusion of early dementia and of moving homes and being in an unfamiliar environment.

"Hi, Tess," Charlie said, glad for the excuse to abandon the rest of her shopping and flop onto the couch.

"*Bonjour, ma chère.* Any more strange visitors?"

"Well, I've been out all day and only just got home, so no, not yet." Charlie looked around her ordinary cottage. There was nothing out of place, no shadows, no glimmering white loafers. "I did get started on the research…"

"Oh, me too," Tess jumped in excitedly.

"Muuuuuum," Charlie heard Leon calling in the background. "Ma! What's for dinner!"

"Hang on," Tess said, putting the phone on mute and the video off. Charlie took the opportunity to hastily make herself a sandwich, her stomach now past the growling stage and gnawing angrily. "Sorry," Tess said. "I swear that boy will never grow up."

"It's okay," Charlie said, hastily swallowing the last bite and once again feeling a pang of sympathy for her friend. Tess had escaped the father but was still stuck with the son. She knew "stuck" was a horrible way to feel, but she'd never been able to like Leon. He'd always seemed so unappreciative of Tess and what she'd given up for him. But that was Charlie, always overprotective. And Tess too, she supposed. Perhaps Tess's own overprotectiveness was part of the reason Leon was still a "boy" with a lot of growing up to do.

"Where were we?" Tess said, flustered. "Oh, yes, what did you find?"

Charlie walked to the table where she'd dumped her photocopying. "Everything actually," she said, bringing the papers back to her couch. "The names of everyone who has ever lived in this cottage. Right back to 1881."

"1881?" Tess asked excitedly. "I thought the house was built in the 1920s!"

"So did I. Maybe there was something else here before the cottage. The real estate agent was pretty firm on the house dating back to the 1920s, and none of the tradesmen who helped fix it up questioned it."

"*Fascinant.*"

"I still need to make sense of it all, but it looks like the house has changed hands only three times, including to me. Then there was a fifth owner of the land before the cottage was built."

"Did anyone die there?" Tess asked, perhaps a little too eagerly.

"Well, probably, yeah." Charlie laughed. "You morbid wretch, you know I live here!" She smirked. "Life was tougher back when the house was built — I'm sure a lot more people died young."

"Okay, okay, I'll be quiet. Tell me everything."

"In the first census record, in 1881," Charlie began, "Henry James Thomson lived here. There's not much detail, so I have no idea if he lived alone. In 1933 a family lived here. William David Evans, his wife Emma, and *six* kids." When Charlie had discovered this, she almost hadn't believed it. She certainly struggled to picture it. The cottage's bedrooms were huge, but still. The Evans must have been a close and cosy family.

"*Oh, la vache!*"

"Tess…"

"*Oui*, sorry. That's just a lot of kids!"

"Yes, well, in 1933 there was ten-year-old Betty, nine-year-old Mildred, six-year-old Marie, five-year-old Alice, three-year-old Florence, and one-year-old Jack," Charlie said in a long-drawn breath, reading from her notes.

"And who died?" Tess couldn't help herself.

"I'm getting to that. It's hard to tell just from the census records, but it looks like there were some deaths. By the time the next census came around in 1947, there was no more Marie or Jack. Betty had also changed her last name to Baxter, and someone called Arthur Baxter had moved in." Charlie looked around her cottage and shuddered. "I can't imagine that many people living in here."

"Poor darlings," Tess whispered, obviously not so morbid now as she reflected on the fact the deaths could have been those of young children.

"By the time the 1954 census came around," Charlie went on, "it was just William, Emma and Florence in the cottage. I suppose the others married and moved out. By the 1962 census it was just William and Emma, and then from 1971 it was just William. So I suppose Emma could have died too."

"In the house…" Tess breathed.

"Tess!" Charlie chastised. "Stop it. I don't know. And let me finish."

"There's more?" Tess asked.

"Yeah, at least one more, I think. After William died, or moved away, a couple called Frank and Linda Forster moved in. No children, and they were in their fifties when they moved in, so I think they might have been retirees. Between the 1996 and 2001 census, Frank either died or moved out because it was just Linda. The previous owner, Rebecca Harper, was listed as living here in the 2016 census. And I know why she sold. She told me it was because she wanted to move closer to Greenfields."

"Okay," Tess said. "I can speak now?" Charlie laughed and nodded. "So, taking count, that's two *bout de choux* — two babies — and probably the mother too. And then who else?"

"Well, we don't know if William died in the house, but I guess we count him until we know. The same goes for Frank and Mary Forster."

"Six suspects…" Tess said thoughtfully.

"Great," Charlie said sarcastically, suddenly feeling tired and emotional, and remembering her anxiety at the post office.

"Sorry, *ma chère*," Tess said, seemingly really meaning it. "You know, I've been meaning to visit for so long. How about I actually plan something?" Charlie's heart warmed like it so often did with Tess, and the corners of her mouth tilted happily. "I couldn't come too soon, not for a couple of months, but let's book it in."

"Yeah, that'd be great," Charlie said, sarcasm gone. "I could really use a visit. And what about you? You said you researched too. What did you find?"

"Oh, *non*, let's not talk about it now," Tess said, obviously worried the conversation had hit Charlie too hard. "Nothing so exciting as you anyway. I'll tell you about it later. Let me bitch about Leon's girlfriend for a while."

Charlie burst out laughing, wiping a tear that had threatened to fall earlier from the corner of her eye. The next ten minutes were a perfect, normal conversation.

# 6

# The Mourning Notebook

The next week passed relatively unremarkably, which Charlie believed was a little to Tess's dismay. Tess had quickly latched on to the idea of a haunted cottage, perhaps to distract from Leon and his girlfriend. The first couple of days that week, Tess had called daily for updates. The only update had been that a mug had possibly moved, but Charlie couldn't actually remember where she'd left it. By the weekend, Tess was messaging instead of calling. Now, on Wednesday, Charlie hadn't heard from Tess since Monday. Charlie had plenty of time to sew, finishing three dresses (one a custom order), two skirts, a pair of culottes, and four more tops. She'd sold as many and more this week too. She thought she would have enjoyed the reprieve from Tess's persistent contact but found herself missing her friend's daily messages.

Unlike Wednesday last, this Wednesday Charlie had woken with the dawn, determined not only to be on time to the grocer but also to start the day right. She now stood on top of the nearest hill, stretching her calves after a steep final climb to the top. She breathed deeply, relishing the freshness in the air. The only scent was from the grass and the trees. Completely clean. She perched herself on a mossy rock, thinking back on the little extra information she had learnt that week.

Charlie had found no records online of the first settler to inhabit this land, Henry Thomson.  Of the Evans family, too, there was no online record. She found Frank Forster in an online obituary for "a life well lived,

1933–2000." Apparently, he'd died peacefully in a nearby nursing home. Charlie was pretty sure she'd found Linda Forster alive and well, in an online newsletter from the same nursing home, smiling sweetly for a family day photo. Linda looked happy, with what Charlie assumed must be children and grandchildren surrounding her. Charlie had stopped digging into the woman's life once she'd realised she wasn't capable of haunting anyone, but she couldn't help Google the person she'd bought the house from, Rebecca Harper. Charlie found her almost instantly on Facebook, wondering if Google had pinged that their phones had been close together earlier that year. Technology was scary that way.

Not much of Rebecca's profile was public, but from the little Charlie saw, it also wasn't remarkable. Rebecca looked to be fresh into her thirties, her profile picture always the same smiling girl with cropped black hair. The only thing this search revealed about Rebecca was that she seemed to like a lot of the local markets' public announcements and often checked into the town's pub – The Grey Gum Inn. Charlie shook her head as she thought how easy it was to stalk someone online these days. Rebecca probably hadn't paid any further thought to Charlie since selling the cottage.

As it tended to do at odd intervals, the wind picked up slightly, howling through the rocks and trees. Charlie cocked her head, waiting to see if the deep thrumming music would start up again; she found herself hoping it would. And just as she'd longed for, the wind did begin to howl melodiously, so soft to begin with she could barely hear it. As the deep, thrumming song wound around with the wind, Charlie relaxed into the stone behind her. "I'm so happy here," she surprised herself by saying out loud.

As if her words had broken the spell, the music faded and all that was left was the sound of the wind. Charlie wondered if Henry Thomson had ever come this way when he lived there and if he'd felt the same way. Maybe even heard the same music. Perhaps the Evans children had played on top of this very hill, climbing the rocks. Charlie liked to think they had. "Right, no more dawdling," she told herself as she stood, staring down over the hills to her cottage. "Time to go."

* * *

This time, Charlie's trip to the post office went off without a hitch — no peanut-wielding toddlers, no near panic attacks. She even stayed in the store to pack her items, rather than hiding in her car, before giving them back to the shop clerk.

"Charlotte White, isn't it?" the clerk asked.

"That's right," Charlie said, taken a bit aback. "I didn't realise you knew my name." Of course, Charlie had seen this man almost every Wednesday for more than half a year now. Feeling a bit guilty she hadn't registered his name, she flicked her eyes down to his name badge. "Tom?" she asked sheepishly.

"Mmm-hmmm. I have a parcel for you this week. It wouldn't fit in your lock box."

"Oh," Charlie said, surprised, wondering if she'd somehow ordered that fabric the other week after all, when the internet had still been dropping out.

"One moment," Tom said, then disappeared into the back room. Less than a minute later he was back with what was indeed a large box. "It's a little on the weighty side," he said. "Just sign here for me." Charlie did as instructed, before thanking Tom and taking what was indeed a weighty box back to her car. As she placed it in the boot, she took the opportunity to look at the "From" section.

"Hollow Tree," Charlie read aloud, with still no clue what was inside or where it had come from. The sticker on the back had a drawing of the Nordic tree of life (a symbol that graced many necklaces, notebooks, art prints, and even garden furniture). If Charlie remembered correctly, the tree was a symbol portraying the connection between all life and all worlds. This drawing was surrounded with star details. A nearby conversation brought her attention back to the path. Seeing an elderly couple walking towards her, Charlie decided she could wait until she got home to solve this mystery. Staying in the post office to pack her items had required enough bravery for one day.

As she started the engine, she checked the time on the dash. She still had ninety minutes before her grocery order would be ready. Enough time to start checking those old newspapers. And she'd come prepared with dates this time. Soon enough, she was climbing the steps to the library, once again loosening her mask as she passed the NO FOOD sign.

"Hi, Trent," she said chirpily as she approached the desk.

"Hi, honey," Trent replied, as if legitimately pleased to see her. He wore his trademark polo shirt and chinos again, and his hair was as unruly as ever. Stubble clung to his long narrow chin, winding its way down to a prominent Adam's apple. Trent's eyes crinkled along well-worn lines as he smiled broadly at her. This time, Charlie didn't flinch at his use of the 'honey' affectation. "I somehow knew I'd see you today. A little earlier than I'd expected, but no point wasting daylight." Charlie guessed in a town this small, there wouldn't be many new people, so perhaps he was happy to see her.

"Actually, I've only got ninety minutes today, but I do have a starting point this time."

"Well, that's handy. What have you got for me today?"

Charlie pulled a slightly creased piece of paper from her pocket. "Can I see the obituaries from the newspaper for these years?" On the paper was written "1881–1921," "1933–1947," and "1961–1971."

"That does make it a little easier," he said. "But there'll still be plenty of papers to trawl through. And the local paper didn't properly establish until 1894. How about I start with 1894–1921 and we can tackle those other dates another day?"

"Actually… Could we start with 1933–1947?" She was more curious about the two children than the first occupier of the land.

"Righty-o." Trent smiled. "Why don't you make yourself comfortable at that desk again and I'll be back shortly."

A short while later, Trent returned with a large box under one arm beckoning to her with his free hand. "Come with me." She followed him to a small, dark and windowless room just past the reception desk. A strange-looking contraption sat on an old desk beside an even older computer. "Our newspaper records are saved on microfilm," he explained, popping the box of microfilm onto the floor. "Pretty easy to use," he said, before fiddling with the wires and cables behind the computer and machine. "Ah, there we go. Loading up now." As the computer pinged to life, Trent took one of the films from the box. "You're lucky we've split the obituary pages out from the rest of the paper already. You won't need to trawl through the whole newspaper." He smiled at her. "Looking up when and how people died is more of a common pastime than you might think these days. So take the microfilm and place it like so in this contraption here. Voilà, here it appears on the screen."

It was a simple process, and Charlie quickly got into the groove after a stern telling from Trent to ensure all microfilms were placed back in the exact chronological order she'd found them. She was motoring through microfilms a handful a minute, her eyes scanning the computer for "Evans." She found none in 1933, but in March 1934 she came across her first name.

*EVANS—Mstr. Jack William, 2, son of William and Emma Evans, died Tuesday at his home in Greenfields, of polio. He was born February 11, 1933, in Greenfields. Brother to Betty, Mildred, Marie, Alice, and Florence Evans. Funeral services will be conducted Thursday at 2:00 p.m. in Greenfields Church under direction of Bishop Archibald Christiansen. Burial will be in Greenfields Church Cemetery.*

There was a photo of the family, dressed in their Sunday best, Jack sitting on his mother's knee, William standing stone-faced behind her, the girls positioned beside them.

"Trent!" Charlie yelled excitedly, forgetting for a moment she was in a library. It barely mattered, as there were only a handful of patrons there that day.

To his credit, Trent came quickly, with not a word of chastisement. "Found something then?"

"This is the family who used to live in my cottage! Can I print this? How do I take a copy?"

"Yep, okay..." Trent leaned over and took control of the computer mouse. "All we need to do is transfer this image to the computer like so...and...send to printer. Voilà!" It really did look simple.

"Thank you so much!" Charlie said, more thrilled to have this piece of the past than she'd thought she'd be. She felt connected to something bigger than herself, even if just for a moment. Her house felt even more special to her, grounded not just in beautiful grassland but in history.

"Was that all you were looking for, honey?" Trent asked.

"Actually, no. I'll keep looking if that's okay."

"Alrighty then," Trent said, rubbing his hands on his jeans. "Just call if you need me."

Over the next sixty minutes, Charlie managed to look through the remaining microfilms from 1934–1936, and the microfilms from 1961–1964, finding both of the other obituaries she'd been hoping to in 1936 and 1964 respectively.

*EVANS—Miss. Marie Patricia, 9, daughter of William and Emma Evans, died Sunday at her home in Greenfields, of pneumonia. She was born March 23, 1927 in Greenfields. Sister to Betty, Mildred, Marie, Alice, and Florence, and to Jack, her brother in heaven. Funeral service will be conducted Tuesday at 2:00 p.m. in Greenfields Church under direction of Bishop Archibald Christiansen. Burial will be in Greenfields Church Cemetery.*

This obituary was accompanied by a new photo, obviously cropped for the obituary, as Charlie could just make out the shoulder of another girl beside her. Marie, wearing a simple dress, pig tails, and bows in her hair, clutched a worn teddy. Her huge eyes gleamed even in black-and-white, instantly drawing her attention. A sparkle of mischief leapt off the page; the way the child held her shoulders shouted defiance. Charlie felt herself connect with the bright-eyed Marie – a kindred spirit.

*EVANS—Mrs. Emma Bernadette, 62, wife of William Evans, died Monday at her home in Greenfields in her sleep. She was born 5 July, 1902, in Sydney, daughter of H. D. and Amelia Morgan. She was married November 11, 1920 to William Evans of Sydney. She had lived in Greenfields since 1924. Besides her husband, she is survived by her daughters Betty, Mildred, Alice and Florence, son in-law Arthur Baxter, and grandson William Baxter. Reunited in heaven with her children Jack and Marie. Funeral service will be conducted Wednesday at 3:00 p.m. in Greenfields Church under direction of Bishop Ronald Baxter. Burial will be in Greenfields Church Cemetery.*

This time there was a new photo of Emma, quite a bit older, sitting side by side with her husband William.

Charlie had walked to her car clutching the papers to her chest in elation. Not only did she have much more information, but she also had their photographs. It made it feel so much more real. She found herself longing to stare at the family photograph again, memorising every detail of the Evans family's faces. She'd resisted, however; this week she was only minutes late to the grocer, much to his approval.

As she started the car up again, ready to head for home, she thought about how excited she was to share her news with Tess.

# 7

# Research

Charlie sat on the dining room chair, pulling the box from the post office towards her. When she got home, she'd tried to call Tess, but there was no answer. Charlie had resisted the urge to open the box long enough to unpack her groceries, but now eagerly ripped off the tape. Inside the box, amongst a considerable amount of packing peanuts, she found several strange objects. The first item she pulled out was a plastic packet with two long metal rods, bent at one end. Confused, she continued digging, pulling out a large pink stone, several smaller stones, and two small brown rectangular packages. Before she could investigate further, her phone rang.

"Hi, Tess," Charlie said, putting the second small, brown package back in the box.

"*Bonjour*, Charlie." Tess smiled. "Sorry I missed you. I took on an extra shift. Not smited yet?" Tess had been working in the same job for more than ten years. Charlie felt a moment of guilt for not knowing exactly what Tess did. All she knew was it involved organising and overseeing the movement of stock between department stores, from before the sun rose to late morning, every day. By the time Charlie had thought to ask more questions, they'd been friends so long it had felt weird.

"Ha-ha, no smiting. It's been a long day for you then! Do you need to head to bed?"

"No, no, no," Tess protested. "You know me, I wouldn't sleep anyway."

THE CORNER OF HER EYE

"Are you ready for some news?" Charlie beamed, reaching for the photo of the Evans family.

"*Oui*, entertain me, *ma chère.*"

Charlie angled the phone camera so the Evans family clearly came into view. She heard Tess make the appropriate excited noises and quickly jumped into the story, explaining all she'd found at the library.

"So the little boy Jack died when he was only two years old, in 1934, at his home. The obituary says it was polio."

"Poor darling. I thought polio only crippled you?"

"I guess not," Charlie answered, making a mental note to continue her online research. "The second child, Marie, also died in the house, two years later, in 1936. She was only nine years old. Pneumonia."

"Pneumonia, I know," Tess said, still subdued. "I can't imagine losing my Leon at that age." Charlie wished she could empathise, but her distaste for Leon kept that at bay.

"The only other death I could prove happened in this house was the mother, Emma. She died in the 1960s. The obituary said she died peacefully in her sleep, but she was only 62 years old. And get this…" Charlie continued before Tess could jump in with her obligatory comment. "The guy who buried her was also named Baxter. I bet you it was her daughter Betty's father-in-law!"

"Oh, yes," Tess said. "The eldest girl, the one who changed her name."

Charlie picked up the picture of the Evans family so she could examine it again, her eyes once again drawn to Marie. "I think it must be one of the children in the house. I just have this feeling. I don't think it's the mother."

"We can find out…" Tess said.

Charlie picked up the phone again. "What do you mean?"

"I saw on the table when you turned the phone…your box was delivered, yes?"

"That was you?" Charlie said. It all suddenly made sense. "The package from Hollow Tree?"

"*Oui.* We never did get around to talking about the research I'd done. I found all sorts of ways to communicate with spirits and to protect you and the home. Although your home seems to have been a bit quiet lately."

Charlie placed her phone back on the table, leaning against the box, so she could use her hands to inspect the items again. "So what is all this stuff?" She pulled the metal rods out first. "This?"

"Copper dowsing rods," Tess said happily as she brushed her dark cropped hair from her eyes. "They're supposed to point to water, but some of those YouTube ghost hunters use them to ask yes-or-no questions. If the rods cross over it means yes, and if they open wide, it means no." Charlie tried to stop her eyebrows from rising but failed.

Coughing loudly, she pulled out the large pink stone next. "This?"

"Pink quartz," Tess said. "It's supposed to be for protection and brings calm back to your home. It's meant to deflect negative energy and attract positive energy. There should be a few smaller crystals too." Charlie pulled them from the box one by one. "They're all for protection. I couldn't choose. Amethyst is supposed to get rid of stress. So is citrine. And the tourmaline is supposed to cleanse bad energy." Charlie rummaged through the box until she found the last stone.

"How do you know so much about this stuff?" Charlie asked, a little overwhelmed. "What do I even do with these? How do I...activate them?" She was a little frustrated when Tess laughed in response.

"You don't need to activate them, *ma chère*. You just put them around your house — I *think* — I've only just started looking into this as well. Is the Ouija board there?"

"Seriously?" With a sigh, Charlie roughly moved her hands amongst the packing peanuts, pulling out a small, flimsy-looking Ouija board, wrapped in plastic. "I am *not* using this."

"It's just for fun, *ma chère*."

"Nope. I've seen enough horror movies. That one is staying shrink-wrapped." As she'd been riffling around for the board, she'd found a set of candles. "Are these for voodoo too?"

Now it was Tess's turn to get exasperated with Charlie's bad humour. *"Pourquoi je m'embête même à te parler?!"*

Charlie didn't understand the words, but she understood the meaning and the frustration behind them. "I'm so sorry, Tess. I'm so grateful to you for getting all this, and for researching, and for even thinking of me at all. I guess this stuff just weirds me out."

Tess sighed and rubbed her forehead. *"Ne t'inquiète pas.* It's okay. I guess I am a little tired." She shook herself off. "I'm just trying to help, *ma chère.*"

"I know, I know. I do appreciate it, I do. What are the candles?"

"Okay, they *are* a little voodoo. They're supposed to be for blessing and protecting your home."

Charlie felt a wave of warmth and gratitude for Tess. "You really are amazing." Tess rolled her eyes in reply. "I mean it — you've gone overboard on the protection, and it's just what I need. You're the best."

"I did go overboard..." Tess said. "What can I say?! There should be a couple more things. A pack of sage for more protection and some tarot cards."

Charlie unwrapped the two brown paper packages, and sure enough, there was a bundle of sage and a packet of tarot cards, with a calming picture of flowers wrapped in concentric circles. "I thought tarot was for witches and fortune tellers?"

"So did I!" Tess said. "But *non*, this website said they can be used for finding hidden answers. There's a guidebook there too."

"Well, it's better than Ouija," Charlie tried a gentle jibe, and Tess smiled in reply. "What should we try first? You want to do this now?"

*"Oui,"* Tess replied, hiding a yawn. "Please distract me!"

"What first?"

"The copper rods looked easy on YouTube. You just hold them loosely in your hands by the handles and clear your mind. If it's neutral, the rods will just stand straight in front of you. You don't hold tight and don't move them. They move themselves."

Charlie was sceptical as she unwrapped the rods, but with what had happened in her house, who knew? Maybe this stuff really did work. "Hang on." She smiled as she stood then jogged a few steps to the kitchen. She returned shortly with a box of matches. "Let's get some of that protection." Tess tried to stifle her smile just as she had her yawn but failed again.

*"Je t'aimerai pour toujours."*

"I'm not hanging up. You're sticking around for this," Charlie said.

"I know, it just felt right to say."

"I love you forever too," Charlie smiled. The candle had a nice soy smell to it, and the flicker was relaxing. "Okay, let's try these rods." She relaxed back into the dining room chair, her elbows by her side, and exhaled as she picked up the rods. At first, they swung in all directions.

"Not too loose, not too firm," Tess said authoritatively. Charlie obeyed and straightened her back, the rods relaxing dutifully into the centre — the neutral position.

"Okay...so...now?"

"Now tell the spirit how they work. Cross over for yes, open wide for no, middle for neutral. And start asking questions."

Charlie cleared her throat. "Ah...did you get that, Marie? We want to communicate with you. To answer, you just have to cross the rods for yes, then open them wide for a no." It felt right to communicate with Marie for some reason. The rods slowly moved to cross in the centre. Charlie felt them move in her grip, like some unseen hand was gently twisting them. "Ah!" she said in shock but also slight elation. "Look!"

Tess made appropriately excited noises, then encouraged Charlie to continue. "Okay," Charlie said. "Marie, my name is Charlotte. But you can call me Charlie. I'm living in your old house. Some weird things are happening, and I was hoping to talk to you about it. If that's okay?" Once again, the rods slowly crossed over in Charlie's hand. Her heart beat faster, her doubt disappearing. She hadn't even thought before addressing Marie; she'd just assumed she'd be the spirit to respond.

"This is good, Marie! This is good! Is it just you in this house?" The rods wavered in Charlie's hands for a moment before very slowly opening wide. A small chill raced down Charlie's spine before the rods slowly returned to their neutral position. "Oh, yes, your brother Jack, right? He's here too?" This time, the rods opened to the "no" position much faster and stayed there. Tess continued to make exclamations under her breath, mostly in French, but otherwise didn't interfere.

41

"Oh, I-I'm sorry. I guess he's…he's in heaven…" Charlie felt disingenuous saying that. With the number of times she'd nearly been killed by a peanut, she wasn't sure she even believed in heaven anymore. The rods stayed firmly in their "no" position. "Can…can you move the rods back to neutral, Marie? So I can ask another question?" It took a moment, but the rods slowly moved back to neutral. "Tess, this is freaking me out," Charlie said, too afraid to take her eyes from the rods.

"*Oui*, but keep going, *ma chère*. She can answer your questions."

"Marie, have you been moving my cups and chairs? I'd really like that to stop." The rods slowly opened to the "no" position. "Oh…no, it's not you or no you won't stop? I'm sorry… I should ask my question better. Is it you?" The rods swung violently back to the neutral position. "I guess that means no answer?"

Charlie wanted to ask who else was in the house. As she tried to think of a way to form the question for a yes or no answer, the rods started moving again. This time they moved together, not into a yes or no position, but as if they were pointing. Slowly they swivelled in unison, then stopped, pointing to the corner of the living room.

"What does this mean?" Charlie asked Tess.

"I-I don't know…" Tess said. "I haven't heard of it doing that before. I'll check. Where are they pointing?"

"To the corner of the room," Charlie said. She realised where the rods were pointing at the same time Tess did.

"Where that thing was standing," Tess breathed, both of them remembering the dark shape Tess had seen in the background of their video call.

"Marie," Charlie said. The rods quickly swung back to neutral. "Am I safe?" The rods pivoted in and out for a moment, as though not sure which way to go, before slowly swinging to the "yes" position. Charlie breathed a slow sigh of relief. "Okay, thank you, Marie." Suddenly, Charlie felt drained through and through. "Is it okay if I talk to you again sometime?" The rods swung back to the yes position. "Okay, that's good. Goodbye, Marie."

# 8

# Haunted by Memories

Before the rods could move again, Charlie placed them on the table. "I'm exhausted!" she told Tess. "I don't think I expected anything to actually happen."

"What did it feel like? Using the rods?"

"Honestly, it was a little surreal," Charlie answered. "The rods never forced themselves in any direction. It's like they were just…drawn where they needed to go. It was thrilling connecting with Marie. But at the same time…"

Tess broke the silence between them by reading Charlie's mind. "Dreadful?"

"Exactly," Charlie answered. "Dread. But not about Marie. It felt nice connecting with her."

"I wish I were there with you for all of this," Tess said wistfully. "I'd love to give it a go too."

Charlie smiled. "You and me both. You know, I think I need to go for a walk. Shake this off."

"*Tres bien*. You do that, *ma chère*."

"Love you forever, Thérèse."

"*Je t'aimerai pour toujours, ma* Charlotte."

Charlie sighed as she hung up. A notification popped up on her phone asking her if she'd like to turn on extreme battery saver; she felt a bit the same about her own body. Standing, she was turning to look at the corner of the living room, where the rods had pointed, before she consciously realised what she was doing. The room looked empty to her. Taking a breath, she hit "ignore" on the phone notification and flipped open the camera app. She looked at the corner again, through the phone camera, and was relieved to see nothing change.

A few minutes later, Charlie was out the door, a warm jumper thrown on. The weather was still unpredictable, and once again, what had started as a warm, sunny day was quickly turning brisk. Clouds hung low in the sky, but it seemed like no rain was looming. Locking the door behind her, Charlie made an unconscious decision not to walk to the hills, like always, but to head to the back of her property. The land in front of her house was a pleasant series of hills. The land behind gently sloped down to a small creek. The creek never normally appealed to her like the hills, but today it seemed appropriate.

"What do you reckon, Marie? Let's give it a go."

\* \* \*

The walk to the back of her property took about thirty minutes, at a decent pace. It was relaxing walking the gentle slope, rather than challenging herself with the hills. In fact, it was just what her body needed. Already she felt revived. Unlike the majority of her property, the trees around the creek hadn't been cleared. Here, the gum trees stood thickly, blocking the brisk wind that always seemed to pick up in the afternoon. With winter so recently passed, the creek was nice and full; in summer she could easily jump over it. Right now, even with her farthest leap, she'd land in the middle of the steadily flowing water.

Charlie made herself comfortable on a nearby patch of thick grass, resting her back against an old white gum tree. These gum trees were her favourite. The trunks were smooth. The bark like paper. Comfortable. The gently flowing creek made a lovely bubbling sound as it flowed over the stones beneath. Charlie wondered why she hadn't come here on her walks before.

She'd known it was here; it had been part of the tour (on the back of the previous owner's 4WD buggy) when she'd bought the property. It hadn't seemed so calm then, though it wouldn't with that engine rumbling.

Leaning her head against the tree, she closed her eyes, enjoying the tranquility. She could afford to rest here a while before walking back before dark.

She'd closed her eyes only a moment when she heard the pattering of small feet. Charlie scrambled to her own feet. It could have been an animal — a wallaby or a rabbit perhaps — but it had the distinct sound of a young child's pattering footsteps. "Marie?" she whispered. Again the pattering feet sounded right in front of her, running past her towards the creek. "Holy fuck... Ah, I mean..." Was it rude to swear in front of a child ghost? One who'd been dead almost a hundred years? She heard another giggle in front of her, besides the creek.

"Marie, it's Charlie. Did you...did you follow me here?" Charlie bent double and slowly walked towards the sound. With sudden clarity, she reached for the phone in her back pocket, fumbling as she unlocked it and opened the camera app. She lifted it to the creek bank and gasped as through the camera she could see not just Marie but another young girl, perhaps five years old. The details captured through her phone weren't exactly clear, but both looked to be wearing pale dresses, one peeking out behind a warm green cardigan, the second behind a thick cream jumper. Both wore stockings with worn boots and had their long dark hair in pigtails. "Marie?" Charlie asked again, but the girls ignored her.

Charlie watched in fascination as the girls laid out an old rug by the creek, neatly arranging a tin tea set, a teddy bear, and what looked to be a new doll. At least the doll was in far better condition than the tea set and the teddy bear, which was missing an eye. The girls knelt on the rug, arranging everything just so, then pulled four arrowroot biscuits from their pockets and gently placed them down in front of the toys. The girls could have been twins, if not for one being slightly slimmer and taller than the other. The taller girl seemed to almost glow a bright blue, while the second was so pale as to almost be transparent, colourless.

"Happy birthday, Alice!" the glowing child said, moving her teddy bear as if it were doing the talking. She looked up to make sure her audience was as captivated by her performance as she was.

The second child giggled, picking up the empty teacup and answering, "Why, thank you!" Thinking of Tess in this moment, Charlie pressed the button on her phone to take a photo, wanting to share this moment with her friend. As the camera noise clicked loudly, the glowing child turned to stare directly at Charlie. The second child, Alice, continued to play, munching happily on her arrowroot. Marie, meanwhile, looked through the camera at her, her eyes just as wide and piercing as they'd been in the obituary photo. She smiled. "Come play with me," she said.

In spectacular timing, the battery on Charlie's phone died in that moment, the phone screen going black, the white pinwheel swirling as the phone shut itself off. Charlie's heart hammered, and it took all her control to keep her breathing even. "Marie?" Charlie said loudly, hating the quaver in her voice. "You stay here with Alice, okay?" She turned and jogged back to the house. She could have sworn there was still plenty of sunlight when she'd set out from the house, and when she'd arrived at the creek, but it must have been later than she'd realised. The clouds must have hidden how low in the sky the sun was, because it was quickly getting dark. And freezing cold.

The jog didn't last long, with the ground uneven beneath her (especially in this light) and the "gentle" slope now working against her. Instead, she struggled at a brisk walk for what felt like much more than half an hour. By the time she reached her door, she was covered in sweat, chilling her even more. With her porch light off, and her phone light not an option, it took her a while to fumble her key into the lock. Finally inside, she slammed the door behind her, using the key to lock it again from the inside. Only then did she flip on the light switch before turning to see that every cupboard door in her kitchen had been flung open. Every mug and glass had also been removed and was balanced on the bench in intricate, stacked patterns.

"Marie!" Charlie yelled angrily. "You stop this now! This isn't a game!"

She cleaned the kitchen so quickly and vigorously that a mug bounced from her hands and smashed on the floor. "Not another one," she mumbled, putting her head in her hands. "Jesus, I'm going mad…"

* * *

That night, Charlie lay in bed, staring at the ceiling. She hadn't bothered to dry her hair after her shower, and it felt uncomfortably cool and soggy against her pillow. The house had stayed blissfully quiet since she'd had her meltdown in the kitchen. She'd stood in the hot shower for at least half an hour, letting her mind go numb. *Am I actually mad?* she thought. *And swept up in my delusions, I've dragged Tess along for the ride?* Charlie rolled onto her side and reached for her phone, now charging on the bedside table. She unlocked it with her code and scrolled impatiently to the photo gallery. "Nothing," she breathed, seeing the photo of the creek. It was an awful photo, dark and blurry. It was also just the creek.

She clicked off the phone screen and rolled onto her back once more. *Come play with me…*the words rang in her head again. In that moment, with her phone choosing to power down, and the dark of night starting to creep around her, she'd been utterly terrified. Now, as she lay awake pondering the words, she realised there'd been no malice in them. They seemed almost innocent. Charlie sat up and grabbed her phone again. "Arnotts arrowroot biscuits…" she whispered, realising the biscuits she'd seen had been far more familiar than she'd first thought. Almost exactly the same as the ones she'd eaten as a child. She typed her query into her phone. The first page of search results was just a long list of places to purchase said biscuits. "…history…" she finished typing.

"Huh," she mumbled, lying back down and scrolling again. The biscuits were first sold in 1888 — originally a staple for sailors, then sold as a first food for babies. Quickly they became a household favourite and treat for all ages. Charlie did the maths in her head as she placed the phone back on the table. The girls had looked around five or six years old when she'd seen them by the creek. Marie was born in 1927, so the flashback, or whatever it was, must have been in the early 1930s. "Those biscuits had already been around forty years." She yawned loudly, wondering how long they'd been

47

around when she herself was a child and if children still enjoyed them as much now. Who knew? The benign thought calmed her, the exhaustion from the day once more creeping in.

# 9

# Unnerved

That night, Charlie found herself back in her bizarre dream world. The grey-white place of endless doors and archways. Again she felt herself waiting. While last time she'd been waiting for her mother, this time she felt something — or someone — was waiting for her.

"Hello?" she said, hearing her voice echo around her. In response, she heard the same giggling she'd heard by the creek. It was just as soft and tinkling as the creek had been, running over its stone bed. "Marie?" Charlie took a step forward and was suddenly standing in the grass fields of her own property. *No,* she thought. Slight differences made her understand it wasn't her property right now — it still belonged to the Evans family. She heard grass move behind her and turned, expecting to see Marie. Instead she saw a large flock of sheep, moving slowly, nibbling as they went, ambivalent to her presence.

"Marie!" a voice called from her left. Charlie turned to see her house — the Evans' house —in the field. The frame was just as it was in Charlie's house now, as was the beautiful deck. But lace curtains hung in the window, and the paint was a slightly different colour. "Marie! Lunch!" After a moment, the woman muttered to herself, but Charlie still heard her as clear as if she stood beside her. "What will I do with that girl?"

The soft giggling started again, and as Charlie stepped towards the sound, the world shifted with her. She found herself at the front of the property near where the gate led to the road. In her dream, the road was still hard-packed dirt rather than tarmac. Along one side of the fence ran a makeshift shelter, a tin roof atop a wooden frame. Beneath that roof was a trough, and by that trough stood a gorgeous, sturdy chestnut horse with white patches on its coat and a caramel mane. A roofless, wooden wagon stood not far from the horse, its harness tossed carelessly inside.

In front of the mare, patting its nose, was Marie. She was still the small, skinny girl Charlie had seen by the creek, but older. By at least a year or two. The horse nuzzled the girl's chest, and as she giggled in response, she wrapped her arms around its neck. The horse lifted its head, pulling the small-framed Marie off the ground. The animal then swung its head, and Marie used the momentum to swing her own leg over the horse's back to sit on its shoulders.

Just as the horse had nuzzled Marie, she nuzzled its back. Somehow Charlie knew that Marie was aware what time of day it was and that her mother was expecting her for lunch. In the same way, Charlie knew Marie would delay as long as she could — as she always did. Whether it was by catching tadpoles at the creek, playing with the caramel-maned horse, or reading amongst the sheep. "I wish she'd let me go," Marie sighed into the horse's neck. "It's so unfair she keeps Alice and me here." Charlie wondered only for the briefest of moments what Marie meant, before Marie's emotions hit her like a wave. Charlie felt the same way she would have if she were at the beach and the surf had struck her, grinding her into the sand.

"Jack..." Charlie breathed. The mother, Emma, kept the younger two children home to protect them, because she couldn't protect Jack. Just as Charlie had understood what Marie was feeling, she knew the older children were at school in town, living with their grandparents during school terms. Marie looked up and peered straight into Charlie's eyes.

"I just want to play." Marie sighed again. The dream slowly washed itself away, everything fading into white. Charlie tried to hold on to the dream to no avail. She then attempted to wake herself, also unsuccessfully, and instead fell into a deep, mercifully dreamless slumber.

\* \* \*

The next three weeks passed as uneventfully as Charlie could make them. She still heard odd sounds in the wind. She still woke to find things had moved in the house — though thankfully not to the same degree as after she'd first spoken with Marie. Charlie also continued to see shapes or movements from the corner of her eye. Even so, she refused to acknowledge they were there. She wanted nothing to do with these weird, spooky occurrences. Charlie even managed to convince herself that how she'd found her kitchen had somehow been her own doing. Perhaps she'd meant to dust the cupboards and simply forgotten she'd left them open. That would explain the loss of time from when she'd talked to Tess with the dowsing rods and when night had descended on her at the creek.

Tess still called or messaged for updates, but Charlie evaded or deflected them. Eventually Tess returned to "normal" conversations about Leon's girlfriend, her current favourite books and TV shows, or planning her visit to Charlie's cottage in November. Tess had also resumed her pattern of only calling once or twice a week. Charlie spent her time in town just at the post office and grocer — each as brief as possible. The library visits, however, were abandoned. She called her mother once a week and messaged her brother reports. Charlie also resumed walking only in the hills, filling the rest of her time with sewing clothes or packing orders.

She expected to return to the same level of contentedness as before, now that she was ignoring the odd happenings in her house. Yet the more the days dragged on, the more unhappy she felt. After throwing on a light jacket, Charlie made her second (and last) trip to the car from the house, carrying two bags of clothes she'd sold to post in town. *I might need to start making two trips into Greenfields each week*, she thought, buckling herself into the car. Sales were booming.

When she was nearly at the end of her driveway, a loud crunch and banging under the car made Charlie swear in shock and concern. *What the fuck?* After putting the car into park, she pushed open the door and ran to the front of her car, expecting disaster and mechanical bills she hadn't budgeted for. Relief swept through her as she realised she'd just run over a particularly large branch, which had cracked in two from the pressure. Pulling the branch out from under her car, she threw it aside. As she stood upright, she remembered Marie with her horse, standing under the tin roof structure. This was exactly the spot where she'd seen Marie in her dream.

Leaving her car running for a moment, Charlie walked through the tall grass to where she'd seen the horse. She scuffed the ground with her foot, trying to break loose the stones and clumps of weed. Her foot met with slightly more resistance, and Charlie bent down and brushed the dirt aside. A large, rusted nail — as thick as her pinkie finger — was unearthed. Charlie grabbed a nearby rock and used it to continue shovelling dirt out of the way. She stopped as the rock hit something else hard and metallic.

"Oh my God…" she whispered, as she unearthed a broken, rusted piece of corrugated tin. The same shape and style as the tin on the roof she'd seen in her dream. She felt another emotion try to break through the unhappiness that had plagued her. Not fear — though she guessed many would find that a normal response. And if she were truly honest, there was a slight pang of dread. More than anything else, though, it was curiosity and a desire to keep digging that tried to break through her forlornness. "I'm not falling for this again." She tossed the piece of tin to the ground and hurried back to her car.

Although Charlie intended to go straight to the post office, instead she found herself driving to the library. She parked (badly) and climbed the steps, neglecting her mask and gloves, and walked straight through the foyer to the front desk. Trent stood there and looked up as she approached. At first he looked puzzled — never having seen Charlie without her mask — but realisation soon dawned. "Charlie!" he said. "It's been a while. I thought you'd given up."

At Trent's innocent words, Charlie burst into tears. Shame and embarrassment burnt brightly, but the harder she tried to keep the tears at bay, the more she snorted as the tears (and snot) broke through anyway. "I-I-I'm… s-s-sorry…" Charlie managed through big sobs, burying her face in her hands, foolishly trying to hide behind her fingers. Trent quickly put his arm around her, guiding her out of the lobby. Through the blur of her tears, Charlie couldn't see where he was leading her, but she soon found herself in an office, sitting on an old, lumpy lounge. Trent was at her side, holding her hand, not saying a word.

After a good five minutes of steady sobbing, Charlie's breath finally slowed enough for her to make a full sentence. "I'm so sorry," she said, tears still flowing down her cheeks. "I never cry."

"I can tell," Trent said in a friendly manner. "Youngest kid here, three older sisters, all tough as nails. They never cry either. Until they do. And then…" He threw both hands out, palms up, in Charlie's direction. The gesture made her laugh, more snot bursting out of her nose.

"Oh, God," she said, covering her nose with her hands.

"Hang on, honey," Trent said, then stood and made his way to the desk. He returned with a box of tissues. "Always prepared. Everyone thinks being a librarian is just about the Dewey Decimal code, shooshing, and chasing late fees. I tell you, we're the philosophers and therapists of the younger generations." Charlie gratefully took a few tissues and cleaned herself up.

"You are so nice," Charlie said through another big sob. "I'm so sorry to come in here like this. What must you think of me?!"

"You don't have many friends around here, do you?" Trent said, ignoring her question. "Greenfields is a small enough town. Everyone seems to know about you, with your odd deal with Emmett, the grocer, and those gloves and mask you always wear. But no one *really* knows you." Charlie just nodded, taking another tissue as fresh tears rolled down her cheek. "Do you want to talk about it?"

She took a shuddering breath, and after a long pause, she actually did tell her story. How she'd been a big shot lawyer in Sydney, with her harbour-view apartment and lavish lifestyle, and how it had all started crumbling down just before the COVID pandemic. All thanks to an adult-onset peanut allergy.

"That's pretty severe," Trent said, having sat in silence for the duration of her story.

Charlie snorted again, this time thankfully without the snot bubbles.

53

"That's a word for it! I guess I hadn't really processed it. Obviously." She laughed, motioning to the tissues on her lap. "This is actually the first time I've had a good cry about it."

"And all your research?" Trent asked. Charlie blew out another deep breath, unsure if she wanted to get into the spooky side of her meltdown. Especially not with the person who might be her first — and only — friend in her new town. "It seems like more than just passing the time."

"My new place…it's been…a bit weird sometimes…" Trent's smile encouraged her to continue, which she did sheepishly. "You know, it's an old place. Odd…noises…and things moving around sometimes. Or at least they seem to. I don't know…"

"Oh, honey," Trent smiled, leaning back onto the sofa. For the first time, Charlie was truly pleased Trent had called her 'honey'. "You don't have to be embarrassed about ghost stories around here. This library is for sure haunted." They both laughed, Trent's rich and full guffaws no doubt echoing through the shelves in the library beyond the door. "The last thing someone like you needs is a ghost making creepy noises and moving your things around."

"Right!" Charlie smiled back at him. "Oh, God I needed this normality. Thank you."

"Anytime," Trent replied. "Anything in particular bring this on today?"

"Oh, right!" Charlie said, the curiosity of the morning breaking through her weakened defences. She told Trent about the dream and her discovery by the front gate.

Trent whistled. "Well, now you've piqued my interest!"

# 10

# A History Lesson

Trent sent one of his staff to the post office on Charlie's behalf to post her parcels. He also called Emmett (the grocer) to tell him Charlie would be picking up her groceries late. Then he gave Emmett a stern talking-to when he tried to complain, emphasising Charlie needed support not a lecture.

Charlie held the sweet, milky tea that Trent had made her, feeling a lot lighter now that the tears had been shed. While she normally had black Russian Caravan, the overly sweet Tetley really hit the spot. It was odd to think that opening up about the weirdness in her house was what had brought her back to a feeling of normality. "I keep wondering what it would've been like living here when they did — the Evans family," Charlie said, sipping from her mug.

"I've wondered the same thing. *And* I can tell you a little bit about it if you're interested. Librarian, philosopher, therapist, and history buff over here. Now…let's see what we know about your Evans family so far…"

"Okay," Charlie clapped her hands. "I have had all this information running through my head on a loop. It'll be nice to finally set it free! Mr William Evans and Mrs Emma Evans built the cottage sometime in the early 1920s. By the time they moved in, they would've probably already had at least one, if not two, children. Betty and Mildred both would've been born in the early 1920s. Marie was the third child and possibly the first one born in that house.

"She also had two younger sisters, Alice and Florence. The youngest was Jack, who died when he was only two years old. From polio. It's always been a huge property, and in my dream — the dream where I saw the same tin I found this morning — there were a lot of sheep. So I'm thinking that's what the property must have been used for originally."

Trent scooted a bit closer to Charlie. "I think that's exactly what they would have had going on. There's plenty of farms around here that still raise sheep, amongst other agricultural endeavours. And that timing…well, it all makes sense. After World War I, a lot of Australians were encouraged by the government to go to the country and make a go of it 'living on the land.' It was romanticised, which may partly be why we still romanticise living in the country today.

"In fact, after the war, the government sometimes gave land away or sold it so cheap they may as well have. The only catch was that you had to clear it yourself. And that was no easy task. We're not talking weeds — we're talking gum trees. There were plenty of young men who worked in the city just long enough to buy their piece of outback so they could live out the Australian dream of having their own farm. Maybe even this Billy Evans? If he moved after he'd already gotten married and Emma started popping out babies, he must have had something else keeping him busy beforehand."

Charlie nodded. "That makes sense," she said, intrigued. A song popped into her head and she couldn't help singing a few lines. "*Give me a home among the gum trees, with lots of plum trees. A sheep or two, and a kangaroo…*"

"*A clothesline out the back. Veranda out the front. And an old rocking chair.*" Trent finished. "John Williamson. We've been idealising the bush for decades!"

"It feels nice knowing the Evans were living out their dream."

"Well, in the 1920s, maybe," Trent continued. "Then the Great Depression hit in 1929, and it hit pretty hard in Australia. Especially here in New South Wales. As a sheep farmer, Billy might have gotten by okay. Wool prices were low, but at least consumption was steady. So long as he knew what he was doing, and he got good quality product, he probably survived the first couple of years okay.

56

"It was in the early 1930s when taxes started going up that things got really desperate. I remember this next statistic because I just can't imagine it happening today. By 1933, one in three Australian breadwinners were unemployed. Can you imagine?"

"I literally can't," Charlie said, finishing her cup of tea. "They'd be burning things down if that happened today. When did we all get so selfish and stupid? Poor Jack would have been born right into the worst of it."

"Well, let's just assume the Evans family got by okay. We tend to look out for each other around here. And by the mid-1930s, wool prices were pretty much the highest they'd ever been. Even higher than before the Depression hit. Demand for wool started growing around then too."

"That does make me feel better." Charlie smiled. "I can picture it. And if they could afford to send the kids to the school in town, then they must have been all right. I even saw…" She was about to admit she'd seen Marie and Alice eating Arrowroot Biscuits by the creek outside of the dream but thought that last revelation might be a step too far. "I even saw Marie with Arrowroot Biscuits…in my dream. They could at least afford those."

"You know, I've got the day off tomorrow," Trent said. "I could take you on a little tour of Greenfields. See the old school, maybe the church too. We might find Marie's and Jack's graves."

A shiver of excitement coursed through Charlie. "I'd actually love that," she said, smiling again.

"Bring your voodoo," Trent joked, referring to the collection of items Tess had gifted her.

"Ha-ha. Okay, I will. Thank you so much for today. I'm such a mess and you've just been the best. Better than anyone could have expected you to be."

"Happy to formally welcome you as part of our little town's family," Trent said. "Let's meet here at 10:00 a.m. tomorrow. I live close by. My partner Brent starts work at 9:00 a.m., so I'll be free as a bird by then."

"Did you say Brent?" Charlie giggled. "Trent and Brent?"

"Don't even start, honey," Trent pushed her shoulder playfully. "I've heard it all before! And besides, there's slim pickings in country towns for *straight* people."

"Okay then." She was still laughing, wiping a tear from her eye. "It's a plan."

* * *

The next morning, Charlie felt animated as she pulled into the library car park just before ten. She'd exchanged phone numbers with Trent the day before. He'd promised there wouldn't be any peanut butter on toast for breakfast, without any nervous prompting necessary on her part. It had felt like an instant and effortless connection between them. And she hadn't realised just how much she'd missed real human interaction, not over a device, and not briefly over a counter and through a mask. Irrationally she felt a pang of guilt she hadn't told Tess yet, but figured she'd call her that night.

Trent gave her a friendly peck on the cheek as he jumped into the passenger seat of Charlie's RAV4. She did her best not to flinch, even though her entire body tensed. *No peanut butter for breakfast*, she reminded herself. *How long has it been since someone pecked my cheek? Nine months? More?*

"Hi!" Charlie said, a little breathless. It wasn't a romantic date, but making friends in your forties sure felt like dating. "Thanks so much, again, for today."

"Are you kidding?" Trent beamed happily. "I never get to do fieldwork, and I never get to meet new people. Thank *you* for livening up my Thursday." From the research she'd done before purchasing her cottage, Charlie knew there were only around eight hundred people in Greenfields. A small town with a grocer, library, small hospital (more of a large health clinic really), pub with dodgy motel rooms, church, post office, a few smaller shops, and of course the school. The school was only a five-minutes drive from the library, on the edge of town. Everything in Greenfields was only five-minutes drive.

"How old is the school?" Charlie asked, to fill the short drive.

"Well, there was what we call a 'bush school' at that site from as early as 1860. It was run out of an old shed by a single teacher. The permanent school only opened in 1921, after the war. It's always been an area school, so we get heaps of kids coming from around here, as far as an hour away by bus."

"I'm ashamed to admit I know bugger all about the history of schooling in this country."

"Is that an invitation to bore you?" Trent teased.

"Only a little…"

"Okay, a history of Australian schooling in two minutes or less…" He took a deep breath dramatically but continued in his even tone. "Us lucky Aussies have had free government-run education since the early twentieth century in every state and territory. Sure, we were still misogynistic: boys learnt geography and science, and girls learnt how to knit and darn. But at least they all got their maths and English. And only the boys tended to get the cane, at least on the regular. Here it is. Turn left."

Charlie pulled up on the side of the road. The sound of children screaming and laughing was audible even this far from the gates. "Shit, I didn't think about that. Of course the school is full of kids."

"And on recess too," Trent said. "I guess two childless adults wandering the grounds might ring a few alarm bells, huh?"

The school, made from red and sandstone bricks, was a decent size. The front office had a high-pointed tin roof, while the rest of the classrooms — surrounding a green oval — were more understated. A sign out front noted it was an "historic" school, operating for more than a century. Charlie tried to picture it as it must have been all those decades ago. Would the kids still make such a ruckus with the cane looming over them? She supposed they would have.

Trent seemed to read her mind. "There were a lot more rules back then. Rules for everything, from how to sit on your bench to how to hold your pen."

"I had rules for my pen too. I even had to get a pen license."

"Sure, but at least you wouldn't have been walloped over the back of the knuckles with a ruler if you didn't hold your pen correctly, sit up straight, or — God forbid — were a leftie."

"What about home schooling?" Charlie asked, thinking back to her dream and her comprehension that Marie had been kept home with Alice and Florence well past the age of six.

"I don't know..." Trent mused, tilting his head to the side. "Ah, you've stumped me. I guess it wasn't really a thing back then. You just went to school."

"And if you didn't go to school?"

Trent shrugged. "I guess you just didn't. Even though it was compulsory, no one really followed up back then. Not in these country areas at least. It was more likely your neighbour would keep you honest than the council. It was easier to get away with keeping your kids on the farm for manual labour." A bell rang and the noise of the kids reached a crescendo as they raced to their classrooms. "On to the cemetery?"

"On to the cemetery."

# 11

## Uncovering the Unseen

For a small town, Greenfields Church had a large cemetery. Hundreds of graves spread out behind the building over several large fenced areas. Charlie never felt so insignificant as when she stared at old cemeteries like these, with not a living soul in sight. Each grave represented a person who'd lived an ordinary life, now mostly forgotten. Charlie had spent most of her life grinding away behind a desk. She had made lasting impacts through her work — she knew that. But no-one would remember them. Her cases weren't exactly history-making. And no one would remember it had been her. It was both a gloomy and a freeing thought. Even the things in life that mattered could rarely be immortalised.

"It's a bigger cemetery than I expected," Charlie said as they stepped out of the car. She took off her cardigan, feeling the warm sun beating down from the cloudless sky.

"And would you believe they closed it to new interments in the eighties? Nowadays, most people get buried in the next town over."

"Good thing I brought us lunch. We'll be here all day!" Charlie felt instantly morbid for suggesting a picnic in a cemetery.

"Good thing I brought us wine!" Trent responded, instantly relieving her of her discomfort. Trent led them through an old metal gate into the first part of the cemetery. "These first few graves will be from the nineteenth century. I guess we'll just split up and go for it."

As Charlie wove through the graves, which did start in the 1850s, she read the names of all those who'd lived and died here so many years before. Most of the older tombstones were so worn she could barely make out the names. Others were leaning or completely worn and toppled. The feeling of insignificance pressed down even harder when she passed these graves.

It was almost twenty minutes before she found them. Her whole body tingled as she read the name "Evans" atop the first tombstone. She inhaled deeply, holding her breath as she took the last few steps to the stone, and bent to brush the lichen and dirt from the inscription: Jack William Evans, 11 February 1932–20 March 1934, Son of William and Emma. It was a simple inscription, but with a beautifully engraved lamb surrounded by flowers atop it. To the right were two slightly taller stones. Darker and smoother but equally as simple. The first read, Emma Bernadette Evans, 5 July 1902–12 October 1964, Wife, Sister, Mother, Grandmother. The second read, William David Evans, 12 August 1900–28 December 1980, Husband, Brother, Father, Grandfather, Great-Grandfather. These two were in better condition than Jack's, though they were still starting to grow lichen.

Charlie knelt as she reached the final grave: Marie Patricia Evans, 23 March 1927–19 July 1936, Daughter of William and Emma. A dove was engraved above the words, just as ornate as Jack's lamb. She was obviously much loved. "Marie," Charlie whispered, placing one hand on the grave. In that moment, she felt such a connection to the history of her house, and to her new town, it was almost like it reverberated through her. To think little Marie's body was laid to rest right here. Just six feet below the surface.

"Have you found them?" Trent called out. He'd obviously looked back and seen her kneeling there.

"Yes!" she yelled. "Yes, they're all here!"

Trent was soon by her side, whistling through his teeth. "Ooh, they got the plots together. They mustn't have been too bad off after all."

"And don't forget they had connections," Charlie said, pulling some of the stray grass and weeds out of the plot. "One of Marie's sisters married the pastor's son. Or at least we think so."

"Looks like Billy was one of the last people buried here too," Trent said, gesturing to the name. "Though seeing how lovingly all these tombstones were carved, I doubt the family would have let them say no." He helped Charlie to her feet, and she brushed the grass and dirt from her knees.

"I can't believe it…" Charlie said. "I never would have found them without your help. I wouldn't have even known their names. Thank you!"

"Somehow I think someone like you would've tracked those answers down one way or another." Charlie gave him a gentle nudge, before taking another deep and calming breath, surveying the graves again. "Let's go back to the car and get the rug and the voodoo." Trent smiled; obviously he wasn't so emotionally connected as Charlie.

"About that…" Charlie said sheepishly. "I was a little embarrassed to bring much… I just brought the tarot cards. I figured that wouldn't look as odd as a giant pink crystal, metal rods, and candles." She scanned the empty cemetery. "Though I don't think it really would have mattered!"

"And tarot works for ghost hunting?" Trent asked sceptically and a little disappointedly.

"Apparently," Charlie answered as they headed back to the car, feeling a bit affronted at the term "hunting," though also too embarrassed to call him out. "I started reading the guidebook last night. It says tarot is for 'uncovering the unseen' and 'revealing what's hidden'. Apparently, the cards can answer questions about pretty much anything you can think to ask."

"Sounds handy to me," Trent said. "Maybe I'll ask a few of my own questions! Honestly I'm just happy not to be gardening or cleaning the house."

They were soon back at Marie's grave, the blanket laid out on the path in front of it. Charlie had picked some of the wild yellow flowers growing by the church car park and placed them tenderly on Marie's grave. Next time she'd bring flowers for all four of them from the grocer. She had no doubt there would be a next time; she wouldn't forget them as long as she lived. She'd also taken photos of the tombstones, which she'd excitedly messaged to Tess with a "look what I found!"

Now sitting cross-legged on the rug, she removed the tarot deck from its case. "You gave me Australian education history 101. Now I get to share tarot 101 with you."

"You sound like an expert already," Trent said, awkwardly shuffling on the rug, trying to get comfortable. Charlie was glad she'd kept herself relatively limber with her regular hikes.

"Oh, I am. I spent an hour studying this guidebook last night. Then I shuffled those cards *real* good! I am so ready. There are five types of cards. Wands, which usually relate to our dreams and goals, and things that haven't started yet. Cups, which are about our emotions and connections. Swords, which are about action, change, power, conflict, and destruction."

"Sounds ominous," Trent chimed in. Charlie raised her eyebrows in response. "Right, right. Sorry, I'm interrupting."

"Pentacles are like the opposite of cups, if I'm getting this right. While cups are still just in the mind, pentacles are manifesting in the world around us. The last type of card is the major arcana. These are like getting a trump card or a wild card in Uno. The guidebook warned me these cards are 'incredibly powerful' and 'not to be taken lightly.'"

"Okay, just talk me through it as we go. How does it work?"

"I need to get the intent and the question straight in my mind. I shuffle the cards until I feel compelled to stop. Then I split the deck into three piles and draw from the deck that calls to me."

"Calls to you?"

"I just won't think about it. I'll go on automatic. The clarity spread is for beginners. You pick four cards — the first is the overall situation, and the next three provide additional information or contributing factors." Charlie took a deep breath, then closed her eyes as she shuffled, trying to still her heart and clear her mind.

"Huummmmm," Trent joked. Charlie opened her eyes with a scolding look. "Okay, okay, I'm serious. Do your thing."

She closed her eyes again and formed a single thought in her head: *revealing what's hidden*. She almost felt a tingle in her fingers when she felt it was time to stop shuffling. Opening her eyes, she let the cards fall into three piles and was immediately drawn to the middle one.

"Here we go!" she said. She placed one card face down on top of the rug and another three face down below it. "Our overarching answer is…" She flipped over the top card. "The ace of pentacles. Right…" She flicked open her guidebook, navigating to the correct page. *"The ace of pentacles represents the power and possibilities of new growth. It is a seed that has taken root, setting your path for the future. You're at the beginning of an important journey.* And pentacles cards are about something manifesting in the real world."

"Like a ghost?" Trent asked.

"Maybe? The next three cards will give us a more rounded-out answer. Ooh, it's a major arcana. *Judgment. Seeking truth. Let go of your fears and opinions. Open your heart, be ready to be reborn.*" Charlie looked up at Trent with an arched eyebrow. "I feel like these cards are a little judgy. I'm working on letting go."

Trent laughed. "I thought this reading was about Marie, not you."

"I guess I didn't really ask about Marie… I just wanted to know what I wasn't seeing in all this." Trent nodded, motioning towards the other two hidden cards. Charlie flipped over the second one. "Another major arcana! This is an important reading then. *The Hierophant. A mentor or teacher will soon appear. Your hunger for knowledge is burning strong, but you've come as far as you can on your own. Be ready.*"

"They're kind of all making sense together…" Trent said, a lot more serious than he had been at the start of the reading. "What's the last one?"

"Another major arcana…" Charlie said, her stomach tightening.

"What does that mean, getting so many major arcana?"

"I don't know… It didn't come up in the guidebook. *The Emperor. He is the father, ever protective, decisive, and reassuring. Clarity of mind is coming. Look to the part of you that stands strong and knows what to do. With help from the sun, the Emperor can see in all directions…* Well, that's cryptic."

"This reading does seem to be more about you than Marie," Trent said thoughtfully. "What do you make of it?"

Charlie looked at the cards all together, took a deep breath, then said what made most sense to her. "I'm at the start of an important new journey. I need to let go of the past and become a new version of myself. I'll need a mentor to help me do this, but in the end, the strength will need to come from within."

"Deep," Trent said.

"Ha-ha, yeah... I guess I didn't know what to expect."

"Me either... Not exactly how I thought ghost hunting would go today." Trent ran a hand through his long brown hair. It instantly flopped back over his forehead. "Well, chuck me the keys, I'll go get us that lunch."

"Yeah..." Charlie said, suddenly feeling drained. "A glass of wine sounds perfect too..."

# 12

# Grey Man

Still fully dressed, Charlie flopped onto her bed. She kicked off her shoes by pushing her heels with her toes, then wriggled up to cuddle into the pillows. After a single glass of wine and half a sandwich, she'd been so tired she could barely keep her eyes open. She'd somehow managed to drop Trent home and make it back to her own cottage, rock music blaring through the speakers to keep herself awake. She'd had to jerk the steering wheel a couple of times when a micro nap had nearly taken her off the road. She blamed the tarot reading; whether from something supernatural or just the concentration she'd put into, it didn't matter: the results were the same.

*I really opened myself up today,* she thought blearily, drifting to sleep. *Look at me, already getting ready for that new beginning...stupid judgmental tarot...* Charlie yawned, rolled over, and fell straight to sleep.

\* \* \*

Slowly she came to, realising night had fallen as she opened her eyes. Groggily she tried to remember what time she'd gone to bed and what day it was. Somehow she'd managed to sleep through the afternoon and well into the evening. Was it already Friday? Or was it still late on Thursday? A creaking floorboard brought her attention to the bedroom door, its outline visible despite the gloom in her bedroom. She realised creaking floorboards were what had woken her in the first place.

Lying still, Charlie strained her ears to hear again. There were definitely footsteps *inside* her house. Very softly, and very slowly, someone made their way down the hall. Occasionally, another floorboard would creak, each time slightly closer to her bedroom. *Fuck... Is someone in the house?* she wondered. She lay as still as possible, willing the sounds to stop, hoping for this to be some horrible dream. She felt panic building — *What do you do in situations like this? Do you confront them? Do you pretend to sleep and just let them take what they want?'* She wished she'd installed locks on her bedroom door, though the thought hadn't occurred to her before now. She also wished she had a second landline phone in her bedroom.

The footsteps stopped right outside her door. From her position on the bed, rolled slightly onto one side, she saw the shadow of two feet behind the door. She squeezed her eyes shut, begging this to be another surreal, vivid dream. *It's just a dream. It's just a dream. It's just a dream...* she repeated over and over.

A squeaking hinge sounded as her bedroom door was pushed free. Charlie's eyes shot open; there'd be no pretending she was asleep. Even though her entire house was dark, she could see clearly enough to find no one standing in the hallway. But someone — or something — had opened her door. Another possibility struck her. *Marie...?* Charlie thought — hoped — as her eyes flicked back and forth across the open doorway.

*No...* she heard a frightened child whisper. But the whisper was only in Charlie's head. So faint she could have imagined it. Perhaps she even thought the words to herself. The fear in that single word certainly matched her own level of dread. Unease built in the room, and Charlie was now sure that whatever was behind the door was not Marie, and it was not human. And it was in her room.

A creak sounded again, this time from the corner. Charlie tried to roll over, to sit, to stare at the corner, but her body wouldn't cooperate. No matter how hard she tried, she couldn't move; she was frozen. The only thing in her control were her eyes. She strained to look as far to the left as she could. Just in the corner of her eye, crouched in the dark, was a figure. Two white pinpricks of light glowed brightly where its eyes should be. Charlie tried to shriek, but it wasn't just her body that was paralysed; no sound left her mouth. *What the fuck?!* screamed in Charlie's head. *Move! Move!* Even though she'd only caught a glimpse of it, she knew. She knew it was the same monster she'd seen in her video call with Tess. The creature that had slunk in the dark corner, with its bright-white and gleaming eyes. Only this time, Charlie wasn't looking through a screen.

She watched in horror as the creature drew itself out of the shadows. It had obviously been hunching, because as it came forward it stood as tall as the ceiling, its pinprick eyes gleaming down at her. It was incredibly thin, its head bulbous on its body. From her position on the bed, everything but her eyes frozen, she couldn't even see if the creature had a mouth. It appeared to only have two large eyes in its oversize head. It took one step closer, and Charlie lost sight of it as it moved behind her. The unease in the room built even further, like a static charge. She could almost feel, even if she couldn't see, the creature circling around behind her.

The bed shifted as something — as *it* — climbed onto the edge of the bed. Charlie tried to scream again, to wrench her body away from it, as she felt it edge closer to her body. She remained still and quiet, as though her limbs were made of stone. She was panting heavily now. Although she couldn't squeeze even a whimper of sound out, her breaths had no trouble rising in a panic. The creature moved agonisingly slowly across the bed, its weight shifting the mattress, until she felt it climb over her. Even though the creature was impossibly slim, as it slithered over her its weight crushed her so much she was gasping for breath.

She flicked her eyes over her shoulder to try to see the creature again and looked straight into its white, piercing eyes. The stress and anxiety she longed to release in a scream boiled inside her as the thing finished climbing on top of her. It looked down on her, its face inches from hers. She could see now that it didn't have a mouth, or even a nose, though the impression of both were there. It was like its grey, wet skin had grown over every orifice. Everything except those eyes.

Desperately, Charlie tried squeezing her own eyes closed, but even this was beyond her. Completely trapped in her own body, she couldn't even blink. The grey man loomed over her for what felt an eternity. Inside her head, Charlie's panic rose to insane levels. She felt as though her mind were coming loose from her body from sheer terror. After the longest five minutes of her life, as she stared directly into its horrible, shining eyes, the creature finally moved. But not away. In its slow motion, its head lowered so close to her face that mere millimetres separated them. It raised its hand, long fingers reaching towards her. Just as Charlie thought her mind would snap, the skin where the grey man's mouth should have been sucked in, forming a large circle, as though it were breathing her in.

The sound it made next was almost indescribable. It bellowed, a horrific sound expelling from its belly in an impossibly deep boom that made Charlies ribs rattle. Although she couldn't physically scream back, her own scream shook in her mind. She wished she would pass out from the fear — anything to remove herself from this living nightmare. Suddenly the creature's hand swiped across her face. The lightning-fast movement was a stark juxtaposition to its previously gradual movements. Its fingers on her skin were like burning ice and fire at the same time. Its sharp nails pushed the sensation deep into her skin. The force of the blow threw her from the bed and across the floor, driving the wind from her lungs as she slid against the wall. In that moment, full control of her body was hers again. She rolled onto her back and scooted onto her bottom, her chest heaving, every limb shaking, tears rolling down her face, whimpers finally escaping her mouth. Her face burned where the creature had struck her.

As Charlie's eyes darted all over the room, she saw it was empty again. The feeling of unease that had reached an unbearable level also started to whither. Without thinking, she jumped to her feet and ran to the bedroom door. She looked both ways in distress and dread before running towards the front of her cottage. Passing the kitchen, she saw in the blurred corners of her eye that once again all cupboard doors had blown open and things were stacked in crazy patterns across the bench and table.

She didn't stop to inspect. She tried to grab her bag, crying out in despair as it fell to the floor. As she bent to pick it up, she felt as though every corner of her house were watching her, pressing in on her. She also felt as though she were moving as slowly as the creature had in her room. Finally clutching the bag, she stumbled to the front door, wrestling with the lock. As soon as she could throw open the front door, she bolted for her car. She didn't bother to shut and lock the cottage behind her. As she got to her SUV, she retched, bile spilling onto the dirt and splashing her feet. She didn't look back as she sped to the road and towards Greenfields.

* * *

The owner of the Grey Gum Inn had looked at Charlie curiously and sceptically as she'd handed Charlie her motel room keys. Her eyes had lingered on Charlie's bare, dirty feet and noted her tousled hair and clothes. "Do you need anything else?" The question came with both judgment and perhaps a little worry — Charlie had needed to call the emergency after-hours number to book a room, which probably hadn't helped with the woman's mood.

"No, no, I'm fine. Thanks." Charlie shivered as she walked away from the counter.

The night had gotten cooler, but it was her body itself that felt like ice — inside and out. By the time she'd gotten to the motel it was 9:00 p.m., earlier than she'd thought. She was still dead tired, despite having fallen asleep in the afternoon. She fumbled her key in the door lock — there were no swipe cards here — and gratefully fell into the room. After flicking on the light, she skittishly scanned every corner.

While there was water damage, dust, cobwebs, and strange dark patches on the carpet, these were problems she happily accepted. These were material, real-world problems. The guests in the room next to her were making reassuring, real life noises as well. Banging and crashing in the kitchenette, while the children yelled at each other and the TV blared. The walls were so thin she could hear — and smell — what seemed to be onions frying.

Charlie sat on the edge of the bed, which somehow was both hard and squishy, and drew in a deep, shuddering breath. The room was the same size as her own master bedroom, but they'd crammed in a kitchenette, TV, and small sofa. *What am I going to do?* Charlie buried her head in her hands, trying to get the images of the supernatural intruder out of her head. Even though the memory was already starting to blur around the edges, the fear was still vivid. Also vivid was the image of the creature reaching its hand out to her, which played on repeat in her head.

As Charlie cupped her face in her hand, she winced. Her right cheek was still sore from where she'd been struck. She headed to the small bathroom and looked in the mirror under the bright yellow light. Across her face were three discernible scratches — red, raised, and ragged. She shuddered again. "I didn't imagine anything..." she whispered, hands clenching into fists.

As delectable smells drifted in from the room next door, Charlie's stomach grumbled. Her stomach, at least, had no concern for the supernatural. As she breathed in the rich, salty smell again, she felt a familiar tingling sensation in the middle of her throat. The tingling was like an itchy, prickling tickle that quickly spread. "Oh, shit..." Charlie ran back to the bed, grabbing her bag and rummaging inside for her EpiPen. The delicious smell was obviously some kind of peanut-based dish. By the time she'd grabbed the pen she was already wheezing, the scratchiness in her throat seeming to grow fingers and tighten around her windpipe. The room was starting to blacken around the edges.

With her thumb, she flicked the blue safety cap from the edge of the pen, then pushed the orange end firmly into her thigh until it clicked. A sharp pain stabbed her. A welcome and familiar pain. Within seconds her breathing started to improve, though it still came in raspy gasps. Thinking of her desperate need to call the hospital, Charlie realised she'd left her phone at home in her haste to escape. The room was now spinning, her stomach lurching. She stumbled to her feet, making for the door. Her vision narrowed as she reached the handle. *I just have to get outside...*

"Help!" she croaked. "Help!"

In that moment, consciousness fled and she crashed through the door.

# 13

# Night Terrors

Once again it was sound that woke Charlie, but this time it was an all-too-familiar one. The beep of hospital monitors. She blinked groggily. Her chest felt crushed, each breath ragged and painful. Her eyes were half swollen shut. Charlie's nostrils were cold and irritated by the oxygen tubes. Her heart thumped so strongly it felt like she'd transformed into one of those cartoon characters with its heart beating out of its chest. To top it off, her mouth was full of a rancid metallic taste.

Lifting her heavy head slightly, she saw a drip in each arm. One no doubt filling her system back up with magnesium — the cause of the metallic taste. The other undoubtedly steadily filling her with adrenaline — the cause of her pounding heart. Unlike most people, once Charlie's body started dumping histamine, it didn't always know how to stop. If she knew procedure — and she knew it well — she'd also be pumped with steroids and antihistamines. At least she hadn't been intubated this time.

As Charlie let her head flop back on the pillow, she felt something she hadn't before — it was like her mind was becoming clearer as she lay there. She was increasingly aware of every part of her body. At the same time, the painful, uncomfortable sensations started to drift away. All sensation except her pounding heart. *This isn't normal*, she thought, looking around the hospital room wide-eyed. Every detail of the room stood out with crystal precision. It was a private room but not in the ICU. She guessed the local hospital didn't have an ICU — and when she was as bad as she was now, it would be too dangerous to move her. The pounding in her chest stopped. She drew a couple of breaths as she lay there, waiting for her heart to resume pumping.

*What...? Is my heart... Is my heart not beating?* Charlie's clarity of mind grew even stronger as the rest of her body turned numb. *My heart isn't beating...* It was her fingers and toes that lost sensation first, the numbness feeling like she was slowly being swallowed whole by blackness. *Why isn't my heart beating?* Next it was her legs, her arms, her stomach and torso. *Why am I still conscious?* As those thoughts raced through her head, the numbness that had overtaken her body started to take her mind as well. She was vaguely aware of alarms sounding, feet pounding, and people yelling. But it slipped away so calmly as blackness swallowed her.

* * *

Charlie found herself back in the dream world, in the land of platforms — the Waiting Place. This time the world was still. There was no mechanical dizziness. No unorganised spinning. Even as she walked through the archways and up the gravity-defying staircases, nothing shifted.

Vaguely she was aware of what had happened to her in the hospital, but that felt like a dream now. And a dream that was slipping away, so hard to remember. Charlie wandered timelessly, and tirelessly, the landscape changing but somehow constant. *I want to see my mother,* she thought. She turned to her left and stepped through the closest archway. She was standing in her mother's nursing home — St Dymphna. Elsa sat in one of the common rooms, by the window. She was hunched slightly, her clothes drooping from her too-thin frame. White, thin hair clung haphazardly to her head, messily caressing the back of her wrinkled neck in a loose bun. Gunk filled the corner of both eyes, and Charlie longed to reach out and clean her weathered face. A cup of warm tea and two biscuits sat on a table beside her. Elsa ignored them. She merely stared out the window.

*Mum,* Charlie communicated without words.

Elsa looked up, confused, staring around the common room. "Hello?" she croaked. "Who's there?" she said a little louder.

"Pipe down, Elsa," another resident complained. "You crazy old bat."

*You're not crazy, Mum. I'm here.*

"No! Get away, get away!" Elsa yelled, drawing the attention of two nearby nurses. "You can't be here! Get out! Get out!!" As Elsa kept shrieking, Charlie took two steps back. Her mother faded from view, and Charlie was once again in her Waiting Place.

Turning, Charlie saw another familiar figure. The shimmering white man with his top hat. He was there only a moment before fading away as well. *You started all this,* Charlie thought. *But all what?* Her thoughts started to become clearer again. As she remembered the white man, she also remembered Marie and her little cottage, the research with Trent, and the "voodoo" with Tess. The memory of the grey man looming over her, reaching for her, also became clear. *I know there are answers here...*

Charlie walked to another archway, thinking of how she wanted to know what was happening to her. She didn't need to step through this next archway to know it led to her bedroom, to the moment the grey man had attacked her. From what felt like a high vantage point, she saw the grey man swipe her, hurling her from the bed and into the wall. After flinging her effortlessly, the creature looked up to where the present Charlie was watching. Their eyes locked and Charlie knew it could see her. Time had slowed to a near stop in the memory that played out through the archway. She watched herself roll in slow motion.

Meanwhile, the grey creature was pulled towards her by some invisible force through the archway and into the Waiting Place. She felt unease and dread again as it drew closer, but not the primal fear that had forced her to flee her home. Here, in this dream place, the grey man was back to being a short, if still slim, man. *What are you?* Charlie wondered.

The creature took a step towards her before answering strongly in her mind, *I am Lam.*

＊＊＊

75

Charlie's eyes fluttered open once again. Her chest still ached terribly and her eyes were still dry, but this time she felt more together. There was no other way to describe it. The clarity of mind was most certainly gone. Although she was bone tired, she could at least keep her eyes open. Breathing hurt but wasn't laboured. And although the cannulas were still in, the drips had been removed.

"Welcome back." At the familiar voice, Charlie turned to see Trent sitting in a chair beside her. "You gave us quite a scare. You really weren't kidding around with this allergy stuff."

"Trent?" she rasped.

Trent stood and handed her a plastic cup from the bedside table. "They told me to try to get you to drink this if you woke up. It's been almost twenty-four hours with only fluid through a drip."

Charlie took the cup thankfully, slowly swallowing with her dry and aching throat. "How'd you know where I was?" she asked, feeling down the side of her bed for the button that would elevate her to a sitting position.

"It's a small town. Everyone pretty much knows everything. Plus, I'm a regular at the Grey Gum Inn." Trent stood and helped elevate the bed. At the same time, he pressed the call button for the nurse.

Charlie heard the bell ringing, echoing in the hallway. "How long have you been here?" she asked, finally sitting, the pillows propped behind her.

"Only an hour or so. Visiting hours are nearly up. I just thought I'd pop in after work, see how you're getting on and—" He paused as a small, plump nurse bustled in. Her blonde hair had so many whites in it, it was hard to tell where the blonde ended and the white began.

"Well, that's a relief." She checked Charlie's vitals on the monitor. "I'm Cathy. Do you know where you are?"

"Hospital…" Charlie responded groggily. "Don't worry, I remember. There were peanuts at the motel."

"You made quite a good mess falling through that door," Cathy said. "At least it was loud enough to alert your neighbours, and you still had the EpiPen in your hands when you fell, which was a good clue as to what was happening. What's the last thing you remember?"

Charlie blinked a couple of times to clear her head. "That's it," she said. "Falling through the door. Maybe glimpses of the hospital. Did-did I die?"

"Not quite." Cathy smiled. "Okay, everything looks good here for now. I'll let the doctor know you're awake and she'll be by when she can." Cathy patted Charlie's shoulder. "You keep drinking. And ring that bell if you need me."

Trent took the cup from Charlie and placed it on the bedside. "I wanted to ask…" he said tentatively. "What were you doing at the Grey Gum? I don't understand. Did something happen?"

"I…" Charlie said, not quite knowing how to explain. "I-I got scared at the house. I thought someone was there."

"Marie?" Trent asked. "Did you spook yourself at the cemetery?"

"No…like an intruder."

"What?! Why didn't you call the police? Why didn't you call me?"

Charlie clenched her hands as she answered. "I… He was… I couldn't see him properly… He looked…supernatural. I didn't know if he was, you know, real." Trent's blank face made her stomach flip. "I'm going completely mental."

"Hey, no way. You're going through a lot — you've just been through a lot. Cut yourself some slack."

"It scratched my face," Charlie motioned to her cheek, which still felt tender. Her whole body did.

"I hate to say this," Trent said. "But you banged your face up pretty good falling through that door. If there was a scratch there, it's covered up with other bumps, cuts, and bruises now." Charlie tentatively put a hand to her cheekbone, wincing as she did. "I talked to your friend, Tess. She's on her way down too. The hospital reckons you'll only need two or three more nights, and Tess will be here before they check you out."

"Tess?" Charlie's heart warmed in her chest. The fear and anxiety she didn't realise she was still holding on to so tightly dissipated a little.

"Yeah, she's your emergency contact. She freaked out when the hospital called apparently. I talked to her just after I got here, reassured her you were doing fine. She said she was planning on visiting anyway, so now was as good a time as any. She's feisty, she is."

"That's my Tess." Suddenly exhausted again, she sank farther back into the pillows.

"You rest," Trent said, jumping to his feet. "Do you need anything?" Charlie shook her head. Trent gave her a quick peck on the forehead as she closed her eyes. She heard his footsteps as he left the room.

* * *

Two days later, Charlie was ready to check out. She had strict instructions on when to return to hospital if anything went wrong, as well as a tapered dose of steroids to keep her airways from collapsing. The discharge papers were ready; the prescription was in a bag by her bed; and the nurse had helped her change out of her hospital gown and into her old, smelly clothes from Thursday. Tess had promised she was only a few minutes away, having driven up from Sydney. Trent had already organised for Charlie's SUV to be dropped back at her place. A pang of anger struck Charlie as she thought of what he had done when he'd left her hospital room two days before. She couldn't wait to get as far from this hospital, and this town, as possible. Amongst Charlie's discharge paperwork was a referral for a psychologist. Trent had told the nurse about Charlie's fear of an intruder. Even though she hadn't asked him not to, she was mortified. The local police had been dispatched to her property, where they'd found the front door flung open but no signs of forced entry. Dining chairs had toppled to the floor, and the kitchen was a mess of crockery, but they'd said there was nothing suspicious. No extra tyre tracks, no extra footprints. Charlie knew they thought she'd had a mental breakdown; in fact, she felt like she'd had a mental breakdown. The doctors had told her it was most likely an episode of sleep paralysis.

Just as Charlie finished brushing her hair with a gifted sanitary kit from the hospital, Tess burst through the doors. She seemed to have dressed hurriedly, her loose top hanging from one shoulder, one pocket untucked in her baggy 'mum' jeans. Instantly the room, and Charlie's heart, filled with Tess's warm, infectious glow. *"Ma chère!"* Tess yelled, running to envelop

Charlie in a hug. "You need to stop doing this to me! I have enough grey hairs." Charlie struggled to see *any* grey in her shiny, dark hair.

"Tess!" Charlie breathed, hugging her close. Relief flooded her — not just that she could leave the hospital but that she finally felt safe again. "I am so, so grateful you're here. I'm not even going to pretend to say you shouldn't have come."

"Ah, it's long overdue," Tess deflected. "Now come on. Let's spring you out of here. God, hospitals are depressing."

# 14

# Douloureux

Tess fluffed the pillows behind Charlie's head before jumping into the bed herself and lying beside her. "Your friend Trent told me you were worried about an intruder, but oh, *la vache*! I never imagined something so terrifying." Charlie had recounted what had happened that night in full detail, leaving nothing out. It was the first time she'd shared the full story with anyone.

"And now you know why I've been referred to a psychologist…" Charlie said, leaning her head on Tess's shoulder. She winced slightly and readjusted so the most painful parts of her face were cushioned. "I'm a complete looney. Their theory is an episode of sleep paralysis and hallucination brought on by stress. I've never had sleep paralysis in my life."

Tess wrapped her arms around Charlie. "What do you think it was, darling?"

"Whatever that creature was, it scratched my face. How is that a hallucination? And I know I fell through that door when my blood pressure dropped, but I saw the scratches in the mirror before the anaphylaxis even started."

"Did you mention this to the doctor?"

"Of course." Charlie sighed. "You know what Trent said? He said maybe I scratched my face when I fell out of bed. I'm the most rational person I know. I've never believed in ghosts or supernatural beings. You know me. But something's going on here."

"I believe you, darling." Tess stroked Charlie's head. "But perhaps now you just tell me these things, hmm? Leave the spooky stuff to me. I'm your research buddy, remember."

"Mmmm," Charlie replied, letting Tess's soothing strokes relax her. She was always exhausted for days after an anaphylaxis episode. "Trent said he believed in the supernatural too, but I guess this was too much even for a believer."

"You're not crazy, *ma chère*, but seeing a psychologist might not be a bad idea. A lot has happened to you, ghosts aside. They may be able to help." Charlie would have sent anyone else daring to suggest such a thing marching from the house, but coming from Tess, it sounded rational.

Charlie mumbled affirmatively as sleep took her.

* * *

"Okay, psychologists or the grey man?" Tess asked. "Your choice. What are we searching for first?" Tess sat on an armchair with Charlie's laptop, while Charlie sat on the couch nursing a fresh cup of Russian Caravan tea. It's light, rich flavour sat delightfully on her tongue.

"Let's delay. Hit me up with the grey man. What does the internet say about him?"

"Hmmm…" Tess said after a few moments typing. "Well, that's not helpful. The first results are all about some ghost haunting South Carolina. Oh, he's friendly, though. He warns people when there's going to be bad weather… Okay…trying a different search… Ooh, Ryan Gosling!"

"Huh?"

"Sorry, sorry… It's a movie…also called *The Gray Man*. Let's try typing in a description instead. You said grey, tall, thin. Anything more?"

"White eyes," Charlie said, shuddering despite the blanket over her knees and the warm cup of tea. "Tall…thin…grey…man… White eyes…"

"Hmm…nothing with white eyes, but the first result is something called *Am Fear Liath Mor*. Ew. A tall, thin creature that hides in fog and shadow and stalks people…in Scotland… Again, not your man. Unless he's on holiday."

They continued searching for several more minutes. Various names for the same creature came up across many different folklore. Some talked about a creature that gave warnings. Others, about a creature that stalked people and brought a sense of unease. The most unsettling was an account of a grey creature that tried to exchange its shadow with that of a living person.

The search soon took them to "sleep paralysis demons," an unsettling — and medical — terminology for hallucinations associated with sleep paralysis. They were far more common than Tess or Charlie had realised, with hundreds of online accounts of strange beings stalking people in their bedrooms. Some were linked to the same folklore and fables they'd already found, and there was mention of them in every culture around the world. But still, none of these cultures had the answers Charlie was looking for — it all just raised more questions.

"There's one more thing we could search…" Tess said slowly.

"Hm?" Charlie answered, placing her empty mug on the coffee table.

"Aliens. Little grey men." Charlie burst out laughing. "Hey! Don't laugh. You got all upset before about people thinking you were crazy."

"Okay, okay, you're right." Charlie wiped a tear from her eye. "Tell me about the little grey men."

"Hmmm…" Tess said after scrolling for a couple of minutes. "According to Wikipedia, it's the most commonly sighted alien… Ah, but black eyes, not white… Ooh, they were first written about by a novelist in 1891. So, they were made up by a white man, typical. The folklore we've found, however, goes back way before then… Ugh, look at this ugly guy." Tess left her armchair and sat next to Charlie on the couch. It was a pencil drawing of a man with a huge head and small eyes. Beneath it was the caption "Crowley's Drawing of Lam." Charlie stiffened, Tess noticing as she did so. "*Que*, you recognise him?"

"No, no, no…" Charlie said, taking the laptop from Tess. "I am Lam…" she repeated. "That's what it said, in my dream…" Charlie typed into the search bar again, navigating through several useless webpages. "Here, the occultist Aleister Crowley claimed to have summoned Lam from another dimension, through a portal, in 1917. Man, they created a whole religion around it."

She kept searching for another ten minutes or so, recounting to Tess what she found. Many others claimed to have come across Lam since the renowned occultist Crowley first spoke about his encounter. The accounts differed widely, and many thought Lam was a type of creature rather than an individual. In all the accounts, one commonality struck her, a singular feeling: terror.

"Okay, I need to stop this now." Charlie passed the computer back to Tess. "This isn't helping at all! There's no consensus on this online, and it *literally* sounds insane."

"*Oui, ma chère,*" Tess put an arm around Charlie's shoulder. "It doesn't matter. I'm here now. If it tries to come back, I'll beat it silly. I'll scare it so bad it never rears its ugly, bulbous head again." Charlie chuckled. "Now…" Tess continued, taking the laptop back. "Psychologists… Not because this isn't actually happening, remember! But because you deserve to be heard and supported. Huh…look, there's an ad for one on your browser. Talk about fortuitous."

"Talk about Google hacking my phone and tracking my every move," Charlie joked. They read the ad together:

*Maryanne Miller, trained psychologist, thirty years' experience. Specialties include trauma, hallucinations, nightmares, feelings of disassociation, terminal diagnoses, and near-death experiences.*

"Sounds like your perfect match."

"Click the link," Charlie directed.

Maryanne's page was simple. A photo of a kind-looking Caucasian woman, her head wrapped in a scarf, sat at the top of the page. While her hair was covered, her eyebrows were dark. They stood out starkly, along with her deep red lips, in a sheet-white face. Below the photo was a short bio, which said she only took appointments via telehealth. The fees tab showed very reasonable — almost too reasonable — rates. An "Enquire Now" button flashed on the right side. "I like that her name is Maryanne." Charlie smiled.

"Reminds me of Marie."

"Enquire?"

Charlie nodded. "What's the harm? Let's do it."

* * *

Charlie hated the tight, pinched feeling in her chest as she walked with Tess down the gentle slope of the back of her property. She still wasn't up to facing the undulating hills. At least not so soon after her medical ordeal. Tess, who had her arm looped loosely through Charlie's, slowed her pace without saying a word. "I love how big your property is!" she beamed, obviously thriving in the clean air and open space. "I knew you said it was big, but I never expected this. You're like a lady of a manor!"

"Ha," Charlie wheezed. "Lady of an old little cottage." She smiled. "But yes, I can't believe it too sometimes. Now can you understand why I moved out here?"

"I'm still not going to forgive you for abandoning me." Tess grinned. "But maybe it'll be *me* moving in with *you* when we're old and grey, not the other way around." They heard the creek bubbling before they saw it through the gum trees. "*Quelle joie!*" Tess glowed as they approached the edge of the creek, colour blooming on her high cheekbones. Already the waters were a little lower than when Charlie had first visited on her own. "It's stunning."

"I still don't know why I don't come here more often." Charlie smiled as she sat by the tree, resting her back against the bark, grateful for the chance to catch her breath. Tess sat next to her and held her hand, the quiet washing over them both. The light filtering through the green of the gum leaves was soft and sparkling with dust motes. It was easy to believe they were the only two people in the world.

"I guess I understand…" Tess said after a long pause. "It's a special place, yes, but it also feels… a little…*douloureux*…"

"*Douloureux?*" Charlie repeated with her awful French accent.

"Painful…aching…sorrowful…grievous… There's no good English word for it."

84

Charlie cocked her head as she took in her surroundings again. A parakeet and its mate sang in a nearby tree, and a slight breeze rustled the leaves of the trees. It was peaceful — there was no doubt about it — but she could understand what Tess meant. *Melancholy* was an appropriate English word for it.

"I guess there's lots of memories here," Charlie said after a moment.

"Maybe not all so good," Tess mused. "Perhaps that's why you never come down?"

"I wonder if it's because of Jack...or Marie. In my dreams she was sad her mother kept her home."

"Because *l'enfant* passed away. She wanted to keep them safe. I understand... But yes, it's sad too." Tess stood up and dusted off her palms. "Enough talk of sad things. Ready to head back?" It hadn't been a long rest, but Charlie was definitely ready to return to the cottage with her friend. She lifted a hand for Tess to help her to her feet.

"You know I'm going to be slower going home — it's uphill," she said. "I might need you to carry me."

*"Tu aimerais bien hein?"*

"I take that as a no." Charlie laughed.

"I've decided something," Tess said as they walked back.

"What's that?"

"I'm going to take you to visit your *maman*."

# 15

# The Crazy Psych

Tess and Charlie agreed to drive to Sydney to visit Elsa that Thursday. It gave Charlie an extra day for the bruises on her face to fade enough for concealer to work its magic. And it meant they could stick to her schedule of a Wednesday trip to town for the post and grocer. Charlie was excited to show Tess the cemetery where she'd found the Evans's graves. As morbid as it sounded to her out loud, it was a connection she wanted to share. In perfect timing, Maryanne, the psychologist, had replied to Charlie's enquiry, saying she'd had a cancellation for that morning.

Tess had given Charlie privacy, leaving to explore the hills Charlie loved. Charlie, meanwhile, sat at her desk, her laptop open, waiting for Maryanne to call her. She felt nervous and clammy, all sorts of tactics for how to approach the session running through her head. She'd thought about leaving out the spooky details and focussing only on her health. She'd also considered going the whole hog and explaining her supernatural theories, even touching on little grey aliens. In the end, she landed somewhere in the middle. She committed to herself that she would tell her experiences in full, but through the lens of rational explanation: night terrors and an old creaky house. See what Maryanne made of that.

The laptop beeped twice, and a notification popped up asking if she'd like to accept a call, which she did. A slowly rotating circle flashed twice before Maryanne's face popped up on the screen. She wore a headscarf today as well, just like in her picture, though a different colour and pattern. She was a little older than the photo too — more wrinkles defining a face that was much thinner than in her portrait. She looked eastern European. Charlie found herself wondering about the headscarf. Did Maryanne have cancer? Was it religious? Or was it merely a style choice?

"Hello, Charlotte," Maryanne said in a calm, authoritative, and soothing voice. "Thank you for taking this appointment at such short notice. I'm Dr. Maryanne Miller. Pleased to meet you."

"Hi." Charlie smiled, adjusting her shoulders as she saw through the camera she'd been slumped. "Thank you for seeing me so quickly."

"I'm glad things worked out. Have you seen any kind of therapist before?"

"A couple of years ago, when I first started having health problems. She was a counsellor though, not a psychologist, and she mostly focussed on mindfulness exercises."

"Your enquiry says you're having hallucinations and processing serious health-related trauma. It also mentions recurring dreams. I can certainly help you with this. I usually like to start with some background on your personal situation before diving into the details. But first, can you tell me what you're hoping to get from these sessions?"

"Well…" Charlie started, thinking out loud. "I recently had a health scare, and the hospital thought it would be good for 'processing my trauma.' My best friend thought it would be nice for me to get some more support. And me, honestly, I'd just love some answers as to what's going on."

"Best friend?" Maryanne said, her tone suddenly flat — even disappointed.

"Yes…?" Charlie said.

"Ah, that's interesting…"

"I'm sorry. Interesting how?" Charlie asked, confused.

"No matter. No concern, dear," Maryanne answered. "Okay, let's get into it. Please tell me about your living situation."

"I live on my own usually. I'm in a cottage, pretty rural, in New South Wales, a few hours north of Sydney. We're talking over satellite connection."

"You're isolated?" Maryanne asked, making notes and tilting her head.

"Yeah, I guess so."

"Mm-hmm, and family? What's that situation?"

"I never married…"

"No kids?"

"No, just me." Charlie felt a little staggered by the barrage of questions.

"Living relatives?"

"My mum and my brother. He has a wife and kids."

"And how close are you?" Maryanne lifted her eyes to stare at Charlie through the screen, pausing her rapid-fire note-taking.

"My mum and I used to be very close. But she has dementia, so it's been a bit harder lately. I still try to keep in touch, but it's not the same."

"No, of course not," Maryanne said compassionately. "And your brother?"

"We used to be closer. Not as close as me and Mum but still on good terms. You know how things are as you move out of home, get your own life. Sometimes you drift apart."

"That's true." Maryanne nodded. "And this best friend?"

"Tess." Charlie smiled. Her stomach fluttered at the mention of her name. "We've been friends for over ten years. And I feel like we've known each other even longer. She's my anchor. She even came down to help look after me after my health scare."

"*Anchor.* That's an interesting choice of words…"

"Is it?" Charlie asked.

"Okay, that's enough background." Charlie found it odd Maryanne wasn't digging any further into her past — it felt surface level. Shouldn't there be some delving into her childhood traumas? Her health journey? Her quick transition from city to rural living? "Tell me what's been happening. Let me know about these hallucinations, these dreams."

Charlie took a quick, deep breath, exhaling sharply. "It started about six weeks ago. I'd been seeing things out of the corner of my eye for a while. But then one day there was this…figure standing in my living room."

"What did it look like?"

"Bright white. Glowing. I couldn't see any facial features. I couldn't even tell if it was a man or a woman. But…" Charlie felt the craziness in her words, though Maryanne's bright eyes urged her on. "But it was wearing a top hat…and loafers…"

"Excellent," Maryanne said, writing furiously on her notepad.

"Really?" Charlie said, starting to feel like maybe she wasn't the one who needed help after all.

"Oh, yes, certainly. Now what else, dear?"

"I've seen a grey shadow in the house, with white glowing eyes. Actually, my friend saw it too. Through a video call. That *thing* was what made me run out of my house and end up in the hospital. The grey man was in my bedroom. I was paralysed in my bed, and it climbed on top of me. After what felt like an eternity, it hit me across the face and threw me out of my bed. I had scratches on my cheek and everything. But I guess I must have hit my face as I fell out of bed."

"Is that what you think?" Maryanne asked. Charlie shrugged, noncommittal. "Okay, well, that's no problem." Maryanne brushed off the grey man encounter like Charlie had told her it would be raining that afternoon. "These dreams, what about them?"

Charlie felt drained by Maryanne's interrogation. She was quiet for a moment then said, "They usually start, or end, in the same place. I'm in this greyish-white place full of arches and stations. It's like a waiting place." Maryanne paused in her notetaking. Charlie tried, unsuccessfully, to decipher the meaning behind the woman's blank expression.

"How fascinating," Maryanne eventually said in a muted voice.

"I guess so… I saw the grey man there and the glowing white figure too. And in this place, I've seen my mum, and also my property, where I live. But not as it is today, back in time. When the Evans family lived here."

"Good, good…" Maryanne wrote on her notepad before slamming her pen down and looking up at Charlie with a smile. "Well, you've certainly had quite a lot happening, haven't you?"

"Yeah. I'd love to know what you think."

Maryanne leant back in her chair, adjusting her tunic top over her not insubstantial stomach. "Did you know anxiety can cause hallucinations?" Charlie shook her head. "Of course, sleep paralysis can be brought on by stress, which has been associated with hallucinations too. And you've certainly had your fair share of stress."

Charlie nodded. "So you think that's it?" she said with some hope. Perhaps it was all just anxiety and coincidence.

"What do you think?" Maryanne asked, folding her hands and resting her chin on them.

"Well…" Charlie mused. As nice as it would be to wrap up her problems so neatly, something didn't quite fit. "I haven't felt that anxious since I moved here. In fact, I'd felt content…but something is obviously happening. I want to know what, and I'd like to try whatever you can recommend."

"Okay," Maryanne nodded. "I can definitely help you. But that's enough for today." Charlie's eyes flicked to the time display on her laptop. It had been barely fifteen minutes. "Are you available this Friday for a follow-up? I have a slot at 10:00 a.m."

"Yes," Charlie said. "Yes, I can make that work."

"Excellent. Same deal as today. Now that we've connected, I'll be able to video call you at that time. Just be ready to accept the call. I look forward to seeing you again."

"Wait, don't you need me to pay you?"

Maryanne waved a hand. "Oh, no, the first consultation is free of charge. It really has been a pleasure to meet you, Charlotte."

"You can call me Charlie…"

"I'll be seeing you, Charlotte."

With that, the line disconnected. Charlie slid back into her chair, staring at the blank screen. She didn't know what to make of the whirlwind appointment. *Was that a normal session?* She wasn't sure what a normal psychology session was. Tess would be gone at least another forty minutes. Shakily, Charlie got to her feet and walked to the kitchen to boil the kettle. *She didn't even ask about the bruises on my face*, she thought as she pulled a mug from the cupboard. *Maybe she sees this type of thing all the time?*

As she sat on the couch with her steaming cup of tea, she pulled out her phone and searched for "Maryanne Miller, psychologist, Victoria, Australia." The first result was Maryanne's website. Charlie added the word "review" to her query, and a selection of Google reviews helpfully popped up, showing an average two-star rating. Charlie didn't know why she hadn't read the reviews before booking; it was very unlike her. The reviews were very much an average because there were only one-star or five-star reviews.

*One Star: Rushed through my first appointment, then was never available again! Waste of my time. Would give zero stars if I could.*

*One Star: My first appointment went great, but then she never returned my booking enquiries. She completely ghosted me. Such a shame as I thought we had a connection.*

*One Star: A bit weird during my first appointment, which was super short, and then I never heard from her again. What the...? At least she didn't charge me. Is she even a psychologist?*

*Five Stars: I don't know what all the negative comments are about. I found Maryanne to be wonderful! So insightful and supportive. She really helped me process the trauma of my husband's death. I would be lost without her. Can't recommend her highly enough.*

Charlie shut off her phone and settled back into her couch, sipping her tea. She didn't know what to make of Maryanne. If the reviews told her anything, it was that she was polarising. *Weird? Yes, she was certainly weird.* But so was Charlie's situation. *Can I really judge her with what I've had going on?* She set her cup of tea on the coffee table and rested her head on the pillow. There was still a chance Maryanne would ghost her too, she supposed. She felt exhausted from all the questions and let her mind wander. In this moment of solitude, it was easy for her to drift off into peaceful sleep.

# 16

## Listen With Your Heart

Charlie and Tess had been driving almost four hours and were minutes from South Sydney, where Charlie's mother resided. Tess had taken first shift behind the wheel — leaving the cottage at 6:00 a.m. while it was still dark — and now slept with her head lolling against the headrest. Charlie was immensely grateful to Tess for suggesting the visit. Tess knew her better than anyone and would know how nervous Charlie would be travelling so far on her own. She also knew how desperately Charlie wanted to see her mother and how broken she'd feel when she did so. Knowing that each time Charlie visited her mum, she'd find another piece of her missing, the person Elsa was gradually fading away.

Charlie flicked the car's indicator and pulled into the driveway of St Dymphna Nursing Home. Well-trimmed hedges lined the curb, with a narrow concrete path leading between them to a single-story concrete building. Blue rendering and dark tinted window took some of the harshness away from the concrete. She still felt her stomach drop the minute she saw it. It was just past 10:00 a.m. — her mum should be in the common area having her morning tea. She took a deep breath, steeling herself to get out of her SUV. She checked her medical alert bracelet was secure on her wrist, then patted Tess gently on the knee. "We're here, Tess." Tess blinked a couple of times, yawned, then squeezed Charlie's hand on her knee.

"Ready, *ma chère?*"

"Never." Charlie chuckled nervously. "But let's go."

Tess squeezed her hand once more and they exited the car. Charlie felt relatively comfortable about the nursing home's strict "no nuts" policy. This wouldn't stop visitors from bringing them in, but it did mean as long as she kept to herself, she shouldn't have to worry. Not unless they spat on her… Which wasn't beyond reason in a nursing home like this one. This 'home' felt more like a waiting room for death. A waiting room for people too far gone to realise where they were.

Elsa paid for her residency through her hard-earned savings. To be more apt, Robert – who managed her finances – paid for it from Elsa's account. Charlie dreaded to think what type of place her mother would have ended up without money scrounged away.

A familiar poster hung on the wall above the front desk: *Listen with your ears. Listen with your eyes. Listen with your heart.* The purple ribbon for dementia awareness was curled in the background. As per normal, there was no nurse at the front desk. A place like this was always too busy for that luxury. Charlie signed them both into the visitor logbook before they walked through the double doors into the large common dining room. The place was packed but relatively quiet. Not everyone in this nursing home had dementia, but most had acute medical needs. Some sat in groups at the tables, nursing cups of tea and munching biscuits. Others sat on the sofas by the window — one smiled maniacally at seemingly nothing. Some looked up interestedly as Charlie and Tess entered the room — likely hopeful to see a member of their own family.

"What's that smell?" Tess whispered, putting her arm through Charlie's.

Charlie chuckled as she leant into Tess and whispered, "Piss, shit, tea and antiseptic."

"*Dégoûtant…*"

"This is what our place will smell like when we move in together when we're old and grey."

"*Non, ma chère,* our place will smell of piss, shit, whiskey, and wine. Do you see your *maman?*"

Charlie looked up to the couches by the window. She couldn't see her mother yet, but if she wasn't in her room, this was where she'd be. "This way." They wove their way through the shuffling residents and quick-moving nurses — each of whom they gave a friendly nod. As they approached the window, Charlie spotted her mother. An odd combination of feelings rose in her: joy, fear, sadness, hope. A nurse was helping Elsa stir sugar into her tea. The woman smiled brightly as she looked up and saw them approaching.

"Hi," she said cheerily. "You must be Charlie. They made a note yesterday that you were coming in today. Best day for it. Elsa's having a wonderful day today, aren't you, sweetie?"

"Hmgh?" Elsa said, looking up from the nurse to Charlie. The lines of her face had deepened since Charlie last saw her, and she'd lost even more weight. She hadn't thought that was possible. It was as if she were a skeleton draped with loose, thin skin. There was no recognition in Elsa's eyes as she looked Charlie up and down. Charlie felt a lump grow in her throat but remembered the importance of staying positive and happy around people with dementia. "Who?"

"You have some visitors," the nurse said calmly and happily. "Isn't that marvellous?"

"Hmgh," Elsa said again, looking back to Charlie. "Hello."

Charlie walked to her mother and knelt beside her chair, taking her wrinkled hand in hers. Her skin felt as weak and dry as tissue paper, and as cold as if she'd been sitting in the fresh spring air rather than the warm common room.

"Hi, Ma." Charlie smiled at her. "It's so good to see you."

The nurse patted Charlie on the shoulder. "I'll leave you to it. Come see me before you go, okay?" Charlie nodded, not taking her eyes off her mother. She could tell Tess was standing awkwardly behind her.

"Who are you?" Elsa asked pleasantly, patting Charlie's hand and smiling.

"I'm Charlie," she said patiently. "I'm so pleased to see you. I've missed you."

"Hmgh... I have a daughter called Charlotte." Elsa smiled, her thin lips peeling inwards to reveal blackened teeth. "You remind me of her. But you're *old*. She's the sweetest thing, my Charlotte. So bright. She's going far, she is."

"That's wonderful." Charlie smiled back. "She's lucky to have you as her mum."

"Aren't you sweet?" Elsa squeezed Charlie's hand, sending a thrill of memories and emotions through her. "I'll tell her I met another Charlie today." Suddenly Elsa noticed Tess standing behind Charlie. "Tess?" she asked, uncertain. Charlie tried not to feel the burning, acidic jealousy as Elsa remembered her friend but not her.

"Oui, *Maman*," Tess came closer, kissing Elsa on each cheek. "It's so lovely to see you."

Elsa laughed, looking between the two of them. "Oh, how lovely. Charlie will be so happy to see you. What have you been doing with yourself, Tess?"

"The same as always, *Maman* Elsa. I'm working all morning and yelling at Leon all afternoon."

"Leon…" Elsa muttered.

"Yes, my son, Leon," Tess said pleasantly, resting a hand on Elsa's shoulder.

"You know, you look like my Charlotte," Elsa said, her attention returning to Charlie.

\* \* \*

After half an hour repeating the same things, Charlie stood to leave. "Goodbye, Mum." She bent down to give her mother a long, tender kiss on the forehead.

"Oh, how nice…"

As Charlie turned to go, another woman sitting by the window caught her eye. She was hunched over, a light-blue shawl draped over her petite shoulders. She was staring at her empty hands. The woman wouldn't have been remarkable, except for a slight purple glow around her. Charlie blinked several times and the glow slowly faded.

"You okay?" Tess asked, laying a hand on her shoulder.

"Yes, yes, let's find the nurse."

They easily located the nurse in the office, hastily trying to catch up on what had to be an endless cycle of paperwork. "Thanks for popping in," she said, the happiness she exuded around the patients now dimmed. In the safety of the office, she exuded fatigue instead. While the nurse was attending to her patients, Charlie would have guessed she was in her late twenties. Here in her office, she looked twice that age. The skin hung from her cheeks like she'd recently lost a lot of weight, and the brown of her hair was as dull as the rest of her. "I'd been meaning to call you, so I'm glad we've got this chance to talk in person."

"Of course," Charlie said. "I'm always happy to talk about Mum." She noticed the name on her badge: Pat.

"Well, there's never any easy way to say this," Pat began. "But I don't think your mum has much longer with us." Charlie's heart dropped, beating hollowly from the pit of her stomach. "I mean, it's not an exact science, and I can't say for sure how long she has. It could be days, weeks, or even months."

"But not longer than that?"

"I don't think so. Elsa has been eating and drinking less. Her mood is improving, but her memory loss is deteriorating daily. And one thing I sometimes notice in other patients — her hands and feet are getting a little cooler." Charlie took a deep shuddering breath, and Tess rubbed her shoulders gently. "I'm sorry. I know it's a lot. But I find it's better to let the loved ones know. Give them some time to prepare."

"No, it's okay," Charlie said, really meaning it. "It is good to know. And I've been grieving my mum a long time now. I just…I just can't imagine life without her. She's always been there. Even like this…at least I know she's still here." Pat gave Charlie a hug, which took her slightly aback. "Thank you," she said, giving the nurse a quick squeeze in return. "It means a lot, knowing my mum has someone like you."

"She's lucky to have you too. It might not seem like she remembers, but she talks about you all the time. She's so proud of her big-shot lawyer daughter. She must have told me a dozen times about how much you loved to sway in the long grass of her favourite reserve."

"That means a lot." Charlie thanked Pat for her time, holding Tess's hand as she left the nursing home.

Sitting in the safety of her car, she quivered, wiping her eyes before any tears could fall. Tess had directed her to the passenger seat without asking permission to take the keys.

"It's okay to cry, *ma chère.*"

"It's just a lot of emotions, you know? A lot to process."

"*Oui.* You two have always been very close."

Charlie rubbed at the snot trying to drip from her nose, then let out a long exhale. "I need to call Robert. Can you get us out of here?"

"That I can do, my darling."

\* \* \*

Tess climbed into the bed next to Charlie, scooching closer to soak up some of the warmth in the bed where Charlie had been lying. While the days were warming nicely, the nights were still cool. Especially when the breeze picked up.

"Thanks for coming with me today," Charlie said, rolling over to look at Tess. "It was long overdue."

"Hey, it was worth it." Tess smiled. "My *old* Charlotte," she mimicked the way Elsa had emphasised the word. "So *old*." Charlie shoved her playfully and the two of them burst into laughter.

"Ah..." Charlie sighed contentedly. "I wish you could just stay. You make everything better."

"Me too, *ma chère*, but Leon needs me back home. And I can only put work off for so long. You've still got me tonight."

"Do you really have to leave tomorrow?"

"*Oui.*" Tess sighed too and rolled onto her back. "Leon has some important dinner planned. He'd better not be proposing to that bitch."

"Tess!" Charlie chastised mockingly.

"I bet that's what he's doing. He couldn't wait another week!"

"Well, let me know. I can't believe you drove all the way back here just to leave tomorrow."

Tess shrugged. "I do what I want."

THE CORNER OF HER EYE

Charlie laughed in reply. "Well, I'm glad... I'll love you forever, my Thérèse."

"*Je t'aimerai pour toujours, ma* Charlotte."

# 17

# The Waiting Place

Charlie stood outside, long after Tess's old, red sedan had disappeared from view, watching the dust settle. She felt sorry for herself. And lonely. Lonelier than she'd ever felt in her cottage. Lonelier than she'd ever felt full stop.

Finally, she strolled down her driveway and back to her cottage, scuffing her feet as she went. She closed the door gently behind her, looking at her empty living room. Tess had been here only days, but the impression she'd made had felt so right. Now everything felt empty without her. A beep on Charlie's laptop brought her attention to her desk. It had just gone 10:00 a.m. Of course, Maryanne, the crazy psychologist, would be waiting for her. She walked slowly to the office chair, took a deep breath, then hit "accept" on the call, trying to fix a neutral expression to her face.

"Hello, Charlotte." Maryanne smiled. She wore a different headscarf today – patterned with beige and maroon swirls. Her tunic was a different colour, too. Other than that, everything was the same as it had been during their last call. Right down to the camera angle. Charlie didn't know whether she felt relieved Maryanne hadn't ghosted her, or not. Who knew what this session had in store for her?

"Hi, Maryanne. Sorry I'm a bit late. I was saying goodbye to Tess."

"Ah, yes, the best friend." Maryanne clasped her hands and leant forward. There was an awkward silence as they stared at each other for a moment. "How have you been since we last spoke?"

"Okay, I guess. It was great having Tess here. We visited my mum in the nursing home. She doesn't have long left, apparently. That was pretty hard."

"Mmm-hmm… I'm sorry to hear that. And anything else happening?" Maryanne dismissed what Charlie had thought was an important comment with a wave of her hand. "Along the lines of what we discussed last time. Any more dreams or hallucinations?"

"No…" Charlie started to answer, frustrated that Maryanne seemed to care so little. "Wait, I guess so. I thought a woman at the nursing home was glowing purple. Does that count?"

Nodding, Maryanne jotted down a note in her book. "Okay, okay. Interesting. We'll come back to that another time." She looked up from her notepad and sighed deeply, then tilted her head as she examined Charlie. "This next bit is never easy."

"I'm not sure I'm following…" Charlie thought back to all the reviews she'd read. Maybe Maryanne had decided not to help Charlie after all. Maybe this was her version of breaking up with her. Charlie's frustration flared close to anger.

"There's nothing wrong with you, Charlotte." Maryanne paused, letting her words sink in. Charlie's anger evaporated in surprise, a slight unease taking its place. "The dreams, the figures you've been seeing. It's not hallucinations. It's not sleep paralysis. And it's not anxiety. I'm afraid it's quite real."

Charlie sat in shocked silence. She believed that to be true, but this was a *rational* psychologist surely? She opened her mouth to reply, but no words came out. Instead, she sat there gaping. *Is this a joke?* she wondered, the anger creeping back. *Is this video call being recorded? Will this end up as a viral video on Facebook? Or is Maryanne insane?* "Are you even a real psychologist?" she finally asked, frustration creeping out in her voice. "Do you get some weird kick out of this?"

Maryanne sighed, putting her pen down, and stared deep into her computer's camera. "I told you this was the hardest part. But I know you won't hang up on me. I know we'll keep talking. Because I know you know it's true." She paused for another moment, looking at Charlie through raised eyebrows. She leant back in her chair. "I am a 'real' psychologist. I've been practicing for over thirty years. And by now I guess you've read my reviews? I take enough clients to keep a living, but my real work is seeking out people like you."

"Like me?"

Maryanne nodded. "Yes. People who can see a bit more than others. People who need to see. I know this'll take a while for you to accept. And I know you'll tell yourself I'm crazy Maryanne, the psycho psych, who you'll never speak to again. But because I've been doing this for thirty years, I also know you *will* accept what I'm saying. And we will speak again. Several times, in fact."

Charlie's heart was beating fast. More than anything, she wanted to turn the call off. The more Maryanne talked, the more the feeling of unease in her chest grew. But she also wanted answers, more than she wanted the feelings of unease to relent. And there was an excitement too. "It is real," Charlie said defiantly. "That grey man scratched my face. Things in my house are moving around. I am a *rational* person. I need to know why this is happening."

"Good," Maryanne said. "And you will. But not all at once. I want to start with what's been happening in your house. Let's see if we can get that sorted first."

Charlie took a deep breath. Maryanne's matter-of-fact approach was both unsettling and reassuring. Charlie felt like she was standing on a precipice. If she took the leap, there'd be no turning back. The tarot card reading with Trent came back to her: *The seed has taken root, setting your path for the future. You're at the beginning of an important journey.*

"I think there's a spirit of a little girl here," Charlie said. "Her name is Marie Evans. She died in this house, in the 1930s, when she was only nine years old. Tess bought all these…things…for communicating with ghosts. And I *feel* like it's Marie. In my dreams, it's Marie. Even one day when I was awake, I saw Marie, with her sister, by the creek. And something I saw in my dreams — a tin shed — I found a piece of it, in the present day, when I had no idea it was there before."

Maryanne nodded slowly as she obviously thought the situation through. "You apparently have a strong connection with this Marie. I can tell you have a lot of questions. Let me just tell you this for today. Whether you're a Christian, a Buddhist, a Muslim, or agnostic, most agree, the human being has a spirit. A soul. Even more simply put, a consciousness."

Charlie nodded. If nothing else, consciousness she could accept.

"Most also believe in the concept of *something* after death," Maryanne continued. "Heaven, hell, reincarnation — even oblivion would be *something*. I can't tell you what it is because I don't know. I won't know until it's my time. What I *do* know is that some people — some souls — aren't ready when they leave this life. They linger. They wait, for lack of a better word."

"Like purgatory?" Charlie asked, trying to conceptualise what the psychologist was telling her.

"I guess Catholics might say so. But time doesn't matter after death. For Marie — who died so long ago to you and me — it likely feels as though no time has passed at all. Eventually, her spirit will move on. They always do. It could take decades, hundreds of years even, but she will, eventually. In the meantime, she's dipping in and out of her Waiting Place, and our own reality."

Charlie thought back to her dream, with its archways and stairs and platforms, and the sense of waiting. "So what does this have to do with me? Why am I seeing her? Why is she pulling me into all this?"

Maryanne leant closer, her eyes narrowing in what Charlie could only read as excitement. "She's not pulling you, Charlotte. You're pulling her. But that's *not* what I want to talk about today. Think of it like this: there's always a sense of order. To life. To death. To this in-between. And for Marie, that order is out of whack. Something hasn't happened as it should."

"She needs help?"

Maryanne nodded. "That's what I believe. I don't have much longer for our session today, so I want to focus on the dreams you've been having."

"The Waiting Place…" Charlie said, thinking of how similar Maryanne's description of Marie's 'waiting place' was to her dreams. "Is it the same place you're talking about?" Charlie asked.

"I don't know, Charlotte. I have a feeling you know better than I do. What I will leave you with is this thought: you don't always have to be asleep to dream. And there can often be a lot of answers in dreams. If you want to connect with Marie, to find out how to help her, that would be a good place to start."

"How?" Charlie asked.

"Trust yourself. Relax your body. Empty your mind. Do what feels right. You'll figure it out," Maryanne replied. "That's my time up, I'm afraid. I have another slot available at 10:00 a.m. on Tuesday. I'll see you then, Charlotte."

"Wait…"

Maryanne disconnected the call. Charlie flopped back in her chair, unsure what to make of the "psycho psych" and her confident descriptions of unbelievable concepts. Wondering, too, why Maryanne was yet to mention payment. "If she's crazy, I guess so am I…"

\* \* \*

Charlie sat in her armchair, with her cup of tea, for almost an hour after her call with Maryanne. She wanted to analyse everything she'd been told, and everything she'd experienced. But the moment she tried to, it was like the thoughts slipped away, and she just found herself staring out the window. She put her now cold cup of tea down on the coffee table. She shook her shoulders to loosen them and stretched her neck. "Okay… let's give this a go…" She let out a deep breath and closed her eyes. "Thank God I live alone," she muttered.

Physically, she had to unclench her jaw, opening her mouth in circles to loosen it. She breathed out again. 'Next my shoulders…' she let them flop loosely and took another deep breath. She deliberately sought out every muscle in her body, consciously ticking them off. 'Loose… relaxed…' Charlie heard the wind blowing at the window and a parakeet chittering contentedly somewhere close by. 'I know what to do…' She thought of Marie, pictured her, and the doubt clicked off in her mind. Innocent, happy Marie, who just wanted to play. Giggling Marie. That was who mattered right now. 'What *are you waiting for...?'* Charlie thought. *'What happened? When did all of this start?'*

With her eyes closed, Charlie felt herself pulled, like she had a string inside her that had been tugged — jerking her from herself. She didn't need to open her eyes. She was suddenly just seeing. While it didn't look like her Waiting Place, it had the same feeling to it. Even disconnected from reality as she was in that moment, it still felt realer – clearer – than the 'real' world. She was in the cottage, but not her cottage. Most certainly, this was the Evans' cottage. She was dreaming.

An extra wall behind her hid where Charlie's kitchen now stood, making the living room feel more enclosed. The floor was covered in a flat rug. The furniture was more modern than she expected. Well-carved oak armchairs, with lime green cushions atop them, matched a low-profile bookshelf along the wall, a square side table, and daybed by the window. The house smelt different too — quite horrible to Charlie, actually. A distinct blend of tobacco, unprocessed wool and horse.

*'Marie...'* she thought, realising as she did so that here it wasn't just a thought. She was calling to her. A giggle brought her attention to the other room. Charlie took a step and was standing where her kitchen should be. *'A dining room...'* Charlie thought, taking it all in. A heavy wooden table took pride of place in the centre, eight well-carved chairs surrounding it. In one corner sat a beautiful matching China cabinet, full of plates and glasses. In another stood two wooden highchairs.

A giggle brought Charlie's attention under the table. Charlie crouched down, and there she was. Tiny Marie, hiding under the legs of the chairs, cuddling a teddy bear with both of its eyes, in far better condition than she'd last seen it. Even if one of those eyes was dangling dangerously by a single thread. This was the youngest Charlie had seen Marie. Her dark hair was cut in a short bob, framing a slightly chubbier face with rosy cheeks. Today she wore a fine, light knitted cardigan over a pale blouse, tucked neatly into a pleated skirt. Her bare feet, however, were filthy, mud and grass seeds splattering up her legs. Charlie smiled as she shifted, sitting under the table with Marie — who thus far seemed oblivious to her presence.

'*Hello Marie,*' Charlie thought happily to herself. She felt a warm glow as she connected. '*What are you showing me today, baby? How did this all start?*'

# 18

# Daydreaming

Still dreaming, Charlie crouched closer to Marie, hiding together beneath the dining table. Footsteps in the living room brought their attention to the door. Through the opening, she saw a woman — Emma — walk across the room, nursing a baby, and settle on the green sofa. Despite how young the babe in her arms was, Emma looked fresh. Her dark, long-sleeved dress was perfectly ironed, and not a single hair was loose. The infant was perhaps only a few months old. *Jack?* Charlie thought. *No. It must be Florence.* William followed not far behind her, his pale trousers stained with grass seeds and mud. From her vantage point under the table she only caught the briefest glimpse of his pale, reddish hair. He'd obviously been wiping at his face with dirty hands, and his waxed moustache was askew.

"Where are the girls?" he asked, disappearing from view but still easily heard.

"With Aunty Alice, washing up before lunch. They're all as filthy as you, Bill. Especially Marie. I don't know where her shoes got to…" Emma sighed, and Marie giggled besides Charlie, who smiled down at her. "Bill…"

"Yes, dear," William said, banging around behind the wall, out of sight. Perhaps wrestling with his boots?

"I really don't know about withdrawing *all* our savings. Is it really necessary? I just feel it'll be safer at the bank than here."

"Hush, Em. You don't want all the stockmen hearing you." Charlie heard

William walk to the window to look outside. "Trust me, I've been following this closely. The Government Savings Bank is going under, ever since the treasury defaulted on its bonds. You know what's happened in the United States. What's *happening*. We need to get ahead of that. Jack 'the Big Fella' is right. Why should we suffer so those rich porkers can stuff their pockets?"

"If you think so…"

"Just for now," William walked over and kissed Emma on the forehead, stroking the back of Florence's head as he did so. "No one will know but you and me, darling."

Charlie didn't completely follow the conversation, and she could tell Marie didn't either. But she felt trepidation and concern flowing from both adults. Marie scooted backwards, crawling out from under the table, and ran through a second door. A door that in Charlie's present day didn't exist. *Where did you go…?'* Charlie shifted to follow Marie and found herself standing in a kitchen. It took her a moment to realise this was the space that had been converted into her present-day guest bedroom. Marie was running through yet another door, then outside onto the deck surrounding the house.

Charlie followed her without needing to move her feet. Marie was now sprinting across the grass, running towards the back of the property. Charlie could see what William had meant by stockmen. The property was a hive of activity, with half a dozen men herding a large flock of sheep, one sitting atop the same chestnut horse from her earlier dream. Charlie noticed that two of the men were indigenous Australian, including the man atop the horse. A woman yelled out after Marie — probably Aunty Alice — but Marie continued her flight, her teddy swinging behind her. The stockmen laughed at the commotion — none stepping in to assist. It was obviously a relatively common occurrence.

Giggling as well, Charlie flew with Marie to the creek at the back of the property. It was barely flowing in this moment in time, dried up from an obviously decent summer. Marie ran with her little legs up to the gum tree Charlie liked to rest her back against. Marie knelt beside it, her poor skirt now in a state worse than filthy. Charlie found herself feeling sorry for this

Aunty Alice, who was busy wrangling the other three girls. Marie rested on her heels, holding her teddy in front of her.

"I'm sorry, Mr Buttons," Marie said in a firm voice — as firm as her sweet, soft, girlish voice could make it. "There's a problem with the bonds. Daddy said so. The banks are going *bust*, and I have to protect you from the porkers." Marie reached over and grasped the loose eye, pulling as hard as she could with her little arm. She grunted as she did so. "Ah..." The eye came loose in her hand. "Don't worry Mr Buttons. We'll keep it safe. We have to bury our treasure so the stockmen don't know, and the porkers don't take it."

Marie scraped the soil out from the base of the tree, digging until a small hole opened up. She pulled a hanky from her dirty skirt and tenderly wrapped the eye inside. Once the eye was safely squished in the hole, she covered it up again, patting the ground down firmly. As she leant back, she sighed happily, rubbing her hands on her skirt. Doing so may, in fact, have made her hands dirtier. "There, Mr Buttons. Now no one can find it." She squeezed the bear happily. A slight breeze picked up, and Charlie and Marie heard the deep chanting starting up in the breeze. Shaken loose from their branches, leaves drifted down to land on the ground beside Charlie and to float in the creek.

"Hello?" Marie said tentatively, scrambling to her feet and holding Mr Buttons close.

"It's okay," Charlie tried to say but found herself unable to form the words. She thought them strongly to the girl instead: *It's okay.*

"Who are you?" Marie asked softly, taking a step back towards the creek.

*I'm here to help,* Charlie said with what confidence she could muster. *I'm a friend.* She wasn't sure if the girl actually perceived her, or if she was just startled by the wind.

Marie squinted in Charlie's general direction. "Come on, Mr Buttons. It's time to go back to the house." Marie ran past Charlie and back towards the cottage.

Suddenly Charlie felt very tired, agreeing with Marie — it was time to go home. Not quite knowing how she was doing so, but trusting her instinct, she started to slowly disconnect from Marie's world, trying to reconnect with her own.

She blinked several times as she found herself back in her own living room, in her own armchair. She rubbed her arms to bring feeling back to them before rubbing her face. "Okay..." she said, testing out her voice, relieved to find she had no trouble speaking. "Okay... That...that was okay..." She looked back out the window. To the right of what she could see, the land would slope down to the back of her property. She wondered if the glass eye was still under the tree. "That was better than okay," she whispered, rubbing her hands together. As odd as all this was, it felt right as well. Like things she'd never wondered about before were starting to click together. She felt giddy, elated. "Okay, Marie," she smiled around the cottage. "Let's go find Mr Buttons's treasure!"

Charlie leant forward to pick up her mug of tea to return it to the kitchen, swearing as the mug scalded her hand. "What the fuck?" She sucked her red fingers, looking down at the steam rising from the hot, *fresh* cup of tea. Her first thought was that someone must be in her house, messing with her. Or Tess had returned. Her next thought was more rational — why make a fresh cup of tea?! Especially if it was Tess and she'd found her sitting in her armchair, unresponsive, staring into space. Charlie fished her phone out of her pocket. It was just before 10:30 a.m. *This makes no sense.* She hadn't even tried to reach Marie until at least 11.30 a.m. She stood up, looking around the cottage in confusion.

*Time doesn't matter after death,* she remembered Maryanne saying.

"Well, shit..."

* * *

Forty minutes later, Charlie knelt by the same gum tree where she'd seen Marie. Carefully she scraped the dirt away, her nerves tingling with excitement and anticipation. Any moment now she should unearth the little handkerchief and the glass bear eye and be one step closer to Marie. She'd actually be able to hold a piece of her history in her hand. Charlie dug for close to twenty minutes, trying other locations near the tree in case she hadn't remembered quite right. She dug deeper as well, wondering if time could have moved things in the soil. Eventually the whole base of the tree was a mess of dirt, bugs, and dislodged stones and grass. But there was no glass eye and no handkerchief. "I was so sure..." she whispered, falling back on her heels just as Marie had done. The vision had been so clear, so *deep*. "It wasn't just my imagination."

Before walking down to the creek, she'd written down everything she could remember. A description of the living room, of the differences in the layout of the cottage, of the odd conversation William had with Emma about a government bank, treasury bonds, Jack 'the Big Fella', and the porkers. While she couldn't make sense of it, she was sure Trent could help. She had a feeling it must be related to the Great Depression. *How could I imagine all of that?* she wondered. Disappointed, but assured of her sanity, Charlie pushed the loose dirt back into the various holes. *Did Marie come back for her treasure?*

Standing, she looked around at the trees and the slowly bubbling creek. Yet again, its flow had slowed and its banks had receded. By the time summer was over, it would be as thin and winding as it had been in her vision. With her excitement and anticipation fading, she began to feel the same emotions Tess had picked up on when they last visited. *Douloureux...* Pain, sadness... *No wonder I never came here before.* Charlie made her way back to the cottage, determined to update Tess now that she'd thought of her friend and to see what she made of all this.

* * *

"Hello, darling," Tess said, a little breathless, as the phone connected. "I don't have too much time to talk. I have to get ready for this dinner."

"Right!" Charlie said, remembering why Tess had left so quickly in the first place. "Of course, I can't wait to hear how that goes. So the drive went okay? You arrived safe and sound obviously."

"*Oui, ma chère.* Sorry for not texting you. The drive was good. I listened to my audiobook and the time just flew. How'd you go with that looney psychologist?"

"*Looney* is the right word. She told me I'm *not* imagining everything, and it's actually all really happening."

"Oh…" Tess said, clearly taken aback and conflicted about how long a decent conversation on this might take. "She doesn't sound like a very good psychologist."

"No, she's absolute shit! But…she told me something, and I tried it, and…I had another dream about Marie. I saw her again, in my house. Well, her house. The layout was all turned around. But it was kind of wonderful."

"You had a dream, during the day?"

"Oh, please tell me you still believe me?"

"*Oui, oui.* It's just a lot to process. And *ma chère*, I really do have to go. I'm so sorry. But I do want to hear all about it after…"

"Of course," Charlie replied, wishing they had more time. "And I want to hear all about this dinner too."

"Hang on," Tess said after a moment's pause, suddenly recalling something. "You should check your paperwork from when you bought the property. If there have been changes to the layout, they had to document that. It's probably in all those papers somewhere."

"Of course!" Charlie said excitedly.

"Okay, *ma chère, abiento.* Talk soon." The phone disconnected before Charlie could say goodbye. She understood — Leon was Tess's world and his girlfriend was the antithesis of that world. Tess would be going through it! And she'd spent so much time with Charlie, only for Charlie to come calling right away as soon as she'd made it home. It felt like Tess had left much longer ago than she had.

"But for now…" Charlie said to herself, looking to the ceiling. "I'm heading to the attic to fetch those papers…"

# 19

# Dark Uninhabited Places

Charlie had retrieved the long-handled hook that would allow her to open the attic manhole. She looped it into the manhole cover, carefully tugging down to release the hatch. As the hatch lowered, a steep staircase unfolded into the hallway. Charlie coughed as dust from the attic settled. She leant the hook against the wall and grabbed the railing, climbing up into the dark room. She'd only been into the attic twice — once when she purchased the house, and the second time when she was moving in. She'd had the manhole replaced with this contraption, thinking she'd make good use of the attic — at least for fabric storage. But then she'd ignored it completely. It's not that there was anything wrong with the space; it was just that no attic was particularly welcoming. There was something unsettling about dark, uninhabited spaces.

Once on the landing, Charlie pulled the string to turn on the light. It was still daylight outside, but the attic windows were so dusty they might as well not have been there. The bulb was centred in the room, its warm glow too dull to light up much, and certainly not the attic's dark corners. "It's just a frigging room," she muttered through gritted teeth as she made her way to the far wall where she'd stacked her boxes. She felt prickles along her back, knowing she was psyching herself up as she knelt to start rummaging through the boxes' contents. The first box was family photos, which she moved to the side.

Before starting on the next box, she looked over her shoulders and into the dark corners. *That fucking grey man would love it up here,* she thought, the prickles tightening. She turned her attention back to the boxes. The second one had her tax records, receipts, and other financial papers — once stacked neat and orderly, now shaken loose by the move. *Ah, shit,* she thought, trying to move the papers back together. She made a mental note to sort through the files in the not-too-distant future. She'd probably never need them, but she couldn't stand the thought of them sitting in disarray.

Charlie looked up at the corner to her immediate left. *Nothing.* The corner to her right. *Nothing.* Slowly she turned to look at the two corners behind her back, her heart pounding slightly as she did. *Nothing...nothing... Stop it. You're working yourself up.* She turned to the next box. This was it: her box of important documents: passport, birth certificate, school records, university degree, tax file number, insurance records... "Aha!" Charlie exclaimed, grabbing the thick folder of documents her lawyer had shipped to her once the property purchase was final.

A scraping noise sounded behind her in what felt like deliberate timing. She turned to see the steps pulling up as the manhole door swung shut, slamming as it closed. "Fuck, fuck, fuck," Charlie whispered, hugging the folder to her chest and hurrying to the manhole. It was even darker in here now that no light was streaming in from the hallway. "Fucking attic..." She pushed on the stairs with one hand to trigger them to release, but without success. After placing the folder on the ground to the side, her phone balanced on top, this time she used both hands. She sighed with relief as the mechanism clicked and the manhole opened again. Her heart beat like a drum as a trickle of sweat ran down the middle of her lower back.

Feeling the urge to look over her shoulder again, she peered at the dark corner behind her one last time. In the gloom, two bright pinpricks of light shone. As her eyes locked with those two white flicks of light, the bulb behind her burst spectacularly. She flinched backwards, yelling as she almost lost her balance on the edge of the manhole. Her arm flailed wildly, knocking the binder, sending it and her phone toppling down the stairs. They bounced several times before launching into the hallway wall

113

and falling to the floor. She looked up again, quickly, to the corner. In the deeper gloom, she saw nothing but blackness; the space was empty.

"Fucking out of here!" Charlie shuddered, making her way down the ladder as fast as she could. At the bottom, she pushed the steps, the mechanism pulling the ladder up and shutting the door with a thud. Charlie let out a long-held breath, watching the manhole suspiciously for a moment. Finally satisfied the door wouldn't swing open the moment she took her eyes off it, she bent to retrieve her phone, which sported a new crack across the screen protector, and the binder, which thankfully had stayed together. "I am never fucking going up there again..." She wiped sweat and dust from her forehead. *Those tax records can rot up there.*

Charlie made herself a cup of tea, shaking so much that the mug rattled as she placed it on the bench. She was starting to get low on Russian Caravan. She should have picked some up on her road trip with Tess. Now she'd have to order another lot online. The local grocer only had Bushells or Tetley's. She started making the order on her phone as she wandered to the table, the mug held gingerly in her other hand. Completing the online order helped bring her pulse down to normal and her breathing to even out. *There's something to be said for the mundane and ordinary...and for retail therapy...*

She pulled the binder towards her and opened it. As she flipped through the dozens upon dozens of pages, she thought just how much trust people put in lawyers — herself included, in spite of her former profession. She should know better. *I don't even remember reading this.* It had been a turbulent time when she'd committed to buy the property. Charlie paused as she got to an addendum, detailing the legality of the alterations to the house. Absentmindedly, she blew on her tea as she read. A nonstructural wall had been removed; the old clay pipes had been replaced with plastic; and fixtures had been moved in the process of relocating the kitchen. Doorways had been moved as well. It did seem like quite a lot of work. The documents indicated the renovations had been made in the early 1980s. Charlie had then had the place freshened and modernised even further before she'd moved in.

On the next page was just what Charlie needed: a visual representation. In the original house design, a wall had separated the living room from what was now an open-plan kitchen. At the time, though, that kitchen had been labelled a dining/sitting room. The old door that led from the dining room into the current guest room (then a kitchen) had been removed and plastered over and was now lined with cupboards, her oven, and the kitchen bench. Charlie found it fascinating that the location of the current fireplace in the guest room — which she'd always assumed was purely ornamental — was the location of the kitchen stove in the original design. The rest of the cottage, aside from modernisation in the bathroom, was still the same.

"See!" She slapped the paper. "Not crazy!" *Even though I just talked out loud to myself...* She glanced around the room, which remained still and quiet. She returned her focus to the binder. She still couldn't believe such a large family had lived here; she supposed the babies would have stayed in the master bedroom for some time, and then the four girls must have shared what was now her sewing room.

Her interest piqued, Charlie flipped through the remaining pages. There were recent maps of the boundary lines, along with an older map showing the property when it was still technically a station — or sheep farm was perhaps the better term. The property was only forty-five hectares — huge by Charlie's standards, but tiny by the standards of Australia's mammoth stations, which were hundreds of thousands of hectares.

She couldn't believe she hadn't taken the time to study these maps previously. About ten kilometres from the main cottage was an area marked "stockmen's quarters" and "wool shed." She'd never been to that part of her property. She'd always headed east to the gorgeous high hills or, more recently, south to the creek. West was mostly flat, with the odd shallow hill and valley. She simply hadn't walked that way because it had looked boring. Just grass. Though apparently not. It should only take her a couple of hours to walk that far cross-country. She looked at her phone; it was getting close to evening. Her stomach rumbled, reminding her she hadn't eaten anything since breakfast with Tess. *Did she really only leave today?*

Charlie wandered to the kitchen to determine what to make for dinner, whilst thinking of the hike she'd most certainly make tomorrow. *Weekend plans are sorted*, she thought as she rummaged in the fridge.

\* \* \*

The next day, luck wasn't on Charlie's side. In typical Australian fashion, the weather had tricked her with warm days and promises of summer, only to flip the cold switch back on. A constant drizzle fell; the low clouds were spraying a fine, cool mist. It wasn't enough to get soaked through, but it was enough for every extremity to be moistened uncomfortably. Undeterred, Charlie dug out her rain jacket and water-resistant hiking boots and backpack and prepared for a full day in the elements.

She locked the cottage door behind her at around 10:30 a.m. *You wouldn't know it's so late in the morning...* With the clouds hanging low, there was a soft gloom to the day. Before setting off, away from the range of her satellite dish, she figured she'd better send a message to Tess — just in case she fell in a hole or something: *Hi, Tess! You were right about the house plans. I found reference to a whole complex of buildings I didn't know existed. I'm walking out today to check them out. About 10 km west of the cottage, on foot. I'm back to fighting fit — don't worry. I should be home by midafternoon. I hope last night's dinner went okay.*

She took a deep breath of the chilly air before setting out, relishing in its freshness. She was very much looking forward to this adventure.

\* \* \*

As she'd hiked out, Charlie had kept a close eye on the time, closely following the compass on her hiking pack. She didn't want to miss the stockmen's buildings. She knew what a mess it would cause being even slightly off course over this distance. The long grass and wet conditions slowed her down, and after two hours on foot she was starting to worry she'd strayed. Turning to look behind her, she saw more of the same grassland stretching out as far as she could see. With the slight peaks and troughs in the terrain, her house had quickly been lost from sight; she couldn't even see the road.

With almost all the trees uprooted, there also weren't very many landmarks to guide her way. She felt reassured, however, by her decision to message Tess her plans, wondering about the accuracy of a compass that came free with an eighty-dollar backpack. Up ahead was a solitary gum tree, for some reason spared from the weeding that had occurred more than a hundred years ago. She made for the tree, figuring it was as good a spot as any to reassess her plans and rest. She pulled a light, water resistant blanket from the side pouch of her pack. It was one of the "compact" purchases that never quite fit back into its bag properly. She settled herself on this mat on the ground, resting her back against the tree trunk, pleased for even a small amount of shelter.

She pulled a small thermos of tea out of her bag and sipped it, grateful for the hot sensation as it made its way to her belly. "Well, Marie," she whispered, looking out through the misty rain and cloud over the grasslands, "looks like a failed adventure this time." She thought about how much easier this would have been with the four-wheel-drive buggy the cottage's previous owner had used, or even on horseback...if she could ride a horse... *It would have been easier if I'd waited for fine weather*, she chastised herself. Charlie pulled out her phone again and opened the photo gallery. Before heading out, she'd at least taken a photo of the property map.

She zoomed in, examining the group of buildings she was hoping to find: the stockmen's quarters and wool shed. It looked significant on the map. The shed was at least twice the size of her cottage, and there were five small shapes where the stockmen's quarters were supposed to be. Charlie zoomed in as far as she could, finding no more helpful details. *No point sitting on my arse in the cold*, she mused. She packed the rest of her tea away and slipped her phone into her pocket, then stuffed the mat back into its bag as well as she could. *Just half an hour more...*

# 20

# Blood and Whiskey

Charlie was soon climbing the next crest, now obsessively checking the compass, the layout of the stockmen's complex running through her head. As she reached the crest she looked out and down into a shallow valley. "Oh my God," she said, looking down the slope. "Oh my God!" She laughed in delight and relief. Before her were the distinct outlines of several ruined buildings. Some stood out proudly from the ground, walls pointed at the sky, while others barely peeked above the knee-high grass. "Yes!" she exclaimed, punching the air with her fist. "Woooo!" Although no one was nearby to hear the commotion, she wouldn't have cared if there had been.

She pulled her phone from her pocket and excitedly took as many photos as she could, along with a short video. She then half jogged, half slid, down the slope, heading for the largest of the buildings. The roof was completely gone, but three of the exterior walls still stood, at least partially. The pale, sandstone bricks were at least the size of her head and quite a different construction than that of her bungalow-style cottage. Charlie laid a hand on the side of one wall, trying to connect to the history. This place had once been a hive of activity but now lay as quiet as the empty grasslands, slowly overtaken by them. She entered the first building, looking through the grass for signs of the original layout, which she found as rubble on the ground. The rooms in this building were far smaller than those of her cottage. Perhaps the stockmen's quarters then?

Charlie spent the next hour exploring the ruined buildings, carefully parting the grass to see if any trinkets might have been left behind. Mostly she just found rubble, bricks, and mortar. The most intact parts of the ruins were the remnants of fireplaces, doorways, and the occasional window. Obviously the roof had caved in first, followed by the walls. The most intact of all the buildings was barely one square metre inside. *Probably the outhouse...*

Broken crockery thrilled her enough that she spent a good fifteen minutes looking for enough pieces to make a full plate. Eventually she took half a dozen random pieces and placed them in her pack before moving on. At the edge of the cluster of buildings she found a large, rusted wheel, which she elatedly photographed from every angle. One building still had a huge fireplace, large enough for her to stand comfortably inside, though the chimney had collapsed long ago. She must have climbed over every building at least three times, using a small notebook to try to sketch out each layout.

With the buildings all well explored and photographed, Charlie sat on her mat again, this time leaning against a broken wall, drinking the last of her tea. She wondered if Marie had ever visited here. Surely she would have, the inquisitive child she was. William seemed like a kindly father — Charlie liked to imagine he'd have indulged her occasionally. Charlie examined the map on her phone again, comparing it to the sketches she'd made. She was pretty sure at least three of the buildings were housing. The one with the huge fireplace she wasn't sure about.

She looked up at the horizon. If she was sitting in the cluster of buildings that made up the stockmen's quarters, then the wool shed should have been directly in front of her, within eyesight. All she could see was more grass. She decided to check the area closely before heading back — as soon as she'd eaten the sandwich she'd brought. The misty rain had finally eased up a little, and she heard a breeze picking up as well. Aside from that, she sat in complete peace. Almost complete quiet. Not even any bird calls — obviously they were smarter than Charlie and sheltering from the weather.

It unnerved her a little. A stark reminder that this place was now far different to how it had been a hundred years ago, when it was full of people.

THE CORNER OF HER EYE

*And full of sheep. At least it smells better today than it would have back then.* Finding her appetite fleeting, Charlie packed the last of her sandwich away and started getting her pack back together. As in the attic, she had the overwhelming desire to look over her shoulder to check if she was being watched. *Not this time, she* thought. *Not falling for that again. Even if you are there, you fucker, I won't give you the satisfaction of a jump scare this time.*

Despite her bravado, Charlie quickened her step as she walked out of the ruins and to the spot where, if she'd read the map correctly, she should have found the wool shed. It still just looked like grass. She walked slowly, head down, obsessively looking for anything that might indicate the former presence of an old building. She was filled with anticipation as she came across a piece of tin sticking out from the dirt. She hurried to the spot, trying to dislodge it from the ground. It wouldn't move. After dropping her pack, she started shifting the dirt from around the tin with her hands and her boots. It was huge!

As she cleared the area around the tin, she noticed other pieces of debris that had, until now, been hidden in the grass or just beneath the soil. Rotten pieces of timber. Old, huge, rusted nails. Smaller scraps of metal. "Looks like I found the wool shed." Sighing happily, she took out her phone to take photos of what she could. "I guess not everything was made to stand the test of time!" Her voice ringing out in the empty grasslands made her feel more unsettled. Resisting the urge to look over her shoulder, she bent back toward the ground to keep removing soil and debris.

Finally, she got purchase under the big piece of tin and pulled, hard. The soil started to give way. The muscles in her shoulders pinched, but she felt the scrap moving, so shifted her full weight into it. Without warning, the tin cracked, flipping through the air, slicing her hand as it did so. "Ah, shit!" She snapped her hand back, holding it tightly as she stumbled and regained her balance. The deep throbbing let her know it was a decent cut.

The tin that had broken free flipped a couple more times before settling on top of a clump of grass. Charlie crouched near her pack, holding her hand tightly. "Shit, shit, shit..." Using her teeth, she bit the cotton scarf around her neck, pulling it several times to loosen it without having to release pressure on her hand. Finally, the scarf came free, and she used her mouth to drape it over her palm. As she released her left hand to grab the scarf, a spurt of blood flowed out, dripping onto the ground. "Ugh…" Opening her mouth in a half retch, Charlie quickly grabbed the scarf and wound it tightly around her cut palm to stop (and hide) the flow of blood.

She let herself fall back onto her bottom, not minding that her pants were starting to soak through. She tested her fingers, and they each moved with no hindrance aside from the pain. She then clasped the scarf with her left hand. *That's good,* she thought with relief. *It can't be too bad then…* She chuckled wryly. *Well, that was stupid!*

Charlie stumbled to her feet to check what had been under the tin. She'd released a nest of small, grey slater bugs. Their pale ribbed bodies scurried on dozens of tiny legs. They were still scattering as she stood to inspect her mess. Aside from the bugs, there were more pieces of rotting wood and rusting nails. A larger piece of metal caught her eye. She walked over to it, the bugs curling into balls as she did so. She used her foot to prod the piece of metal and shift it loose. *Perhaps this injury wasn't for nothing,* she thought as her foot dislodged the object, which was almost as long as her forearm. She picked it up with her good hand and wiped it on her jeans to dislodge the larger chunks of dirt. On one end were large, rough metal clippers. On the other end was what looked like a metal elbow, sticking out at a ninety-degree angle.

"Definitely the wool shed," she mumbled. The throbbing in her left hand was making her feel woozy. She crouched again and, with her left elbow holding the bag straight, opened the pack and dropped the clippers inside. Swinging the bag onto her shoulders, she decided it was high time to head home; that was enough exploring for one day. Turning to take one last look at the ruins, Charlie thought she saw movement behind one of the walls. Blinking to dislodge the fine misty rain that had started falling again, she squinted at the ruins again. *Nothing.*

* * *

By the time Charlie approached the cottage, it was almost 4:00 p.m., despite having picked up the pace on her return. She let the pack slide to the floor, cradling her hand as she made her way to the bathroom and her first-aid kit. She'd lost a little feeling in her fingers, which were freezing cold, but put that down to the weather. She brought the first-aid kit back to the kitchen, where, before doing anything else, she grabbed a squat square glass and her best whiskey. "No better time," she said, pulling the cork out with her teeth.

She shot the first pour in one gulp, then poured a second glass so it was ready when needed. "Okay…" She gritted her teeth as she started pulling the scarf from her hand. The blood had soaked through two layers, effectively gluing the scarf to her flesh. "Gargh," she yelled through clenched teeth, flipping the tap on — hot — as she built up the nerve to remove the scarf. She held her hand under the hot water, retching as the pain flared again — sharp and raw. "Okay, okay…" She breathed shallowly through gritted teeth, downing the second pour of whiskey. With a loud groan she pulled the scarf from her hand, slowly and steadily. Fresh blood poured from the wound as the scarf came free.

She flipped the tap back on, holding her now-shaking hand underneath, panting from the pain. Her vision went white at the corners, so she grabbed the whiskey with her good hand and took another swig straight from the bottle. Steadied, she patted the wound dry with a large strip of gauze from the first-aid kit. The next step was pouring Dettol antiseptic over her hand. "Fuuuuuck!" The stinging was so deep she almost felt it reverberating in her eyeballs. Holding the gauze loosely in her hand to catch more blood, she sifted through the first-aid kit for a nonstick dressing. After finding a decent-sized one, she ripped the packet open with her teeth, placed it on her palm, and wrapped it tightly with a bandage. She dropped the bloody gauze onto the bench with her scarf, rewarding her handiwork with another swig of whiskey.

As Charlie leant her elbows against the bench, holding her throbbing hand, a creaking sound came from behind her: the front door was opening. Even through her whiskey haze, she felt the mood in the room shift, discomfort building. Slowly she turned. Stooped in the doorway, its white eyes drilling into Charlie, was the grey man. They eyed each other in silence, the thing's shoulders moving up and down as though it were breathing — despite the absence of a mouth or nostrils.

Behind it, Charlie saw the rain had picked up and was whipping around into a decent storm. Her emotions blurred from the pain and the whiskey, Charlie was numb as she stared back. She felt the unease continuing to build in the room, but neither it — nor any terror — was able to pierce her fog. "Fuck…off…" she said quietly. Anger burst through her haze. *"Fuck off!"* she screamed. The creature continued to stare at her for a moment before giving a slight shudder and fading into nothing. Only the storm was left visible through the doorway; the rain started to form a puddle at her front door.

She stomped to the door, slammed it closed with her shoulder, and locked it with her good hand. She then rested her forehead on the wood, sighing loudly. Exhaustion washed over her, and perhaps a little of the terror was creeping in. The handle rattled soft and slow. "I said *fuck off*!" As the handle silenced, Charlie's sense of unease finally faded.

She trudged back to the kitchen, where she took a strip of codeine from the first-aid kit and the whiskey bottle back to her couch. She knew she probably needed stitches, but with this weather and the whiskey already in her system, that would have to wait until morning. Resigned to being stuck in her cottage, she popped two pills into her mouth, swallowed them with whiskey, then lay back on the couch, her hand elevated on her forehead to help with the throbbing.

*I told that grey creep who's boss,* she thought as her eyelids grew heavy and she drifted to sleep.

# 21

# The King of the Idiots

The next morning, the first thing Charlie felt was the pounding in her hand. She blinked groggily. It wasn't just her hand that was pounding. Her head throbbed in rhythm, no doubt helped along by the crick that had developed in her neck from sleeping on the couch. As she rolled into a sitting position, she groaned, holding her hand against her shoulder.

Stunned by her rough awakening, she stared around her gloomy cottage. It looked early. She fished her phone out of her pocket, which was down to 20 percent battery. Without unlocking it, she saw the time blink onto the screen: 7.00 a.m. She examined her hand more closely— her fingers were swollen and tinged purple. The tingling also persisted despite warmth having returned to her extremities. Gingerly, Charlie loosened and unwound the bandage to relieve some of the pressure. Despite being "nonstick," the gauze pad was fixed firmly to her hand, and blood had oozed through the material. *That is some good swelling...*

She rewrapped the bandage with less pressure, then stumbled to her feet and to the kitchen for a glass of water. She scowled at the whiskey bottle as she passed it. Her phone pinged as she went for her second glass of water. *Why aren't you answering?! I'm starting to get worried*, the text message read.

*Crap*, she thought, rubbing her forehead as she unlocked the phone. Three missed calls and four messages from Tess. As she went to return the calls, her stomach heaved, and she vomited — spectacularly — into the kitchen sink. Her hand throbbed in sympathy with her stomach. *Hospital first,* she thought, stumbling to the cupboard for a bottle of water. She grabbed her handbag from the hook by the door, and the keys from the bowl, before heading out to her SUV. The air was still chilly and moist after the storm the night before. The birds — especially the parakeets and cockatoos — were chirping happily now that the weather had passed. Crickets joined in the chorus.

Before starting the engine, Charlie plugged her phone into the car charger, and messaged Tess. *So sorry. I'm okay. I'm heading to the hospital to get some stitches for a cut on my hand. Long story. I'll call in 15 when I hit signal.* She stared at the message, feeling unsatisfied, but not in the right headspace to retype it. "That'll do," she muttered, pressing "send" and starting the ignition.

* * *

Charlie's phone pinged again as she reached signal. She used her bad hand to pressed the "Tess" favourite button on her car dash before returning it to rest in its new favoured position on her shoulder. The phone rang once before Tess answered.

"She lives…" From Tess's tone, Charlie could tell she wasn't impressed.

"Hey, Tess," Charlie said, dreading the lecture her pounding head wasn't prepared to receive.

Tess paused before answering. "You sound awful… What the hell were you doing?"

"I found the plans, like you suggested, and there were a bunch of buildings called stockmen's quarters and wool shed on the original property plan. It was only ten kilometres from the house, so I checked it out…" Charlie had rehearsed what she would say for the first fifteen minutes of the drive.

"*Andouille…* You just got out of the hospital, *ma chère.* When you didn't get back to me I was so worried. I was ready to call the police!"

"I'm sorry. I didn't mean to worry you. I really am feeling much better. I just…I got a bit carried away. You know me. I don't do well sitting still. I found ruins, Tess. There's this whole ruined complex on my property. It

125

was amazing! Then I found the wool shed, but it was in a bad state, and when I tried to lift this big piece of metal, I sliced my hand open."

"*T'es vraiment naze…*" Tess sighed. As usual, Charlie didn't know what she was saying, but she heard the affection in her voice — despite being sure it was also an insult. "That is exciting, darling, but I just wish you'd waited. And why didn't you call me back?"

"Okay, so this next part, I know you'll understand… it was a big cut — I know I need stitches. I was trying to clean it, and it was deep, and you know I don't like blood…so…I had a little whiskey to help with the pain…" After a brief silence, Tess burst out laughing. Charlie joined her.

"*Oui,* that I understand. Ah, but you really freaked me out. Don't do that again, okay?"

"Okay." Charlie smiled. Rather than making her head worse, as she'd feared, the conversation actually helped. "It's not all about me, though, okay? I *need* to hear about Leon's big dinner."

"*Ne me lance pas… Leon est le roi des idiots*! *Con comme une valise sans poignée!*" Not only was Tess speaking in French, not only was she speaking a million miles a minute, but her voice was also getting increasingly shrill.

"Tess…"

"That idiot kid of mine asked her to *marry him!*"

"Oh, boy…"

\* \* \*

By the time Charlie pulled up to the hospital, she was starting to feel relieved — guiltily — that she had such a good excuse to end the call. Tess had broken into her native tongue a dozen more times. Charlie was pretty sure she'd heard several new ways to insult someone in French. No doubt after the next phone call she'd have them memorised. One particularly good insult she heard several times in reference to "the girlfriend" was *pompe à chiasse.* This one she understood. While she knew Tess was calling her "full of shit," it literally translated to "diarrhea pump." *Why do people think the French language is so romantic anyway?*

126

As it was a Sunday morning in a small town, no one else was waiting in the emergency room. However, as it was a Sunday morning in a small town, Charlie still had to wait for the doctor on call to be woken, to shower, and to head into the hospital to start his shift far earlier than he'd planned. How nervous the nurse had been to call him should have prepared Charlie. When he arrived, he communicated mostly in grunts, and she felt sure he knew more ways to insult someone than even Tess. He stabbed the anaesthetic needle into her hand harder than necessary, she was sure. Poor bedside manner aside, his stitches were excellent, according to the nurse who was watching closely. While he sewed her up, Charlie examined the stains on the wall. And at least the nurse was the one to administer her tetanus shot, far more gently.

By 10:00 a.m., sitting in the car — with her freshly cleaned, stitched, bandaged hand — Charlie wasn't ready to head home. She thought of Trent, the only person with whom she had even the beginnings of a relationship in this town. She hadn't exactly left things on the best of terms with him. She'd been so angry with him after her hospital visit that she'd returned his several missed calls and messages with a blunt *I'm fine. Tess is here. Busy.* She clenched her teeth and grimaced as she remembered it — he hadn't deserved it.

Five minutes later, Charlie was climbing the steps to the library. She pushed the door and rebounded heavily. *Locked?* She peered through the window, seeing the lights were off. She walked around the side of the building, where she looked through another window. This one was so dark she couldn't see anything. "What...?" Charlie mumbled, trying to angle for a better look.

"What, what?" Charlie shrieked and jumped as Trent spoke behind her.

"Oh my God!" she said, breathing deeply. "You scared the shit out of me!" Trent tried to hide his smile, poorly.

"Sorry, I didn't expect to see anyone here today either. Least of all you. It's not even Wednesday." He looked her up and down, his eyes lingering on her hand. "You okay, honey?"

"Yeah, I am...and look... I'm sorry for how shitty I was after my stay at the hospital. You were just looking out for me, and I totally proved you right by freaking out so hard."

"I get it…" Trent said after a pause, looking her up and down again. "That's a crap thing to go through — it was bad enough seeing you go through it, let alone how you must have felt. It was probably really frightening, and then this guy who hasn't known you all that long gets the cops called on your place. I didn't mean for things to escalate to therapy. I was just worried, you know? That someone broke in or something."

There was another awkward silence and then Charlie threw herself at Trent, hugging him tight around the waist. "Thanks, Trent," she said, muffled into his olive green, slightly ribbed jumper. She sighed deeply as she let him go. "I hope that was okay?"

Trent responded by giving her another tight, long hug. "Of course it's okay, honey. What are you doing here anyway?"

"I'm coming to the library…you know, to research."

Trent burst out laughing. "It's Sunday, Charlie! Library's closed. You're not in Kansas anymore."

Charlie's cheeks burnt red. "Ah…yep, going from city living straight to hermit has its drawbacks. What are you doing here?"

Trent shrugged. "Brent has the flu, so I popped in to get some work done. I'm hopeless around sick people. After your hospital visit surely you realised that already? Come on, let's get some breakfast, and you can tell me what research was so exciting it couldn't wait until Wednesday."

# 22

# Destitution Is the Worst of Vices

With her allergies, Charlie had been reticent to go to a café, but Trent had convinced her with an outside table and promises he knew the owner. She'd told him all about the ruins at her property over a huge stack of pancakes and a soup-mug-size cup of coffee — eating out was a treat she hadn't been able to enjoy in more than a year. Her fear of peanuts had seen to that. Trent did the honours of cutting her pancakes into bite-size chunks for her, as her left hand was still too tender to hold a fork.

"And I took so many photos," Charlie said around a particularly large mouthful. Trent's version of "bite size" was a little larger than Charlie's. She pulled her phone out of her handbag to show him. "This is actually the first chance I've had to look at them too. Sorry — there's so many of them!"

She passed the phone over, then ravenously returned to the pancakes, more than making up for the little she'd eaten over the two previous days. Charlie heard him play the short video she'd taken from on top of the hill before moving onto the photos. "Huh," he said as he flicked through. "You're a really shit photographer."

"Hey!" Charlie said, taking a slurp of her coffee to wash the pancakes down. "I'm no pro, but I am *not* shit."

"No, seriously," Trent turned the phone around to show Charlie. "They're all blurry and dark. What were you doing? Taking action shots?" Charlie took the phone from Trent. She could tell what this picture was supposed

129

to be of: it was the first building she'd entered — the largest — with the three partial walls. She remembered taking this photo. Carefully lining it up. It had looked perfect through the phone screen at the time. Even though it had been overcast, there was much more light than what she could see in the photograph. It also looked like she'd been shaking the camera, with blurred edges and streaks across the photo. She swiped through several more, each one the same, before zooming out to the picture gallery to look at the pictures en masse.

Almost every photograph was alike. Dark, blurry and poorly focussed. The first picture and video from on top of the hill were the best. Some of the close-ups of the windows and things like the crockery and wheel were okay. The photos of the rubble from the wool shed were also perfect. But the rest were trash. When she zoomed out, another commonality across the photos made the pancakes turn to stone in her stomach. At the corner of each and every photo were two bright-white pricks of light. *I guess the feeling I was being watched* wasn't *all in my head.*

"What is it, honey? Are you okay?" Charlie looked up at Trent and passed the phone back to him.

"Tell me what you see in common in each of the crap photos. Tell me I'm not crazy." Trent stared at the phone, zooming in on some photos, and swiping across to others. "The same thing in each photo, despite being in a different location," Charlie emphasised.

"Are you talking about the white flicks?" Trent asked.

Charlie nodded. "Two, exactly the same width apart, in every photo. And what caused more than half of the photos to turn all dark and blurry like that? I swear I was holding the camera still."

Trent shrugged. "I dunno. Maybe the phone overheated? It is weird, though. Ooh," he exclaimed as he was swiping through. "That's great!" He flipped the phone around so Charlie could see the wheel.

"Yeah, I thought that was great too. Do you think it was from a cart or something?"

"Probably not a cart," Trent said, zooming in. "I'd say it's more likely from a horse-drawn buggy. Now *that* I'd like to see. What else did you find?"

"I wish I'd brought my pack," Charlie said. "I found bits of crockery, but the most interesting thing were sheep shears, I think. It had clippers on one end and this knobbly, metal elbow thing on the other."

"Probably were shears." Trent smiled, handing the phone to Charlie. "Sounds like it might have been from a mechanical shearer, if the elbow you're describing is what I think it is. Hey…" He paused, wringing his hands together. "I don't suppose I could come out and see the place, could I? This type of history fascinates me, and the idea of any kind of fieldwork just blows my mind."

Charlie perked up. "Yeah, that'd be great! I'd love to pick your brains on the history of the place. It's partly why I was coming to the library. I want to know everything I can — the fact that there were all these buildings on my property and I didn't even know! And…" She paused, remembering what Tess had said to her about sharing the "spooky" stuff only with her. She'd been about to tell him all about her latest waking dream and the notes she'd taken. "…I've been doing some internet research, and I have a few questions about the Great Depression."

"That, I'm sure, I can help you with. Is this afternoon too soon?" Trent asked sheepishly. "It's totally okay if it is! I mean, it's just kind of perfect timing, with Brent out of action, and your hand and all. I could help out. Cook dinner or something. As friends, you know."

"I do have a spare room…" Charlie said, thinking out loud.

"Oh my God, an adult sleepover!" Trent clapped his hands together. "And we can take my car. We have a *proper* 4WD, so we can drive out to the old station instead of trudging it."

Charlie smiled. "This plan is sounding better and better."

\* \* \*

They'd stopped at Trent and Brent's place so Trent could pack some essentials — underwear and wine, he'd informed her. He'd actually come out of the house with a full overnight bag slung over his shoulder and *two* shopping bags, one in each hand. The house was exactly as she'd pictured – white all over, with a high pointed roof, large bay windows, and neat green garden.

Brent had stumbled to the door, wrapped in a white blanket, despite the warmth to the air that day. He'd looked like death, his skin the same colour as his sheets, aside from redness at the tip of his nose and purple bags under his eyes. Even with his eyes and nostrils caked in bodily fluid, Brent was handsome. Trent was charming enough in a 'boy-next-door' kind of way – even though his stomach poked slightly over the edge of his pants, his chin hung a little loose, and he never seemed able to catch all his stubble. Brent, though, was classically handsome. Charlie could picture him in an old Hollywood movie; he would have glistened in black and white.

Trent had jogged up to the car, asking Charlie to message Brent the address of her house — so he'd have both her address and her phone number — pleading embarrassment at Brent's overprotectiveness. This had actually made Charlie feel better about inviting a near stranger to her house, alone. She'd taken the opportunity of the drive home to call Tess and inform her of her plans as well.

Trent was now sitting at Charlie's dining table, turning over the sheep shears, having already briefly inspected the pottery. It felt good having Trent in the house. Like Tess, he filled it with something she'd been missing. While she didn't mind her own company, it was nice to have a little extra *life* in the space.

"Definitely mechanical shears," Trent said, smiling up at Charlie. "Wolseley shears to be precise. I can't say for sure, but I'd say they're from around 1930, maybe a bit later, probably electric. Your Bill wasn't mucking around. He had some good equipment. And this is a great piece."

"What about the crockery?" Charlie asked, joining Trent at the table.

"Not all that interesting I'm afraid," he answered. "Maybe if they'd been intact... Maybe if I knew more about this stuff... Honestly, I can't even tell which era they're from. They could be from the twenties or from the forties. It's hard to say." He looked up and around the cottage. "It looks so different on the inside to the outside. You've done a great job doing this place up." He'd already had the tour when they'd arrived, with Charlie talking him through how everything had changed since the original plans.

(And sheepishly hiding the half-drunk whiskey bottle she'd left out on the kitchen bench).

"We'd better get going to the station, don't you think?" she asked, looking at her phone to see it was already pushing 1:00 p.m.

"Let's do it." Trent jumped up excitedly, grabbing his keys from the table. "Can we bring the plans this time?" He nodded to the binder on the table. "They might help me figure out what's what."

"Absolutely!" Charlie bundled them up, along with her pack, in which she'd chucked a couple of bottles of water, some fruit, and a few muesli bars. "And I'm going to pick your brain on the way. I have so many questions."

Driving in Trent's "proper" 4WD, and with Charlie's handy compass, it would only take fifteen minutes or so to reach the old stockmen's quarters. Charlie had her notebook and a pen handy, and peppered Trent with questions as soon as they were on their way.

"So, the Great Depression," Charlie started. "I remember you saying it hit hard in 1929 and got bad enough that one in three people in Australia were unemployed?"

"Yeah…" Trent began, slowing down as the car rolled down the first shallow hill. "It was tougher than most people now could even begin to imagine. Hungry, humiliated, angry and afraid — that's how I picture most people back then. The whole government split over how to handle it. Charity groups couldn't keep up with demand, and there wasn't the unemployment benefits we have today. Sure, the States had their sustenance payments, but people could barely get the necessities. And so soon after the Great War, it broke a lot of people. We're a tough nation, though, so we made it through. I'd like to think we're just as tough now, but I really don't know."

"But some people did okay, like maybe the Evans family? They probably kept working throughout?"

Trent nodded vigorously. "Oh, yeah, I'd say so. In fact, they probably had a lot of people coming through the place looking for work. You've heard of the swagmen, right?"

"*Once a jolly swagman…*" Charlie replied, quoting the country's unofficial anthem.

"The swagmen were unemployed men — and the occasional woman, to be fair — who travelled the country during hard times, looking for work. Even if they couldn't work for money, they'd work for food and shelter. That's what they'd usually find at the farms. They'd walk tens of kilometres every week, with nothing but their swags on their backs. It started in the first depression of the late nineteenth century and really picked up again during the Great Depression in the thirties. They're icons of Australia but somehow largely forgotten by the current generations. A tragedy really."

"So these swagmen would have come to the Evans farm?" Charlie prodded.

"Almost certainly," Trent said, hitting the accelerator a little harder as they climbed the other side of the shallow dip. "I think it's crazy how many Aussies know the words to the song 'Waltzing Matilda,' but how few know what it actually means."

"I have to admit I'm one of the many," Charlie said, the words to the song running through her head. She sang part of the song out loud — badly. *"Once a jolly swagman, camped by a billabong, under the shade of a coolabah tree. And he sang as he watched and waited till his billy boiled, you'll come a waltzing matilda with me…* That part's easy. Camped by the water, boiling his kettle. Never knew what 'waltzing matilda' meant though."

"'Matilda' was slang for the swag they used to carry on their back," Trent informed her. "Usually their bedroll, basic supplies, including their 'billy' — or kettle — and their 'tuckerbag,' which was what they'd carry their food in."

"Ah yes — he *'shoved the jumbuck in his tuckerbag'* — a jumbuck is a sheep, right?"

"Bingo! You're not too bad after all. A male sheep to be precise. The *'squatter mounted on his thoroughbred'* is the farmer on his horse, and the troopers were the local coppers. That's us Aussies for you. We can't just call something what it is — we have to have a nickname for everything."

"Bill the squatter…" Charlie smiled.

"That's the one, honey!"

Charlie looked through her notes, thinking back to her dream. "Was the Depression bad enough that people would, I don't know, withdraw all their savings?"

"You mean make a run on the banks?" Trent asked. "They certainly did in the US, and elsewhere in the world, but the banks stayed relatively stable in Australia. Sure, there were a lot of worried people, and I'm sure some folks lost trust in the banks — especially when the Government's Savings Bank went under — but for the most part, we fared okay."

Trent had just answered a lot of Charlie's questions in one go. "And who was 'Jack the Big Fella'?"

"Specific questions today!" Trent said, eyeing her curiously for a moment. "That's a bit of an odd question, honey. If you know his nickname — 'the Big Fella' — I'd have thought you'd have known who Jack Lang was. He was the premier of New South Wales and one of our most famous politicians. He opposed the federal government taking out so many loans and laying off so many civil servants after World War I. And when the federal government got the states to repay the loans, he defaulted, on purpose. He wanted every state to default. He even withdrew all the state's funds to prevent payments being made. It was such a big debate the whole Labour Party split, and there were concerns the Commonwealth Armed Forces would openly fight the New South Wales police. A really interesting time in Australia's history."

Puzzle pieces were starting to click together in Charlie's head. Bill Evans was obviously a supporter of the Big Fella, and worried enough about the impacts of the Great Depression that he'd at least considered removing all his money from the bank. "Did indigenous Australians work on the stations?" she asked, reading her last note from her dream.

"You're all over the place today!" Trent laughed. "But great question… Absolutely they did! In fact, we wouldn't have some of our most important stock routes if not for their contributions. They really opened the outback to us. Their connection to the land and their understanding of the seasons and cycles were invaluable — so much so that farms with higher proportions of indigenous workers usually sold for half as much again as farms without."

"Could they have had indigenous workers here, on the Evans' farm?"

Trent nodded. "It's definitely a possibility. I can find out, probably, with a bit of time at the library."

Charlie felt emotional. Her own connection to this place was growing deeper; it felt epic. "I think it's just over this next rise," she said as the car started its climb. They'd just passed the gum tree she'd rested against the other day. She felt the excitement flowing off Trent in waves now as well. "You're gonna love this!"

# 23

# A Spider on the Ceiling

For more than an hour, Trent had excitedly exclaimed over — and climbed over — the ruins on Charlie's property. At first Charlie had followed him through every room, asking him questions. Eventually, when she had to repeat her questions several times, she decided he was in the zone and to leave him to it. He'd carried the binder with him, obsessing over it almost as much as the ruins. Eventually he returned to sit with her at the edge of the complex, balancing on his car bonnet.

"What do you think?" Charlie smiled up at him as he joined her.

"I'm in heaven!" Trent smiled back, leaning against the car and throwing his arms wide.

"Any theories yet?" She nodded to the binder.

"Plenty. This complex is definitely older than your cottage. If I had to guess, I'd say 1880s maybe."

Charlie remembered the first day she'd met Trent, when she was looking through the census records, and how she'd discovered someone had lived on her property before the cottage was supposed to have been built. "That's right…" she mused out loud. She'd been so obsessed with the Evans family she'd forgotten. "Someone lived here before the cottage was built. What was his name…?" She opened her notebook, flicking back until she found the printouts from that first day. "Henry James Thomson," she read. "His name was recorded in the 1881 census."

"Am I good or what?" Trent said with a grin, slapping the binder with his hand. "I was close! At least the 1880s then, maybe the 1870s. There were no national census records between 1828 and 1881... I bet I can find out from local records, though..."

Charlie also tapped the binder, which was open at the original property map. "What about the buildings. Do you know what's what?"

Trent pointed to the first building, with the most intact walls. "That would've been the overseer's house, I'd guess. He would have managed all the other workers at the station. The other two next to it would have been quarters for the stockmen and their families." He swept his hand over to the ruins with the largest fireplace. "This would've been the kitchen, perhaps a communal dining area, and come with me..." He jumped to his feet and made his way to the kitchen. "Careful now," he warned, taking Charlie's elbow and judiciously making his way to one side of the ruin. With his foot, he tapped the ground next to the wall, and part of the soil crumbled and gave way. "This would have been the larder or the cellar," he explained. "You need to watch your footing here — one wrong step and you'll crumble into this hole. What I wouldn't give to dig this up a bit."

Trent pulled her towards the square metre-size building. "This I can guess," Charlie said before Trent had a chance to explain. "The toilet, right?"

"That's right, honey!" Trent took a deep breath and exhaled happily. "You can really feel the history of this place. There are so many similar ruins around on private property — so much untapped history."

"What about your wheel?" Charlie asked, motioning towards the rusty object. "Is it from a buggy like you thought?"

"Yep, that's my best guess. Probably used to ferry goods, and sometimes people, to and from the main cottage. Most of the stockmen would have ridden on horseback."

"And maybe to take the kids to school?" Charlie asked, picturing Marie and her sisters.

"Nah." Trent dismissed the idea. "The Evans family almost certainly would've had an automobile for trips to Greenfields."

Charlie felt her cheeks flush. *Of course they would have*, she thought, dismissing her romantic notions of horse-drawn carriages.

"There's something else interesting..." Trent said, motioning to the wool shed where Charlie had cut her hand. "Come on..." She had to jog to keep up with his long legs. Trent stopped, kneeling down to fidget with the grass. "Here," he said, crouching and pointing to a dark patch in the ground with fragments of old wood. "Can you see?"

"I'm not sure what I'm looking at," Charlie admitted.

"I'd bet you five hundred bucks this shed burnt down. See the dark patches, and the black on the wood? And also how little wood is left? I'd guess this place burnt down at least sixty years ago."

"And it had all been forgotten until now... I wonder what happened..." Charlie rose to her feet, looking out over where the wool shed would have stood.

"I'll find out what I can this week," Trent promised, a fire lit behind his eyes.

Charlie grinned. "I bet you will."

\* \* \*

The whole drive back to the cottage, Trent theorised about how many men might have worked on the station, how the fire might have started, and when the property had transitioned to just a residence. Despite the excitement of the day, and of the conversation, Charlie's eyelids drooped. They'd achieved a lot in such a short time, and the effort was catching up with her. She was very glad to make it back to the cottage in such good time.

With Trent still nattering in her ear, Charlie unlocked the cottage and pushed the front door. Something resisted as she tried to open it.

"Everything all right?" Trent asked, noticing Charlie straining.

"Yeah...it's just a bit stuck..." She felt as though someone — or something — was pushing on the door from the other side. Eventually the door gave way, and she stumbled inside. She blinked as brightness hit her. Every light in the cottage — of which there was a substantial number — had been turned on. If she hadn't been so drowsy from the drive, she might even have noticed through the window before she'd gotten to the door. In the middle of the floor, near the door, sat Trent's overnight bag.

"What the fuck?" he said, walking past her to pick it up. "I put this on the guest bed…" He trailed off, looking at the lights. "I swear these lights weren't on."

Charlie — who was experienced with these strange occurrences, even if not used to them — felt a pinch of nerves but not the panic she saw creeping into Trent. "This sometimes happens here…" she started.

"Someone *did* break into your house, didn't they? They're messing with us. Why would they do this?!"

"No," Charlie said, walking up to him, holding on to his forearm with her good hand, trying to soothe him. "You said so yourself… When the police came that day, they found no sign of forced entry. It's just an odd house." Charlie watched as the colour drained from Trent's face, her spirits dropping as she wondered if Trent would renege on his offer to stay the night. "Maybe you just forgot to put your bag in the guest room," she said, trying to appease him, Tess's wise words to leave out "the spooky stuff" ringing in her head.

"Fuck, it really is haunted," Trent said, clasping Charlie's hand, which had remained on his arm. "I'm sorry I didn't really believe you! This is insane!" He opened his bag, looking through it to see if anything else had been tampered with. Seemingly satisfied nothing was missing, he hurried to the guest room, Charlie following him tentatively. The room was just as they'd left it, except for the lights being on. Even the bedside lamp glowed brightly. Charlie was relieved to see the smile on Trent's face as he swivelled around. "Can we talk to her? To the ghost kid?"

"I…I guess we can try…if you want," Charlie said, feeling slightly uncomfortable at the proposition but not able to put her finger onto why.

"With your voodoo." Trent clapped his hands together. "But not the cards this time, yeah?"

"Um…" Charlie paused, finally swayed by Trent's puppy-like eagerness and not wanting to disappoint him. Or for him to find a reason to leave. "The dowsing rods worked pretty well last time," she said. "We could give those a try. And light some of the candles." She'd feel better with as much protection as she could get.

* * *

Trent and Charlie sat on the sofa, the remains of the fabulous steak dinner Trent had cooked them sitting on the kitchen bench, empty red-wine-stained glasses on the dining table, and candles lit around the room. Charlie had left the lights on as well, as apprehension had built in her chest like the bile had built in her stomach. The dowsing rods rested on the coffee table in front of them.

"Ready?" Trent whispered.

Charlie nodded and picked up the rods, exhaling strongly and holding them loosely in front of her. Her bad hand twinged slightly but held on to the rod well enough.

"Marie?" she asked gently. "It's Charlie. This is my friend Trent. We'd like to speak with you if that's okay. Do you remember how the dowsing rods work?" There was a brief pause, like the room itself was holding its breath, and then the rods slowly moved to cross over. It felt like the same electricity powering the lights was crackling in the air around them and through the dowsing rods.

"That means yes, doesn't it?" Trent whispered, the hairs on his arms visibly rising. Charlie nodded.

"Marie," Trent said after the rods had swung back to neutral. "Was that you who moved my bag?" The rods slowly moved to the "yes" position. Charlie recognised the same excitement and nervousness in Trent that she'd seen in Tess that first time.

"Okay, thanks for letting us know," Charlie said, her back stiff and straight, every part of her body on edge. Slowly the rods swung back to neutral. "Did you turn on the lights too?" Again the rods answered yes. As soon as they crossed over, the bulbs glowed even brighter for a moment, crackling. The static made the small hairs on the back of Charlie's neck tingle. "We can leave some of the lights on tonight, sweetie. I like the light as well." The lights faded back to normal, the hum dimming.

Trent shuffled slightly closer, now barely making contact with the couch. "And did you hold the door closed? Do you not want us here?" The rods shook but didn't move. "Do you not want *me* here?" The rods swung into the 'no' position. The hairs remained stiff on Charlie's neck.

"I think maybe…maybe we should stop?" Charlie asked timidly, looking up at Trent as the buzzing sensation in the room continued to build. The rods opened wider into the "no" position.

"No," Trent agreed as the rods returned to neutral. "It's okay." Charlie's unease continued to build as she felt a lump in her throat. "Why were you closing the door on us?" Trent asked. "Did you want to keep us out?" The rods swung to "no" again. "Did you want to keep *me* out?" The rods stayed in the "no" position.

"You wanted to keep *it* out…" Charlie whispered, barely audible, thinking of the grey man. The rods swung violently into the "yes" position. A chill settled over her as the rods shifted back to neutral; she felt the energy coursing through them.

"Keep what out?" Trent whispered back. After a moment, the rods did what they had that first time with Tess, spinning together to point at the corner where she and Tess had first seen the grey man. "What does that mean?" he asked. Charlie was about to answer when the rods moved again. Trent's and Charlie's eyes followed, both sitting in stiff silence. Trent put his hand on Charlie's shoulder. The rods finally stopped, pointing to the entryway.

A loud bang sounded at the front door, and Charlie, in shock, dropped the rods, which clattered against the coffee table before falling to the floor. More loud thumps sounded, one after the other, the front door shaking, as though someone — or something — were banging against it with all its force. Trent shifted his hand from Charlie's shoulder to grab her in a terrified embrace. The sound built until it seemed louder than any knocking should be able to sound, the walls reverberating around them.

Charlie wrestled her arms up through Trent's titan grip to cover her ears, squeezing her eyes shut. A groan escaped her like a whimper, inaudible over the din.

"What the fuck is happening?" she barely heard Trent yell. He released her and sprang to his feet before running to the window and peering behind the curtain. As soon as he did, the thumping ceased. Trent twisted the key in the lock to open the door.

"Wait, no!!" Charlie yelled, too late.

Trent wrenched the door open. The energy that had been building in the room dissipated in an instant. At the front door, a large puddle of water had pooled, but nothing else was on the landing. And there was no sign there ever had been.

"Where did this water come from?" Trent asked.

Charlie leapt to her feet and ran to the front door, slamming it closed and turning the key. She was panting, despite the limited effort. "Please, keep the door locked…"

\* \* \*

Charlie lay on her back in bed, staring at the roof. She felt a little tipsy. She and Trent had eased their nerves by finishing off a second bottle of Trent's wine – a delicious and rich cabernet sauvignon from the Barossa Valley. Despite Tess's advice and her better judgment, she'd confided in him that the fear that had driven her from her house that night had been due to this sleep paralysis demon — this grey man. Now Trent lay beside her, snoring lightly. She didn't blame him for not wanting to sleep on his own in the guest room. To be honest, she was glad to have him there too.

The hallway light seeped in from under the door. Every light, except the bedroom light, had been left on to appease Marie. Charlie wasn't sure how long she lay there awake, watching the light beneath the door. Her eyes had drooped closed several times, heavy with exhaustion, but always popped open again as soon as she remembered the thundering at her front door. She sometimes could almost hear it again, the knocking coming from deep inside her head. Sleep viciously eluded her.

A drop of water fell on her forehead, rousing her again. Confused, she tried to move her hand to wipe it away, but it wouldn't respond. She tried to sit, but again her body wouldn't react. *Oh, no*, she thought, remembering her last bout of sleep paralysis. The fear built against her will before she even saw *it* this time.

The light behind the door in the hallway flickered and surged a couple of times before fading completely, plunging Charlie in darkness. Her breath quickened. Once again, only her breathing and her eyes were in her control. Lying on her back, she strained her eyes to examine every corner of the room, searching for the grey man she knew must be there. She couldn't see anything but darkness, even as her eyes adjusted.

Another drop of water fell on her forehead, and Charlie turned her eyes up to the ceiling. Hanging there, its limbs twisted behind it like a grotesque spider, was the grey man.

# 24

# Lock Your Dreams At Night

Charlie tried to yell, to exclaim, as she realised the grey man was hanging from her ceiling. Its limbs twisted and its head cocked to the side, its white eyes glaring down at her. A puddle of water had pooled behind it, supernaturally, on the ceiling. Another drop fell, splashing near her eyes, which she now couldn't even blink. She tried to yell again — to tell the grey man to fuck off like she had the day she'd cut her hand — but her voice had disappeared, leaving her helpless, unable to do anything but stare up at it.

Slowly it lowered itself towards her, the skin where its mouth should be once again hollowing out in a large O as it neared her. *Noooo!* Charlie screamed in her head as it came closer. Her chest now strained with deeply panting breaths. In moments the thing would be on top of her again, smothering her, pressing down on her. She recalled the sensation the first time, her fear of this moment coupling with her fear of the anaphylactic reaction that had hospitalised her. She couldn't stand the thought of the grey man touching her again.

Its face hovered inches above hers. The guttural sound again emanated from its absent mouth, building in intensity just as the knocking at the door had done. In her head, she heard its voice taunting, *Marie. Is. Mine. Marie. Is. Lam's.*

Trent rolled over in his sleep, his arm flinging through the air and over Charlie's chest. As his arm arced towards it, the grey man disappeared. The

145

panic building in Charlie's chest released painfully, a sob escaping her lips as it did. Her fingers twitched as sensation slowly returned, a tear leaking from her eye as she could finally close them. She tried to sit up, to shake Trent awake, but her body still wouldn't fully respond. She felt herself sink back, her eyes drooping, despite how hard she fought.

\* \* \*

Charlie was back in the Dream. The fear that had sat on her chest like a crushing boulder was still there, but numbed, as if felt from a far distance. She could look behind her, through the archway, and see herself lying in bed next to Trent, her eyes open and vacant. At least this time, as she examined the archway, there was no sign of the grey man.

A sobbing drew her attention back to the dreamscape. It was distant and low, but even from so far away, she felt the pain behind the cries. *Marie?* she wondered, thinking how terrified the girl's spirit had been to lock the front door and turn on every light in her house. She took a step and shifted to another archway. This one looked down on the master bedroom in her house too, also in the dark, but a much different scene. Instead of Charlie's king-size bed, a large wooden bed stood in the middle of the room. In one corner was a dresser with mirror and chair; in another, a white metal crib.

Emma Evans lay in the bed, her body curled around the much smaller body of Jack, who lay completely still. Stiff and still, as though his limbs were made from wood. Little Jack gasped desperately as Emma sobbed into his chest. Bill paced in the corner, tears streaming down his face despite his obvious efforts to conceal them. His lips trembled as he chewed at his knuckles.

Emma looked over her shoulder at him, "Are they coming soon?" her words quivered as much as Bill's lips.

"They said they would come as fast as they could, darling…" His pacing increased in speed. "I've a mind to take him to town myself."

"Can we move him?"

"No, no, no…" Bill muttered. "They said not to… Damn it, I can't just do nothing!"

Emma turned her head back to Jack's chest, her sobbing continuing. Bill marched quickly out of the room, down the hallway and through the door to the veranda. Charlie followed him with almost as much anxiety as Bill himself. The First Nations man Charlie had seen in her last dream — seemingly not aged a day — was waiting on the veranda. He sprang to his feet as soon as he saw Bill.

"How is he, Bill?" he asked in a soft, deep voice, his hands wringing his hat as he spoke.

"Not good, Kapiri," Bill answered, clasping the man by the shoulder. "I need you to ride as fast as you can towards Greenfields. Find out what's taking that blooming Dr Archer so long. Tell him to hurry." Kapiri nodded, then turned and ran towards the property's front gate. Charlie fled back into the house as Bill stood there, gripping the veranda railing until his knuckles turned white.

After moving past the master bedroom, Charlie lingered in the doorway to what was her sewing room in the present but in this moment housed four single beds, a sitting chair, and two dressers. In the chair was a slim First Nations woman about the same age as Kapiri — though Charlie found it hard to determine exactly what age that was. White tinged the corners of her hair, so perhaps she was in her sixties. A toddler lay asleep in her lap — *Florence*, Charlie thought. Lying in one of the beds, obviously fast asleep, must have been little Alice.

Marie sat upright in a second bed, her face pale and clammy. "What's happening to Jack, Aunty Alice?" she quietly asked the woman.

*So, this is the Aunty Alice whom Marie was evading last time*, Charlie thought, willing herself to sit on Marie's bed, which she instantly did. Charlie wondered if the little Alice sleeping in the bed across from her was Aunty Alice's namesake.

"Don't you worry your pretty head," Aunty Alice said gently, stroking Florence's hair. "You need your rest, young miss. Dr Archer is on his way for your brother."

"But the doctor said Jack and me are fine," Marie persisted. "Just a flu. Am

147

I going to get sick like Jack too?"

Aunty Alice stood carefully, carrying Florence to one of the empty beds and tucking her in gently. She came to sit on Marie's bed, passing through Charlie as she did so. For a moment she felt both everywhere and nowhere. Aunty Alice shuddered, looking about her, startled. Charlie, who'd also found the experience unsettling, stood by the wall instead, watching Aunty Alice closely. "*Yaree yarwoo*," Aunty Alice whispered before turning to Marie and hugging her. "Lie down, Marie," she said kindly. Marie obliged, and Aunty Alice felt her forehead. "You'll be fine, darling. You've been sick longer than Jack. If you were going to get worse, you would've already. See? Your fever is breaking."

"But what about Jack?" Marie persisted. "Will he be better by my birthday?"

Aunty Alice sighed as she tucked Marie in and stroked her hair too. "Let's pray he will be." Marie nodded and squeezed her eyes tight. With Marie's eyes closed, Aunty Alice examined her. Obviously satisfied, she opened her mouth and began to sing. The sound was deep and thrumming, the vowels held in beautiful harmony — much like the gorgeous music that flowed through Charlie's hills. Her native language rushed from her like poetry, like a river to the sea.

While Charlie didn't understand the language Alice was singing, its meaning swept through her without effort. *Hail! Dawn is shining with glory. The sun blazing with warmth. Night moving... Men stirring... Children are restless. Women thinking by the fire. Birds singing. Animals awakening. Camp noises grow.*

A gut-wrenching wail interrupted Aunty Alice's song. The woman tensed on the bed, her hand holding Marie down. The wail rang out again, piercing Charlie's stomach and heart with its agony. Little Alice stirred in her bed and sat up, rubbing her eyes. Aunty Alice walked to the bedroom door, shut it quietly, and sat cross-legged on the floor in front of it. Marie had swung her legs out of her bed, and Florence was also stirring now as the cries rang through the house. "Come here, my babies," Aunty Alice said gently, opening her arms wide. "Come to Aunty Alice." As the children tottered over to sit in her lap, or to lean against her on the floor, Charlie willed herself back to the master bedroom.

The source of the wailing, as Charlie had guessed, was Emma, who'd thrown herself on top of a now motionless and silent Jack. Bill knelt by the bed, one hand on his son's head, the other on his wife's shoulder. Though Bill was silent, the agony creasing his face hit Charlie just as hard as Emma's bellows. As the pain and sadness washed over her, Charlie felt herself panic, her breaths coming ragged and hard. She urged herself back to the present, back to her bed — away from this devastation. She felt herself pull away in excruciatingly slow jerks. As she pulled herself away, another figure glistened into being in the room. One long arm reaching out towards Jack… He glittered in the dark, his full body gleaming white, a top hat perched perfectly on his head.

* * *

Charlie sat bolt upright in bed, tears rolling down her face. It was one thing to know Jack had died at two years old. It had been something else to sit at his grave. It was excruciating, though, to have witnessed the moment he passed away and the moment his family and those closest to him had lost him so unexpectedly. Trent snored loudly beside her, rolling over but otherwise undisturbed by Charlie's sudden awakening and mourning. A small sob escaped her as she grabbed her phone from the nightstand and tottered out to the hallway. The light, which she had left on in the hallway, was now off. However, the light in the kitchen still glowed brightly, illuminating her way back to the living room.

As Charlie entered the kitchen, she rubbed the tears from her eyes, then checked her phone to see it had just gone 5:30 a.m. Working on automatic, she boiled the kettle, making herself a cup of Russian Caravan tea. She sat at the island bench, furiously tapping into the search bar on her phone, looking for as much information as she could on polio. *How could this have happened?* she wondered. *How could he have died so quickly? Why didn't the doctor help him?'*

A plethora of information swamped her phone. Charlie clicked on the first link and skimmed the information.

*Poliomyelitis... Highly infectious viral disease... Mostly affects children under five... Only one in four cases shows symptoms... Most who are symptomatic only have mild symptoms, including sore throat, fever, and other flu-like symptoms... In severe cases, the virus affects the nervous system. Paralysis and even death can occur in just hours.*

She placed her phone on the counter, the tears finally starting to dry on her face. *Poor Marie,* she thought. *She must have brought the virus home from school. And poor Jack. No wonder Emma kept the younger ones home,* she thought, remembering Emma's wails and the depths of pain that had hit the Evans' house — her house — that night.

# 25

# More Questions Than Answers

On Monday, as soon as Trent left, Charlie crawled back into bed, where she spent most of the day. While she hadn't known Jack personally, the experience still hit her deeply. She felt as though she were mourning someone she'd known far longer and far more intimately. Emma's wailing kept echoing through her head, mixing with Aunty Alice's stirring singing. At dinnertime, Charlie surfaced to eat, then went to bed early that night, exhausted. The dreamless night was blissful.

On Tuesday morning, she sat at her dining table with her notebook, making a list of questions for Maryanne. *What is the Dream? How do you control it? What is the grey man? What does Lam want with Marie? How do I stop it? Who is the white man? What did the white man do to Jack? Why is he wearing a hat? How do I help Marie? What did Maryanne mean when she said that I was pulling Marie to me? How do I make all this stop? Do I have a choice? How many other people has Maryanne "helped"? What's the point of all this? What is the "order" Maryanne mentioned? How is it out of whack?*

As the clock approached 10:00 a.m., Charlie sipped her tea and reread her questions. It felt like she'd barely begun to scratch the surface — she knew there was so much more she wasn't seeing. A notification popped up on her screen. Charlie answered Maryanne's call before it even had the chance to ring.

"Hello, Charlotte," Maryanne said, the same scarf on her head, the same tunic across her torso, the same mask of a smile on her face. "How are you today?"

"I have a lot of questions for you," Charlie tried to wrestle control of the conversation by ignoring the psychologist's pleasantries. "And I don't want you just running off and ending the call when you feel like it. I need answers this time."

Maryanne nodded calmly and slowly, tilting her head as she examined Charlie. "I knew you'd have a lot of questions for me today." The way she took her time with her words frustrated Charlie. "But before we get to those, why don't you tell me what's happened since we last spoke? So I'll have the full picture. How did it go with the Dream?"

"No, I want my answers first."

"Charlotte," Maryanne said tolerantly, "I'll be able to help — I'll be able to answer your questions better — if I know what else has happened since we last spoke."

Charlie conceded. She thought back through everything that had occurred since their last appointment; it seemed like so long ago. "It worked," Charlie said shortly, wanting to recap quickly so she could get to her questions. "When I tried to enter the Dream, I did. I saw Marie and her parents in this house, but almost a hundred years ago. The layout was different, and when I found the original layout of the property, it proved what I'd seen was real." Maryanne didn't respond, so Charlie kept talking. "But I couldn't control it. I couldn't choose what I saw — it just took me to a random point in time. And the strangest thing was I could swear I started trying to reach out to the Dream at 11:30 a.m., but when it was all finished, it was back to 10:30 a.m. And my cup of tea was hot again."

"I did tell you time doesn't matter after death," Maryanne said.

"Does that mean I'm *dead* when I go into the dream space?" Charlie asked a question she hadn't even thought to write on her list. And the idea terrified her.

"Was that the only time you went back to the Dream?" Maryanne deflected.

"I need some of these questions answered!" Charlie yelled, thumping the table with her hands — her sore hand throbbing in protest. To her credit,

Maryanne didn't even jump.

"I will, Charlotte, but tell me what's happened first. It'll help. Was that the only time you went back to the Dream?"

"Okay, fine." Charlie sighed, flopping back in her desk chair. "Yes, I did return to the Dream. But not by choice. The grey man returned Sunday night. I was paralysed again; I couldn't stop it; I was helpless. It told me Marie was his — Marie was Lam's. And then I was sucked into the dream place and I had to watch Jack *die!*" She sobbed the last word out, tears flowing again, the pain fresh in her chest.

Maryanne's mask cracked, genuine sympathy peeking through for just a moment. "I'm sorry Charlotte," she said. "That must have been difficult for you to experience. And I *know* you didn't just see it — you *experienced* it. All of it. All the emotion, all the confusion, all the pain…" It was like Charlie was speaking with someone completely different, just briefly, and then the rational Maryanne was back. "What I'd like to focus on in today's session is —"

"No!" Charlie thumped the table again. "What *I* want to focus on in this session is getting some answers to some goddamn questions."

Maryanne sighed, rubbing her temples. "I'll try to answer your questions, Charlotte, but I don't have all the answers. And I need to give you more context before some of my answers will make sense. That's why I do this in a strict and careful process."

"What is the grey man?" Charlie asked stubbornly.

Maryanne sighed but nodded. "The grey men were human once. Do you remember when I said some spirits linger after death? Types of spirits — types of creatures — exist in the Waiting Place, periodically re-entering our world until they're ready to properly pass on. The Greys are one such type. They're usually people who experienced significant pain and fear at the moment of their passing or in the lead-up to their deaths. I believe this is partially why they have trouble moving on. They need to process this pain and terror, and in doing so, it consumes them. It becomes their very being, their purpose. They're drawn to it and crave it."

"That's so fucked up," Charlie breathed. "So this Lam, is he one person or a type of spirit?"

"That's an interesting question," Maryanne smiled genuinely. "I prefer to call these spirits the Greys. Some call them Lams, and that isn't necessarily wrong. I like to think of Lam as the spirit responsible for keeping the Greys in balance, in *order*, in the Waiting Place. Like their spiritual leader." Charlie took a deep breath of frustration as she struggled to understand what Maryanne meant. "See, Charlotte? This is why I like to do things in order…"

"Wait, no, I have more questions. So this grey man, it's not Marie?"

"No," Maryanne answered patiently. "I'd say there's another lingering spirit. What its connection is to Marie, I can't say. It's not common for Greys to hunt specific individuals — not unless they were linked to them in life."

"So I need to find out who this Grey is…" Charlie pondered.

"The dreams can help," Maryanne said after a short pause. "That's what I want to talk to you about today. There's nothing random about what you see when you will yourself to the Dream. If you saw Marie in her house with her parents, there must be a connection to your *intent* when you entered the Dream. What was your intent?"

Charlie thought hard about how this first dream had begun, her head beginning to pound. "I wanted to know how all this began," she said thoughtfully.

"Then there must be a connection," said Maryanne. "You should practice. Be very clear with your intent each time you do this, though."

"Is it safe?" Charlie asked, already knowing the answer deep inside. *No.* "How do I protect myself?"

"You have more control than you think. If you come across the Greys, tell them to leave. Keep yourself calm and unafraid, and command them to go. They will."

"But how?" Charlie asked. "I can't speak in the Dream. I especially can't speak when I'm paralysed in my bed!"

"You don't need to speak with your words," Maryanne answered. "Use your voice but not your words. *Think* what you want to say strongly, just like you think where you want to go, or what you want to learn, in the Dream." Charlie nodded, Maryanne's words starting to make sense. "I have an open slot at 10:00 a.m. on Friday—"

"Wait!" Charlie said. "No, I have more questions!"

"I'm afraid that's all the time I have for today."

"Wait, no! Who's the white man?"

The question made Maryanne pause, her hand hovering above her keyboard, as she obviously wanted to end the session. "He's another spirit, Charlotte."

"Connected to this house?" Charlie asked desperately. "Please, I need to know. I need to know what he did to Jack."

"No," Maryanne said. "Not connected to the house. Connected to *you*. I have to go. See you Friday." She hung up the call.

Even though Charlie had some answers, they had only raised more questions. *Connected how? Why is the Grey hunting Marie? Why can I only find answers in the Dream? When will all this end?*

One question stood out the most to Charlie: *Who the hell is the grey man? I need to know how he's connected to Marie.*

# 26

# The Links of an Anchor

That afternoon, Charlie lay in bed, trying to clear her mind and relax her body to enter the Dream. Every time she managed to relax one part of her body, though, her mind wandered. Questions were swirling in her head, all leading back to the Grey and to the fear he sparked in her. She was pretty sure it was a "he." As her thoughts strayed, she always ended up in the same place: *I want to talk to Tess.*

She sat up in frustration, deciding today wasn't the day she could find the calm she required to enter the Dream. She grabbed her phone from the bedside table and dialled Tess. The last time she'd had a *proper* conversation with Tess had been when they were last together, in this house.  Since then, life had been so busy on both ends that their conversations had been fleeting.  Tess hadn't had the time to fully invest in Charlie's odd, crazy life. And Charlie hadn't had the time to properly console Tess over Leon's engagement.

Evidently, Tess was already home from work and answered the call quickly. "*Bonjour*, darling. How are you? Not smited yet?"

The familiar words and warmth flooded Charlie from her heart to all her extremities. She leant back against her pillow, a contented sigh leaving her, along with a lot of her stress "Hello, Tess." Charlie smiled before they launched into the deepest, warmest conversation they'd had in days. Tess told Charlie all about her fight with Leon after the engagement, her promise

156

to try to reconcile, her realisation that perhaps she was holding on too tightly. Charlie told Tess all about her adventures with Trent, her conversations with Maryanne, and her latest encounter with the Grey.

"It all sounds too fantastic to be real, doesn't it?" Charlie asked, finally finished recounting everything in more detail than she herself had yet had time to ponder. "The Waiting Place — a purgatory — where souls who aren't ready to move on can wait, dipping in and out of our reality without being bound by the confines of time."

"There's a beauty to it too though, *non*? And I understand. Death is the biggest change of them all — it's scary, it's hard to accept. It's almost comforting to believe that no matter what the afterlife is, if you're not ready, there's a place to wait until you are. To process everything that's happened to you. Where you can still have some contact with the people — the places — that mattered most to you. And if time doesn't matter after death, perhaps there is no separation from your loved ones. I've always liked to believe that when I die, everyone I've ever loved will instantly be with me. Even Leon — even after he lives a full life. Hopefully with some grandchildren who'll take after me and not *her...*"

Charlie laughed before sipping the tea she'd made herself partway through the conversation. Her phone was now on charge on loudspeaker too; she was grateful the initial issues with her satellite uplink had finally resolved themselves. "That's just how Maryanne described it to me. Even she said she doesn't know what happens after death. That no one can really know until it happens to them. She insinuated that I know — or at least I will know — more than she can. It's a lot to process, but it's a lot easier to process with you. Thank you, Tess. Really."

"Pah." Tess dismissed Charlie's affection. "You know it's not a chore for me, *ma chère*. Now let's talk about this grey man. This *Grey*. Who do you think he is?"

"That's the question going round and round in my head. I have a strong feeling it's a man. I don't know how to explain it, but the last couple of times he's visited me it's become clearer. Hang on…" Charlie picked up her cell phone and flicked to the gallery. She selected a few of the photos of the ruins where the eyes were most prominent and messaged them to Tess. "I just sent you some photos. They're of the stockmen's quarters. I think the camera mucked up because of the Grey. I believe it's connected to these ruins somehow. Either a stockman or maybe the overseer himself."

Tess made the appropriate surprised noises as she scrolled through. "That makes sense," she said after investigating the photos. "And it's probably the Grey that keeps opening your front door — or trying to. And that's where you told it to fuck off, right? I'm proud of you for doing that by the way!"

"I think being a bit drunk helped." Charlie laughed. "Trent said he'd try to find out more about the ruins, so hopefully that'll be a good starting point. Whoever it was, they must have died scared or in pain. Or both. It's Wednesday tomorrow... I'll pop into the library and talk to him."

"I can't believe we've been talking for hours," Tess said. "I should start getting dinner ready. Leon and Ella will be home soon."

Charlie gasped mockingly. "You named *the girlfriend*!"

"Yes, well. She's *the fiancée* now. And this is me trying."

"I'm proud of you," Charlie said. "Okay, I'll let you go. Thank you for this."

"And no more ghost hunting today, okay?" Tess said firmly. "Go sew some culottes or something."

Charlie laughed for what felt like the thousandth time during the call. "I'll see if my hand is up for it. I love you forever, Thérèse."

"*Je t'aimerai pour toujours*, Charlotte."

\* \* \*

Charlie pulled up in front of the library. She hadn't needed much time at the post office that morning. Sales had dipped a little with her being offline and not adding new stock; she'd made a mental note to try to remedy that. She was now also on a first-name basis with the grocer, Emmett, who'd told her to send him a message when she was on her way from the library. This meant time wasn't such a limitation today. She felt a thrill of satisfaction with herself for *finally* starting to integrate into this little town. She almost had a spring in her step as she strode up to the library.

Trent was at his usual spot at the front desk. His eyes lit up when he saw her. The night before, she'd sent him a message to check he'd be at work, so he knew she was coming this time. "Charlie!" he said excitedly. "You're going to *gush* when you see what I've found. Wanna grab a coffee, honey? We can talk about it over cake."

A familiar bubble of anxiety and fear popped up in Charlie at the thought of going to a café, especially without her gloves and mask, but the familiarity she was gaining with the town gave her the small confidence boost she needed. "As long as we can sit outside and you word up the owner again, that sounds great."

In no time at all, Charlie and Trent were sitting at a small table out front, a soup-mug-size coffee in front of each of them. The café was named a very unimaginative 'Greenfields Café'. Though Trent had informed her all the locals simply called it "Dot's" anyway, after the owner. Unfortunately there was no guarantee the selection of cakes didn't have trace nuts, so Trent had abstained in sympathy. "You can get cake if you want to," Charlie tried again. "As long as you don't spit it in my mouth, we'll be okay!"

"Trust me, this is a good thing. Brent will thank you. He's been complaining I'm getting pudgy." He pulled his satchel onto his lap and removed a small sheaf of papers. "Get ready to gush! I found the records for your property all the way back to 1880! That's when the stockmen's quarters and overseer's cottage were first built." He extracted photocopies of handwritten notes that she couldn't decipher. Handwriting had certainly changed a lot in the last hundred or so years.

"That's amazing!" Charlie patted his shoulder affectionately as she looked over the papers. "But you'll have to decipher all this for me, I have no idea what I'm looking at."

"Henry James Thomson," Trent said, tapping the piece of paper. "He acquired the property in 1880 and constructed the overseer's cottage, kitchen, outhouse, stockmen's quarters, and wool shed. There should also be stables somewhere on the property. At the time, the overseer's cottage was *his* cottage. He had three full-time stockmen living at the station and working for him, including two First Nations people. Someone whose name is recorded as Jacob Smith — though I wonder if that was his real name — and someone called —"

"Kapiri," Charlie whispered, only the hint of a question in her tone.

Trent looked at her with surprise and question. "Ye-yeah…" he said slowly. "How did you know?"

"Spooky stuff." Charlie dismissed the question with a wave of her hand. "His wife was Alice, right?"

"That I can't say," Trent answered. "I only found the names of the men who worked the station, though they often had their wives and children living with them, and the cottages certainly would've been big enough for small families. Seriously, though, how did you know about Kapiri?"

"Promise you won't refer me to any more psychologists?" Charlie joked, but it obviously cut deep, as Trent grimaced and slumped his shoulders. "Sorry, I didn't mean anything by it. I was teasing… Well, it'll sound a bit weird, but I've been having dreams about the cottage and about the people who used to live there. Kapiri was in one of the dreams."

Trent's mouth dropped open. "Now that *is* spooky. If I hadn't experienced what I did at your place, I wouldn't have believed it. Surreal."

"Who was the third stockman?" Charlie asked, tapping the papers and bringing Trent's attention back.

"John Garrett," Trent said after a moment.

"I think the grey man is someone who lived at the stockmen's quarters," Charlie said. "Maybe even died there. Not of natural causes too, probably a nasty death. Which is why he turns up when there's fear or pain."

"Are you saying I was scared at your place?" Trent mocked.

"Yep!" Charlie laughed, then took a slurp of coffee. At that moment, the café's owner, Dorothy — Dot for short — bustled out with a small stack of pancakes. She wore a well-made brightly coloured dress, garishly paired with a multi-patterned apron.

"I'm going to get some nut-free options here soon, darl." She smiled as she plopped the pancakes down. "In the meantime, enjoy these, on the house. I was so sorry to hear about your hospital stay recently." The whole town seemed to have heard about it. "I do hope you've fully recovered." Dot was about a decade older than Charlie, greying at the temples, and nicely rotund around the middle.

"That's so sweet of you!" Charlie said, feeling the homeliness click even more. "You didn't have to, but I really appreciate it. Thank you."

"Just don't let him eat all of it," Dot said, motioning at Trent with her thumb.

He threw his hands up in faux defence as Dot walked away. "Want me to cut that up for you?" Trent asked, motioning to Charlie's hand.

"Nah, I got this today." She halved the pancakes and made a start on them. Dot really was a fantastic cook.

"Do you know if any of these guys died at the property?" Charlie asked around a mouthful.

Trent shook his head. "Not yet. But I can find out. I can tell you who *didn't* die at the property, though." Charlie raised her eyebrows. "Henry Thomson. He died in 1901 during the Second Boer War, in South Africa. He went off to serve his country and never came home. I don't know how he enlisted – he would have been 37 years old when the war started. Anyway, that's when the property became vacant and presumably went up for sale. The Evans Family bought it in 1922 and the cottage was constructed by the mid-twenties, as you already know. It must have stood empty all those years in-between. I can't find any record of what happened between Henry's death in 1901 and the Evans Family purchasing it in 1922."

"We know Kapiri stuck around..." Charlie mused, finishing off her coffee.

"Maybe he even kept the place going when Henry was away and before the Evans family bought the place," Trent thought aloud.

"What about the others? What were their names again?"

"Jacob and John. Jacob most certainly did stay on — but not John. Looks like Billy Evans had a few stockmen come and go over the years. He never had more than four at a time, though."

Charlie thought back to the Dream — there had been at least six men. "That's not right... There were more than that in my dream."

"Probably swagmen or temporary labourers." Trent shrugged. Having already finished his half of the pancakes, he leant back in his chair contentedly. "It wasn't uncommon for extra hands to come on board when it was shearing time. And swagmen would have been pretty common during the thirties. Even if it was just menial labour in return for meals."

Charlie sighed. "This is feeling more and more like a needle-in-a-haystack situation!"

"Don't worry." Trent patted her hand. "I'm on the case. I'll see what I can dig up."

# 27

# Sweet Dreams

Charlie spent the afternoon cleaning her cottage, unpacking groceries, and sewing. By the end, her hand throbbed a little, but she found that ache, as well as the ache in her shoulder muscles, satisfying. She'd achieved a lot that day, and it felt good. She sat on the couch with a hot cup of tea as she tapped on her phone to edit photos she'd taken of the clothes she'd sewn that day. By the time she finished her tea, two tops were up for sale, and it was approaching 10:00 p.m. Feeling relaxed, she decided now was a good time to try to access the Dream again. At least once more before heading to bed for real dreams.

She sat back in her armchair, getting into a comfortable position and slowly relaxing each of her muscles as she breathed in and out. She heard the insects outside her windows chirping their music, as well as the wind gently blowing through the grass. *Intent...* Charlie thought strongly. *I need to know who the Grey is. Show me who the Grey is...* Frustratingly the Dream continued to elude her — she felt it just out of reach.

Just as Charlie's frustration threatened to break her calm, she felt another presence join her; in fact, she sensed the figure standing beside her. A slight fear coursed through her but nothing like she'd felt with the Grey. It was more innocent, and there was something else too...a cheekiness. *Marie?* she probed gently. *It's okay — I'm going to help you. Show me who the Grey is, darling. I'll stop him from hurting you. Show me...*

Feeling the familiar tugging, Charlie sighed in relief as she allowed herself to be drawn into the Waiting Place, into the Dream. She opened her eyes and found herself in the living room, the decor the same as it had been in Marie's time. She was sitting in the green-upholstered armchair, daylight streaming through the windows. Hearing sounds coming from the kitchen, she willed herself to the doorway. Emma had rolled up her sleeves and was kneading dough on top of a wooden counter. Working besides her was Aunty Alice, her own sleeves rolled up, flour sprinkled across her apron. The two were engaged in a deep, friendly conversation.

Hearing more noises outside, Charlie willed herself to the front of the cottage. A small table had been set up on the veranda with four seats. On one seat sat a middle-aged Caucasian woman. Two young girls Charlie recognised as the youngest Evans girls — Alice and Florence — also sat at the table. Both were older than Charlie had seen them before, perhaps six or seven years old. Each had a chalkboard in front of her, learning their letters from the older woman. A third chalkboard sat unused at the fourth empty place. *Of course, Marie is off hiding or making mischief*, Charlie thought, amused.

*Marie?* Charlie called out. *Where are you, darling?* Feeling a light tugging, she let it pull her. The world blurred, and then she found herself standing somewhere she didn't recognise. There was a large clump of gum trees, and just beyond them, stretching as far as her eye could see, stood a property fence, made of wooden stakes and wire. A group of men were replacing the fence — Kapiri, Jacob, and three Caucasians she didn't recognise. As Charlie stepped closer to investigate, thinking one of these *must* be the Grey, Kapiri stood and turned. He stared directly at her. Charlie stopped in surprise — if he were seeing her, this was the first time it had happened in the Dream. Aside from her strange moment with Marie at the creek — and she wasn't sure Marie *had* actually seen her. She tilted her head as she examined Kapiri back. Although he stared in her direction, his eyes weren't fully fixed onto her.

Charlie looked behind her to see empty grassland before turning back to Kapiri. "What do you see?" asked Jacob, the first to notice Kapiri had stopped working. The other three turned to look as well, obviously happy for any small distraction from their jobs.

"I'm not sure," Kapiri replied in his deep, smooth voice. "I thought I saw a shimmer in the light, just for a moment. But it's gone now." Shocked by the thought that Kapiri had caught even a glimpse of her, Charlie fled to the gum trees, determined not to alter time in any way. She'd always assumed she was a silent observer, not something that could be touched or seen. Marie was the only one she'd ever interacted with. "Whatever it was, it's gone now," Kapiri said, turning back to the fence.

Jacob passed Kapiri a water skin. "It's hot today," he said.

"Let's stop for a break," Kapiri ordered. "The squatter will be coming by soon to check on our work."

The others threw down their tools without any further encouragement, wiping dirty hands on even dirtier trousers. A snapping sound brought Charlie's attention to the branch above her head. Lying across the branch, her dress hiked up to her waist to reveal stockinged legs, was Marie. If it had been possible for Charlie to laugh out loud in the Dream, she would have. Marie had obviously followed the men out to the fence, rather than do her schoolwork. As there were no horses in sight, they obviously weren't too far from the cottage. How they hadn't seen Marie following them, Charlie didn't know. The grass was long enough to crouch behind perhaps. And her white dress would blend in perfectly. This Marie certainly was a troublemaker.

"Start us a fire then," one of the Caucasian men called, wandering to a large pack leaning near the fence. "I'll boil us some tea."

"You've got everything in your bluey, you have, Tom," said a second man.

Tom opened his bag — his "bluey," as it had been called — and pulled out a billy, two cups, and a tin of tea. Charlie recognised the name Bushell' on the side of the tin and smiled to herself. *They still only sell Bushells or Tetley's in the local grocer!* she thought. *So Tom must be one of these swagmen...* Marie scooted a little closer, farther down her branch; Charlie felt excitement and curiosity seeping out of her.

"Tell us a story, Tom," one of the others piped up as they set about boiling the billy. "How far did you walk this week?"

"Too far," Tom answered in a gruff but friendly voice. "There's too many swaggies on the roads now. Not enough work to go round. My stories would bore you all to tears... It's not so easy for some. The whole country's gone bung." He poked the fire with a stick. "Well, most of it," he added, motioning around him. "You blokes are lucky." He grunted as he stood, then walked back to his swag to search for something else. He came back carrying something wrapped in a wet cloth and a small tin. "You boys hungry?" Not waiting for an answer, he fished a knife out of his pocket and went to work on the tin. Charlie realised it was corned beef as the lid popped open to reveal the bright-red meat.

Tom removed the billy from the fire then poked the sticks a bit more until it died down. He unwrapped the other item and removed a lump of dough, which he placed in the dying fire. "That damper'll take time to cook," one of the other men piped up. "Come on, cobber, tell us a story."

Marie's leg dangled down from the tree, and Charlie could almost hear her excited pleading. *Come on, cobber,* Charlie heard Marie thinking. *Tell us a story, please.*

"All right," Tom conceded. "It's March now? Well, almost four years ago to the day you know where I was standing? Sydney Harbour. And you know what I was seeing? The Big Fella opening the Sydney Harbour Bridge," Tom sighed, then laughed gruffly. "Well, it wasn't him that opened it, was it? Some Irishman rode out of the crowd and slashed the ribbon with his bloody sword." Tom laughed harder, the men joining in. He poked his damper with a stick, smiling as he remembered. "The police dragging him down off that horse was one of the most exciting parts of the whole day. Then, of course, they had to retie the ribbon for the Big Fella."

"What I wouldn't give to have been there," one of the men said, making tea with the boiled billy.

"You could barely move for the number of people there that day," Tom said. "But I had one of the best seats in the house. Right under the sign for Clements Tonic. Natures great remedy! Dressed in my best suit... And when Jack Lang cut that ribbon, a rocket shot up into the air, and there was fire across the sky and flags flying everywhere. And then the parade! Oh, ho, the float full of Australia's surf girls… Cornstalks, the lot of them!" Whistling, the men clapped Tom on the back.

"Ah, but that's all behind me now." He rubbed his face. "Now the most I can look forward to is a dry night's sleep, a good day's work, and some tucker with good men."

"Cheers to that, Tom," Jacob said, passing him a mug of tea.

"That's not all some can hope for," one of the stockmen piped up. "I hear Bill has boxes of pounds buried somewhere on the property. He doesn't trust the banks. Always rattling on about the porkers, like he's as down on his luck as the rest of us."

"That's enough of that," Kapiri interjected. "Tom, we've got to fix the full property fence. Why don't you stay on a few months? At least see the other side of winter with us. It'd be better than humping your swag through the frost and rain."

"Don't you have to ask the squatter?" Tom asked in his hoarse voice.

"Bill will see the worth of it," Kapiri said. "Here he comes now anyway." Kapiri nodded. In the far distance a horse could just be seen trotting towards them.

One of the stockmen spat on the ground before practically growling at Tom, "The squatter is one of these Aborigines Progressives types." The tension built, but Tom quickly offered to tell another story, and the atmosphere died back down.

Charlie looked up at Marie, who was happily watching the conversation, then back to the men. *One of you is the Grey*, she thought. If she stayed long enough, she might just find out the names of the other two stockmen. Maybe that racist spitter…

A tremble ran through Charlie's sternum. She shuddered, looking around her. The tremble ran through her sternum again, almost like bubbles rapidly popping in her chest. *Something doesn't feel right…* She tried to pull herself out of the Dream and felt a little resistance. Again, she pulled back as she'd done the first time, but something held on to her. *Marie…* Charlie thought, realising it might have been the child holding her back. *Marie, I need to leave…* Charlie tried a third time and, blissfully, felt herself surge back.

She gasped as she became aware again, sitting in her living room chair. Her mouth felt sticky, her head was pounding, and she found it hard to focus on the room around her. It was still dark, so she couldn't have been in the Dream for long, but her whole body felt stiff. It wasn't just her mouth that was sticky — her whole throat and chest felt gummy and achy. Quickly she realised she was *thirsty*. *So thirsty!* Charlie stood up and stumbled. It felt as though her legs had fallen asleep. Her right leg shook as she groggily walked to the kitchen where she filled a glass with water.

She drank it greedily, despite the pain in her throat as she swallowed. She downed a second glass more slowly before thinking to check the time on her phone. 3:00 a.m. But not 3:00 a.m. on Thursday — it was 3:00 a.m. on Friday… She'd been in the Dream all Wednesday night, all through Thursday, and into early Friday morning…

# 28

# Truth Gives a Short Answer

Remarkably, Charlie wasn't tired after her days in the Dream — just sore and bewildered. Shocked and alone, she switched into pragmatic mode, running through practicalities and setting about achieving them.

*Dehydrated: make a bottle of Hydralite from the medicine cabinet and add an extra tablet of dissolvable magnesium and other vitamins I have for use after anaphylactic attacks.*

*Stiff and sore: take some ibuprofen and slowly stretch out and rub my muscles.*

*Hungry: warm up a tin of vegetable soup and toast some bread. Take it slow.*

*Bewildered: check my phone for news to ground myself back in reality and write everything down in my notebook.*

Leaning against her kitchen bench, Charlie felt slightly better with the beginnings of her plan enacted. Her muscles felt better too, the ibuprofen kicking in. She carried her soup and drink bottle to the dining table, where her notebook and phone waited for her, and started checking back in mentally. A message from Trent read, *Dot tells me she's found an excellent nut-free cake recipe. Let me know when you're popping into town next, and we'll grab a slice.*

There was one missed phone call from Tess, as well as a text that read, *Sorry I missed you, darling. Just checking in.* There was also a message from her brother, Robert: *I've just popped in to see Mum. She's not doing too well, Lottie. Give me a call when you can — we should talk next steps.* Like Charlie, Robert was ever the realist and pragmatist. Still not quite 4:00 a.m., and none of the messages needing an urgent reply, Charlie placed the phone aside and set to work recounting everything she could remember from the Dream in her notebook.

* * *

Charlie's phone alarm pinged at 9:15 a.m., rousing her. Even though she'd felt quite alert at 3:00 a.m., by the time she'd finished her soup and her notes, the reality of the past couple of days had fallen on her heavily, and she'd collapsed into her bed. She stretched, reaching for her phone. The message from her brother was still open when she unlocked it, so she went about replying to messages. She promised Robert she'd call him that afternoon. She assured Tess she was fine, just "lost track of time" (she laughed at her own pun). She paused over Trent's message, which she took a bit more time with.

> *Cake sounds great. Maybe even this weekend. I think I've got a lead for your research too. I'm pretty sure the Grey is either Kapiri, Jacob Smith, or one of the two stockmen Bill would have had working for him in March 1936.*

Charlie had researched the date of the Sydney Harbour Bridge opening on her phone at three thirty that morning. *Anything you can find on a swagman called Thomas who might have passed through town around then would be useful too. I'll explain over cake!*

After running to the bathroom — feeling relieved the dehydration was passing — and having a quick shower, Charlie sat at her computer, waiting for Maryanne. Unlike last time, when she'd written too many disjointed questions, this time Charlie only had three. She hoped by narrowing her list she'd be able to pin Maryanne down on the answers she needed.

*How do I get more control over the Dream, especially time?*

*Why am I finding it harder to enter the Dream?*

*Who is the white man?*

Charlie felt in control. She'd prepared as best she could. She'd taken charge in a weird, startling situation. She was ready.

She answered the phone call as the notification pinged on her screen. Maryanne's familiar face popped onto the computer. "Hello, Charlotte. How are you today?"

The simple question overwhelmed Charlie. A torrent of emotions burst through her control like floodwater through a dam. She erupted into tears, holding her face and sobbing. "Charlotte? Charlotte?" She was aware Maryanne was trying to break through, but could barely hear her over her sobs. Her chest hurt as it heaved, snot dripped from her nose, and every time she tried to open her mouth to speak, she wept instead.

After a few minutes, her hands gripping the edge of the desk, Charlie found enough composure to raise her eyes and look at the screen. She half expected the crazy psych to have disconnected rather than sit through her emotional outburst, especially once she had gone silent.

"I'm sorry," she mumbled. "I always do this. I pent everything up and then it just explodes out of me!"

Maryanne hadn't left the call. In fact, she was looking at Charlie with concern, and the most genuine sympathy she'd seen from Maryanne since they'd met. "It's okay, Charlotte," she said. "Tell me what's been happening."

"My brother messaged and I think my Mum is dying. *Actually* dying this time. Robert never messages me. And I got trapped in the Dream for almost two days — what if I'd been trapped in there longer? Would I die from dehydration without even realising it? I'm starting to try to settle into life in town, but I'm still so scared. Dot from the café says the cake is nut free, but is it really? I can't stand living every day so terrified of a *peanut*. So afraid that any moment I could spontaneously combust. Do you know how terrifying that is? Can you even imagine? I *know* when it's going to happen now. It's not the smell. It's not the tingle. It's literally a sixth sense. Can you explain what it's like to see to a blind person? Or what it's like to hear to a deaf person? I *can't* explain it. But I know, and by the time I know, it's too late. Every time I hope it won't progress to full blown anaphylaxis, but it does. *Every. Single. Time.* Fighting just to breathe. Fighting just to stay awake. So afraid that if I lose consciousness, I'll never wake up again… And then wouldn't it be easier to not wake up? To stop fighting… But every time it happens, I have no choice, I just fight. And I am so tired of fighting."

Maryanne didn't interject this time, didn't tell Charlie that's not what she wanted to focus on this session. Instead she let Charlie talk — rant really. She asked prodding questions at random intervals and gave assurances at others. Maryanne ended with an informative, comprehensible discussion on how the human brain processes trauma — that "fighting" and stress were all completely normal responses. As were the emotional reactions that came afterwards. Her "paranoia," as Charlie had described, was actually a rational response from the brain trying to understand what the danger was and to keep her alive. Something that was programmed into the human body and not a conscious response.

As the clock ticked past 11:00 a.m., Charlie sighed, looking at her unanswered questions. "You probably have to go…"

"No, Charlotte, I have some time," Maryanne answered. "It'll come as no surprise to you that I know what I'd like to focus on this session, but…" She sighed, her mask cracking and slipping again. "What do *you* want to focus on today? I know you have questions prepared."

Charlie looked again at her questions, then back to the screen. "It's okay..." Her outburst had washed some of the frustration and anger away. "You start..." she said. "I'm sure there's a reason you're doing it the way you are."

Maryanne nodded and smiled. "Thank you, Charlotte. What I want to discuss is what I know about the types of spirits you've been seeing." Charlie perked up, grateful for the distraction and eager to hear what Maryanne had to say. The tarot reading popped back into her head. The *Hierophant*. The mentor. Someone coming into her life when she'd learnt all she could on her own and needed someone to help her the rest of the way. The message that had come with the reading also repeated in her mind: *Be ready*. Had she been? Was she now?

"That would be great," Charlie said. "Please."

"We've already talked about the Greys. Last time I told you they aren't the only type of spirit in the Dream. I don't have experience with every type of spirit — there are dozens. But I can tell you about some of the more common ones. The Greys, as you know, are those who've experienced significant pain and terror. There are also Blues, who are generally youthful spirits, cheeky, and like to play games. The Purples are generally described as *alluring*, eminently attractive and sexual. Temptresses or sirens. Of course, these are accounts from *men*..."

"Wait..." Charlie interjected, trying to take notes while also comprehending what Maryanne was telling her. "Spirits have colours?"

"That's how people who've entered the Dream have perceived them in the past," Maryanne said patiently. "I've never seen them myself, at least not in colour. Most spirits who dip in and out of our world aren't perceived in colour, the same way someone like you can see them. Some, however, like the Greys, certainly can be. You've heard of Black Widows? Or the Lady in Black?" Charlie nodded, thinking back to the various horror movies that had focussed on this trope. "The Blacks are spirits who have endured great betrayal or abuse. Not all female, but certainly a high proportion are. And unfortunately they're as common as the Greys."

"So the man in white..." Charlie started, trailing off and looking at Maryanne expectantly. "The Whites?"

173

"Yes, you can call them that," Maryanne nodded. "The other term I use to describe them is *Keepers*. I told you about the balance to the Dream, to the Waiting Place. Each spirit who lingers has something they need to do — or process — to find their own balance before they can move on. It's also important that no single type of spirit has dominion over another. If the Greys had their way, everything would be pain and fear. If the Blues had their way, everything would be fun and games. And the spirits who don't want to move on...sometimes need a nudge. As I understand it, the role of the Keepers is to *keep* this balance. To maintain it."

"And the top hat?" Charlie asked. "*Why?*" Maryanne burst into delightful laughter. A genuine sound that lit up her entire face and made Charlie smile back unwittingly.

"It happens sometimes," said Maryanne. "Some Blues have objects that defined them in life. Especially children. A ball, a doll, cute ringlets for hair. Some Greys bear the physical scars of what happened to them in life. I'm sure you've heard of Blacks wearing veils. I suppose for this particular Keeper you're seeing, there's a connection to that *hat* from its human days." The rational description was a relief to Charlie — humanising something that had been too fantastic to process before now.

"We spoke about spiritual leaders last time," Charlie said. "Like Lam..."

"Yes," Maryanne answered. "With the balance to the Dream also comes a hierarchy. I don't pretend to fully understand it, but I'll describe it as best I can. I've always understood Lam to be the spiritual guide, or leader, of the Greys. I believe there's more than one Lam — there would have to be with the sheer number of them — but they each have the same purpose. To keep the Greys in check. Each other spirit has their own leader or guide as well. The Blues, the Purples, the Blacks... As I've told you before, I'm a Seeker. It's my job, my purpose, to seek out these guides in this life and help them come to terms with that purpose, set them on their way. And there are *a lot* of them. Population control, I suppose. The irony is that when we start the process, I'm the teacher. But when we finish, they know far more than I could ever begin to comprehend."

"Do the Whites have a guide?" Charlie asked.

174

Maryanne nodded. "Yes, I believe they do. But I've never met one. In fact, I rarely meet a Keeper."

"What about Marie?" Charlie asked. "Is she one of these guides?" She remembered how Marie had helped her in and out of the Dream.

"No, dear. She's a lost spirit. Whether she's a Blue, or something else, I can't say. But that's why I think you're connected to her. You need to help her find her balance before she can move on."

"Something else?" Charlie asked. "Like what?"

Maryanne paused for a moment. "Like a Grey, Charlotte. Perhaps that's why it pursues her."

Charlie felt her blood turning to heavy ice in her veins. "No, not Marie," she whispered. "Not her."

"Charlotte, I'm afraid I do have to go. I have another client waiting for me."

"Wait!" Charlie said, thinking how all her conversations with Maryanne ended the same way. "One more question..." Maryanne nodded. "If these spirits are so common, why don't more people know about this? Why don't more people talk about this?"

"*That* question requires a much longer answer than I have time for, I'm afraid. Next appointment, Charlotte, let's discuss this. Tuesday, 10:00 a.m. See you then. Goodbye."

Charlie stood, pacing the floor, all the new information running through her head. She grabbed her notebook, determined to make as many notes as possible. Before she could find her pen, her landline phone rang. She stared at it dumbly for a moment; it had been so long since that phone had rung. Before she'd gotten satellite internet, it was usually only Tess who'd called that number.

She walked to the phone and answered it. "Hello?" she answered.

"Charlie, it's Pat, from St Dymphna Nursing Home. I'm calling about your mum, Elsa." Charlie recognised her as the nurse she'd spoken with when she visited her mother with Tess. Immediately she felt lightheaded, a large fist clenching her chest.

"Oh my God..." she breathed. "Is she...?"

"She's alive, Charlie. But she's very distressed. I think it's best you come as soon as you can."

"Of course, of course," Charlie said, already making a mental list of what to grab before racing to her car. "Distressed how?"

"She was having morning tea, and then she just started yelling. She's been talking about a glowing white man. We can't get her to calm down. We've got her into bed, and she's not shouting anymore, but she's still muttering about him. I do fear it's a sign —"

Charlie's heart pounded. "I'm on my way right now."

# 29

# Don't Wake Up

Charlie had driven far too quickly from her house to the nursing home. Along the country roads, she was soaring at over 120 kilometres an hour. When her phone had signal, she made the important calls. Robert first, who had also just received a call from the nursing home. He told her he'd arrive there later that night. Tess second, who had offered to drop everything and come with her, but then understood when Charlie said no. When Charlie didn't have reception, she ran through mental lists. She thought about her mum's friends, and how she'd get in touch with them. Did her mum still have her phone book?

Of course, her thoughts kept returning to what Pat had told Charlie. The white man. The Keeper. If Charlie'd had Maryanne's direct number, she would have phoned her as well, seeking as much information as she could. *What does it want with Mum? And why is she so afraid? What does the balance have to do with Elsa? With Jack? With Charlie?*

Charlie pulled into the first available car park, ripping the hand brake up and unbuckling her seatbelt. She looked at her reflection in the rearview mirror and took a deep breath. *Is this it?* she wondered. As she tried to process how she felt about that, numbness hit back. Of course she didn't want to lose her mum, but in many ways, she felt she'd already lost her to the dementia.

Charlie got out of her car, slammed the door behind her, and hurried to the entry, and through the lobby. Pat was at the check-in desk this time. She looked up at Charlie with a sympathetic expression as she recognised her. "How's Elsa?" Charlie asked, a little breathlessly, as she approached the counter and picked up the pen to scrawl into the visitor book.

"She's settled," Pat said in a reassuring tone, the edge of sympathy still strong. "It's good you've been able to come today. Is there anyone else you'd like us to call?"

Charlie had thought this through in the car in agonising detail. Elsa didn't have many friends left alive, and those who were also weren't in a good state. Aside from her and Robert, there was no family. Her Mum had been an only child. Even Charlie's Grandma hadn't had any siblings. And last rites? No…her mum had never been religious. "Robert should be here tonight," Charlie said, forcing a smile. "There's no one else Mum would want here, I think." Finished scrawling her details in the book, she plopped the pen down. "Can I see her now?"

Pat nodded, patted her on the side of the arm, and turned to lead the way. As it was midafternoon on a Friday, there were a few more visitors in the nursing home today. Charlie found herself wishing she'd brought her mask but reasoned that was no way to greet her mother. Especially not if she was already afraid. *How many other guests are here to see their loved ones for the last time?* she thought. Arriving at her mother's room, Charlie opened the door a crack and peeked through. Elsa was lying in bed, covered in a white blanket up to her chest, hooked to monitors checking her vitals. That was new. She took a deep, shuddering breath.

"Do you want me to stay?" Pat asked.

"No…no…" Charlie whispered, squeezing Pat's hand, which was still on her shoulder. "Thanks, though." She pushed the door open and walked in, taking long strides, making her way to the bed with as few steps as possible.

Elsa stirred as Charlie arrived by her bedside, looked up and groaned. She called out in a weak, gasping voice, "No! No! Get away! I'm not done yet, you bastard!" Charlie knelt, gently grabbing her mother's hand to stop her swatting.

"Ma, Mum, it's okay. It's me. It's Charlie."

Elsa stopped tossing and groaning, and harumphed as her eyes refocused on Charlie. She let out a short, shallow cry of delight and squeezed her daughter's hand. "Oh, Charlie," Elsa said, her mouth shuddering upwards into a smile. "Oh, my Charlie, it's so, so good to see you. I thought it was *that thing* again…" Charlie's heart fluttered like a bird in her chest. Her mum had remembered her, had called her by her name. A tear fell from her eye before she could catch it.

"Mum, yeah, it's me. I'm here." She kissed her mother's hand.

Pat was suddenly behind her, pulling a chair across for Charlie to sit on. She hadn't even realised Pat had come into the room. "I'll be going now," Pat whispered, as Charlie stumbled to sit in the chair, not letting go of her mother's hand. "It's good she remembers you. This often happens at the end." She patted Charlie's shoulder one last time. Charlie smiled and nodded as Pat left.

"Robert is coming down too, Mum," Charlie said, now sitting more comfortably by her mother's side. "As soon as he can."

"That's good…" Elsa said weakly, struggling to keep her eyes open. "I'm not ready to go, Charlie. I'm just not. I-I'm scared… What if all those hell-raisers were right? That—that *white creature* — it won't leave me alone…"

Charlie wanted to ask her mum all about the white man, to dig out as much information as she could while she could tell her. Instead, hearing the fear in her mother's voice, she ignored those impulses and kissed her mum's hand again. "You were too good, Ma." She smiled. "Even if they're right, there's no way the Devil would take you. You're the gentlest person I've ever known, and the fiercest. There's no place in hell for you." Elsa chuckled, looking up into her daughter's storm-blue eyes again.

"I'm not exactly the white robe and halo type though, am I?" she said. More tears spilt from Charlie's eyes — this time tears of such bittersweet joy. This was the first time in such a long time she'd had a real conversation with her mother. Just like they always used to have. Her memories returned in a flood — memories of talking to her mother for hours on the phone, of drinking wine together in her apartment, of watching movies on the couch with popcorn as a teenager, and right back to her childhood…sitting on her mother's lap while she cuddled her and Charlie bugged her with a million questions.

*Perhaps your life doesn't flash before your own eyes at the end,* Charlie thought, *but before the eyes and over the hearts of everyone who's ever loved you.* "I think you could pull off a robe." Charlie chuckled. "You looked pretty good in a toga." Her mother laughed so hard that she coughed, obviously remembering Charlie's fortieth birthday toga party. It was so refreshing to see her mother's memories weren't gone — they'd just been lost for a while.

"Ah, I'm not ready to leave you and your brother," Elsa said, closing her eyes again.

"We'll never be ready to leave you either." A little sob stuck at the back of Charlie's throat. She remembered what Tess had told her during their last phone call. "But you know what? You know what I think? I think that the moment we pass away, time is meaningless. It doesn't exist anymore. I think that when you pass over, we'll be together again. Straight away, no waiting. And I'll have lived a full life, and so will Robert, and your grandchildren. But we'll all be together. No pain, no weak bodies giving out on us."

Elsa breathed out long and slow. Her breathing was becoming shallower, with longer and longer gaps between each breath. "That's nice…" She smiled. "Oh!" Elsa blinked as she looked over Charlie's shoulder. Charlie wondered if Robert had made it earlier after all — it wouldn't be long now. "It's back… the glowing man…" Charlie let go of her mother's hand, spinning around, standing as she did so to glare behind her. She couldn't see him, but it did feel as though they were no longer alone.

"Fuck off!" Charlie yelled. "Get out of here! Leave her alone!" She felt her mother's hand knocking at her leg, reaching for her.

"Charlie…" Elsa said softly. "Charlie, it's okay." Charlie sat down, taking her mother's hand again. "I'm not afraid anymore. I'm ready. Thank you, Charlie." Her mother smiled weakly at her one last time, then she looked up over Charlie's shoulder and a tear fell from her eye as her hand went limp in Charlie's.

"Mum…?" Charlie whispered, kissing her mother's hand again. Her mother's eyes remained open, but something had left them. She could already see her eyes changing. Elsa's chest also no longer fell. All that moved was her last tear, rolling down her wrinkled face. "Ma...?" Charlie asked again, her voice shuddering. She knew she was gone, deep in her heart, but she couldn't stand to admit it yet. "Ma...?"

\* \* \*

Tess's front door swung open mere moments after the knock. She'd been expecting this, ever since she'd gotten Charlie's call. It was nearly 9:00 p.m. — earlier than she'd expected. Sure enough, it was Charlie standing by her front door.

"She's gone," Charlie whispered, her head hanging. She sobbed as she breathed in and looked up into Tess's eyes. "She's gone, Tess." Tess threw her arms around Charlie, holding her as tight as she could as Charlie whimpered. "Can...Can I stay here?"

"*Oui, ma chère. Oui.*"

# 30

# The Shadow of Your Smile

The next four days passed in a blur. Charlie didn't know what she would have done without Robert and Tess. All she wanted to do was mourn, but there were death certificates to issue, service providers to notify, funeral arrangements to be made, legal processes to commence, and friends to inform.

Robert and Charlie divided and conquered, with Charlie leaning heavily on Tess. Robert arranged the death certificate and the will, and notified the banks, Electoral Commission, Taxation Office, and all other arms of government that had anything to do with Elsa's life. He also agreed to write and present the eulogy at the funeral.

Charlie made all the other arrangements for the funeral service, cleaned out her mother's final possessions, and notified her mother's friends. It was also her job to write the obituary for the local newspaper, with a notification of the funeral date. The nursing home had been wonderful, assisting with the death certificate and even offering to pack her mother's belongings. Charlie was relieved her mother had sold off all her property and assets before moving into the nursing home, only retaining a small china cabinet and two boxes worth of trinkets and photo albums. She kept her mother's locket and wedding rings, a silver framed photo of her parents together, a couple of photo albums, and her mother's phone book. The rest she had delivered to Robert's house, with his permission. Elsa's grandchildren would probably want something to remember her by.

Tess had helped Charlie make her way through the phone book, calling Elsa's various friends — not all of whom were still living. When they had been able to contact old friends, however, they'd all been long phone calls. The stories they shared of her mother both lifted and weighed down Charlie's heart. The funeral home did its best to make the process as easy as possible, but the number of decisions still overwhelmed her: would the funeral be livestreamed? What type of service did she want? Did she want full transport for the body? Did she want a viewing of the body at the mortuary? What clothes would her mother be buried in? Would she like make-up and how heavy? How should her hair be done? Which coffin? Cremation or burial? Or cremation and burial? Cremation before or after the funeral service? Which officiant? Which photo for on top of the coffin? Which music, hymns, or readings? Would she like a slideshow of photos or videos? How would she like the service booklet printed?

The blessing of it all was that all decisions were made quickly, and Charlie had the luxury of not worrying about the cost of each service provided. Any decision she could make and then outsource, she did. She chose the flowers — daffodils and tulips — but someone else would arrange them. She chose the music, but someone else would organise that for her. She picked her mother's clothing, then left that to others to finalise. Her mother had plenty of money squirrelled away to cover her funeral as well as leaving a decent inheritance for her children and grandchildren. Not all were so lucky in this situation.

Before Charlie knew it, it was Monday afternoon, and the deadline for a Tuesday obituary was looming. The newspaper — the South Sydney Herald — knew it was coming, and it had to be in their inbox by five that night to make the print run. Her mother's funeral had been booked quickly for Wednesday, to accommodate Robert's family. Tess had rescheduled Charlie's appointment with Maryanne for Friday rather than the following week, figuring counselling sooner rather than later would be a good thing. Tess had also updated Charlie's various business pages and socials to advise there would be a shipping delay due to bereavement. Trent had sent roses, which sat on Tess's dining table, along with a note that read, *Cake and distractions when you get back.*

Charlie stared at the blank Microsoft Word document in front of her, the vertical line blinking mockingly. Tess put a cup of Russian Caravan tea in front of her and rubbed her back affectionately. "It doesn't have to be a masterpiece, *ma chère*. Just make it factual. The picture you've chosen is beautiful. It says more than you need to." She kissed the top of Charlie's head and walked back to the kitchen. It was her favourite photo of her mum, taken ten years ago. The wrinkles around her eyes hadn't been so deep yet and her cheeks hadn't been so hollow. Most importantly, her brilliant smile was on full display. A smile that touched every corner of her face.

Charlie sighed and pulled her notebook out of her bag. She flipped to her clippings of the Evans' family's obituaries. Charlie had connected so fully to this family through these small snips of paper. Perhaps it really was this simple... She began typing, following the same format.

*WHITE—MRS. Elsa Heather, 82, wife of Albert Donald White, died Friday at St Dymphna Nursing Home in South Sydney, peacefully with her family. She was born 30 November 1941, in Sydney, daughter of Frank and Sarah Hammond. She was married 16 April 1966, to Albert Donald White of Sydney. She lived in Sydney all her life. She is survived by her son Robert Donald, daughter Charlotte Heather, and grandchildren Mia and Ava. Reunited with her loved ones, forever at peace. Funeral service will be conducted this Wednesday at 1:30 p.m., 9 Adelong St, Sutherland.*

Charlie reread the words several times. She'd borrowed "reunited with her loved ones, forever at peace" from the epitaph that would eventually grace her mother's headstone. Would anyone ever track her mother down using these words? Would this simple paragraph sit in someone's notebook in one hundred years' time? Charlie submitted the email to the newspaper with an hour to spare and closed the laptop.

\* \* \*

Charlie sat at the front of the funeral home, next to Robert, his wife Bron, and their two children. Tess, Leon, and Ella sat in the row behind them. Around thirty people had attended — more than Charlie had expected. She dreaded having to speak to any of them afterwards. "I hate these things," she whispered to Robert, her hands tense in her lap.

"You've done a beautiful job, Lottie," he replied, patting her hand affectionately. "Simple and elegant, just like Mum. She'd have loved it."

The service itself only took forty minutes. The officiant kept it short, sweet, and respectful. Robert's eulogy had everyone in tears, remembering his mother through her early days, their childhood, and into her final years. One line stood out strongly: *When Dad died four years ago, he took a piece of Mum with him. Now they're back together, and Mum is whole again.* Charlie sobbed loudly as Robert choked the words out.

Charlie read one of her mother's favourite poems, "A Psalm of Life," by Henry Wadsworth Longfellow. It represented her mother through and through. Elsa had always focussed on life and living, not on what waited at the end of the journey. She'd always taken common phrases and turned them on their head. *You think I'm dust,* she could almost hear her mother saying, *That's not who I am!*

> *"Tell me not, in mournful numbers,*
> *Life is but an empty dream!*
> *For the soul is dead that slumbers,*
> *And things are not what they seem.*
>
> *Life is real! Life is earnest!*
> *'And the grave is not its goal;*
> *Dust though art, to dust returnest,*
> *Was not spoken of the soul....*
>
> *Lives of great men all remind us*

*We can make our lives sublime,*
*And, departing, leave behind us*
*Footprints on the sands of time;*

*Footprints, that perhaps another,*
*Sailing o'er life's solemn main,*
*A forlorn and shipwrecked brother,*
*Seeing, shall take heart again...*

Charlie had removed some verses, needing to keep her speaking time short so she could get through it. But these were the verses she most remembered her mother reciting.

The coffin had been carried out, Charlie and Robert leading from the front, with Andy Williams's "The Shadow of Your Smile" playing. It had been her mother and father's wedding song and seemed apt for this day as well. Charlie would certainly always remember the shadow of her mother's smile. A smile so big it filled her up from her chin to her eyes, throwing a delightful shadow over them all.

She placed her hand on her mum's coffin, in the back of the hearse, before it was driven away. In the afternoon, they'd head to a nearby pub called The Goose and Gander — the garden courtyard so Charlie could avoid the smells from the kitchen — to raise a toast. Right now she wanted to take a moment, as quietly as she could make it, before launching into the obligatory social gathering. "Goodbye, Ma," she whispered. With everything that had been happening to Charlie lately, she'd so feared that her mother hadn't been ready to move on in the end after all. That she might linger. But as Charlie stood there, saying a final goodbye to the body that had housed her mother, she didn't think so. In fact, she felt very strongly that Elsa was truly at peace.

*Dust thou art, dust returnest, was not spoken of the soul.*

# 31

# Leave a Light On

Charlie slowed down as she approached the turn to her driveway. She'd taken her time driving home, in stark juxtaposition to how she'd left. It had been less than a week since she'd sped off towards Sydney, but it had felt much longer. That morning — the day after the funeral — had been blissfully normal. She'd slept until 8 a.m., woken by Tess with a cup of tea. They'd sat in bed together for almost an hour, scrolling through dumb Facebook reels. Then Tess had forced Charlie out of the house to drive her to some of Charlie's favourite fabric shops. Her mask secured to her face, Charlie had spent hours browsing various fabrics, feeling the texture, taking photos of stock numbers, and purchasing enough to keep her busy for the rest of the year. It had been hard to leave, this time her turn to drive away as Tess waved at the gate.

She flicked her indicator on, even though she was the only one on the dusty country road. It was dark, and why take the chance when it was so easy to flick her wrist? As she started down her driveway, her house came into view. She gasped. It was lit up brilliantly, every light blazing. *I didn't leave the house like this,* she thought, swallowing hard. She slowed down, approaching the house at a crawl, eyes peeled for any movement. She *felt* the electricity zinging in the air as she approached. "Every fucking light…" Charlie breathed shallowly as the car drew closer to the front of the house. The porch light was almost buzzing, it was blazing so brightly.

She unbuckled her seatbelt and cautiously stepped out of the car. She made the conscious decision to leave her bag and keys in the car in case she needed to make a quick escape. As she took a step towards the cottage, every hair on her arms stood up straight.

"Marie?" Charlie attempted to say confidently and calmly. *Attempted* was the key word. Her voice came out as an uncertain whisper. The porch light blazed brighter and the bulb burst spectacularly. Charlie threw her arm up to shield her face as glass shards exploded outwards. "It's okay, Marie," she said from behind her arms. "I'm back. I'm here now. You don't have to be afraid."

She remembered Maryanne's warning: perhaps the reason the Grey was pursuing Marie was there was a chance Marie could become a Grey herself. Lam's torment also replayed in her head: *Marie. Is. Mine. Marie. Is. Lam's.* Charlie took a deep breath, trying to empty her head of emotions, especially fear, and willing the tension to ease from her body. When she closed her eyes, the bright light of her house still pierced her eyelids. *Relax my face... Relax my neck... Relax my shoulders...*

"Marie, it's Charlie, I'm here now. There's no need to be afraid," she repeated. "It's important you're not afraid, sweetie. That's what it wants." She stepped onto the veranda, trying to feel for Marie's spirit. It was so much easier in the Dream to just will herself to Marie's side. Standing on the porch, Charlie saw that her front door was wide-open — that certainly wasn't how she'd left it. She saw the door handle had twisted and was hanging loosely. Forced entry... She wondered if this might not be a supernatural force after all — or at least not fully — and if someone might be in the house. When she pulled her phone from her pocket to call Trent to warn him someone might have broken in, her phone showed no signal. No Wi-Fi. The satellite must be down. *Of course it is*, she thought angrily. She tried to stoke the anger, to keep the fear at bay.

"Marie, I'm coming in. Please don't be afraid." Slowly, Charlie pushed her front door open. It creaked loudly, the only other sound the buzzing of the lights inside the house and the door handle rattling as it swung. The house was chaos. Dining room chairs were stacked on top of one another in precise patterns, but all her living room furniture had been upended violently. Every door, every cupboard had been thrown open, so viciously that a couple of her kitchen cupboards were hanging from their hinges. Some of her crockery had been stacked in delicate towers, while others had been smashed across the kitchen floor and bench top. No corner was untouched. Papers had been tossed all over her desk, the desk chair upended, every drawer open. She was relieved to see her laptop looked to be in one piece.

Fear crept into the pit of Charlie's stomach like a cold, wet worm and wound its way towards her chest. She took a deep shuddering breath, trying to push the fear back down. Fear was what the Grey wanted — it wanted her terror. "Marie," Charlie said, more confidently. "Where are you, sweetie? I can't see you right now, but I'm here. I'm with you. Show me where you are."

*I'm scared*, she felt rather than heard Marie whisper, from just in front of her and to the right. From the kitchen. *I didn't mean to, Daddy. I'm sorry.* Charlie tried to keep a level head, which was increasingly difficult with the hum of the lights and a sense of unease so strong it turned her stomach.

*Be rational, Charlie*, she thought. *It's not the kitchen — it's Marie's dining room. She's hiding under the table again.* She got down on her hands and knees, trying to remember the layout of the dining room in comparison to her kitchen. Slowly she crawled forward, trying to exude as much love and calm as she could towards where she expected Marie was cowering. "I'm here, sweetie," she said over the hum. "Your Daddy loved you...*loves* you." The correlation to her own mother stung, mixing with the sick feeling in her stomach and almost bringing a tear to her eye.

*I didn't mean to*, Marie wept. *I just wanted my own story...like the swaggie. I just wanted my own story. I just wanted to have an adventure.* Charlie sent another wave of love towards where she felt Marie was speaking from. She glimpsed her very briefly, at least nine years old, the age she'd been when she passed, hunched in as small a ball as humanly possible. Hugging her knees, her chin between them. Swirls of blue and grey battled one another around her small form. Then she was gone — visibly at least. Charlie crawled the rest of the way to where she'd seen Marie, huddling in her own ball beside her.

"I'm going to help you," Charlie said, stronger, more assured. Determination built, replacing the fear. The humming sound also built in intensity, Charlie's long red hair now standing on end with the static. Although she put her hands over her ears to try to keep out the thrum, the vibrations coursed through her whole body.

*He's here!* Marie screamed in Charlie's mind, and then every light in the house exploded, the same way they had on the porch. She pulled herself even tighter into a ball as the house was plunged in darkness and showers of glass rained on top of her. Her hands still clasping the back of her head, Charlie looked up, staring through the gloom. Standing in the middle of the chaos of her living room was the Grey. His head scraped the ceiling, his shoulders heaving as though he were breathing heavily. His piercing white eyes glared at Charlie through the darkness, the skin over where his nostrils and mouth should be sucking in deeply. Water dripped from him, forming a puddle on the hardwood floor.

"You can't have her!" Charlie yelled, still crouched in a ball. "You ca—" Her voice was stuck in her throat, the familiar sensation of paralysis locking her in place. Her mouth was open, partway through her shout. She tried to close her mouth, to force out the words, but she was frozen again. She sensed Marie beside her, tightening further, becoming even smaller.

*No!* Charlie screamed in her head, remembering Maryanne's advice that while her words could be silenced, her voice couldn't be. The Grey bellowed its deep, guttural noises, building from its stomach and roaring outwards. *You can't have her! You hear me?* The Grey took a shuddering step towards them. *Fuck...off,* Charlie thought viciously towards it. *You fuck off.*

The Grey faltered, shimmered, moaned one last grunt, then vanished. As it did, Charlie could move again, collapsing back onto her heels. The unease in the room dissipated, and with it the build-up of energy — which must have been Marie's. Both Marie and the Grey were gone.

* * *

After the ordeal, Charlie stayed in her house, despite its disarray. She pulled her mobile phone from her pocket, turned on the flashlight, and found the candles in the kitchen, lighting enough of them to illuminate the living room. Despite how raw the pain of losing her mother was, this rawness — this pain — she felt in her home was deeper. Her mother didn't need her any longer, but Marie did.

Using her phone's light, she discovered the satellite had been disconnected and went about fixing it. Next, she swept up the larger shards of broken glass and crockery, rearranging her furniture as she went. While pulling out her vacuum cleaner, she found a single spare light bulb, which she replaced and turned on in the kitchen. Not only did it help illuminate her work, but if this was Marie's hiding place, Charlie wanted to ensure she had the light she obviously craved. It was 11:00 p.m. when she had finished cleaning the kitchen and living room as much as she could. With glass shards still sprayed over her bed, she decided it would be best to sleep on her couch. Closer to Marie and closer to the light. Before letting her heavy eyelids close, she messaged Tess to say, simply, *I'm home safe. Sorry for the late message. Weird things happening in the cottage again. I'm okay. I'll call you tomorrow night to update you.*

She then messaged Trent. *Can we catch up tomorrow afternoon? I'll be in town after lunch.* After placing her phone on the floor beside the couch, she closed her eyes in exhaustion, sending one last burst of love out to Marie: *Don't worry. I'm here. I'll help you.*

\* \* \*

Charlie woke around eight the next morning, having slept better than she'd expected. She sat up, looking around her house now that daylight streamed through the window. She'd done a good job of tidying her living space. Some cupboard doors still swung on their broken hinges; she saw a few shards of glass glimmering on the floor, which she'd obviously missed; and her study space was still a mess. Otherwise it wasn't too bad. The rest of the house, though, she had yet to investigate.

She was grateful to see her sewing room had been left in one piece, aside from the burst globe. The guest room and bathroom were also fine — again, except for the glass. It took Charlie the better part of an hour to remove all the burst globes, change the bedsheets, unscrew the damaged kitchen cupboard doors, and sweep up the rest of the glass — including the shards on her porch. By the time she'd finished tidying her desk and had a load of bedsheets tumbling in the washing machine, it was nearly time for her call with Maryanne. She made a cup of tea and sat patiently, waiting for the psychologist to connect.

"Hello, Charlotte," Maryanne said in her familiar greeting. "I'm sorry to hear about your mother. How are you?"

"It sucks, but I'm actually doing okay, I think," Charlie replied. "I will miss her *terribly*, but I've been missing her for a long time now. And I have a feeling she's okay. She was calm towards the end."

"I'd say you had something to do with that." Fine smile lines creased Maryanne's face, and Charlie wondered if perhaps Maryanne was 'normal' in her own life — beyond the screen. "It's good you could be with her when she passed."

"Yeah," Charlie replied, then quickly shifted to the topic she most wanted to discuss. "Something happened at the cottage while I was away." Maryanne's interest piqued, Charlotte recounted what had happened the night before in as much detail as she could remember, drawing from her notebook as needed.

"It does sound like the theory that Marie could become either a Grey or a Blue is correct," Maryanne said after a moment's pause. "You did the right thing, Charlotte. I'm impressed with your progress."

"So," Charlie said, rearranging herself in her office chair, "what do you want to discuss in this session? What's next?"

"Well, I haven't exactly done things in order with you."

"I know, and that's my fault," Charlie responded. "But I'm ready now, I promise. What's next?"

Maryanne tapped the table in front of her with her pen. "I think it's time I tell you what your role in all this will be." Charlie's nerves bubbled as she waited for Maryanne to continue. "You, Charlotte, are going to be a Keeper."

Charlie was dumbfounded. She tried to reply but lost her words. "Wait…" she said, rubbing her temple. "What? Like the guy with the top hat?"

"That's right," Maryanne answered patiently. "That's why, I expect, you have a connection with him."

"But…" Charlie struggled for words again. "But… What? No, you said Keepers only existed in the Waiting Place. Not here."

"I also said Keepers were once human," Maryanne replied. "And I said you *will* become a Keeper. You're not one yet."

"I still don't know what that means," Charlie replied, the nerves turning to bile in her stomach.

"You will help keep the balance. You asked what the Keeper was doing with Jack? I think he was helping him move on. Not all spirits are trapped — some move on straight away, but others need a little push."

"My Mum…?" Charlie asked tentatively.

"The same, I expect. You said she wasn't ready to move on? And now you tell me you think she's okay? I'd say the Keeper had a role there." Maryanne took a deep breath. "I believe this is also why you have a connection with Marie. She's not moved on, and she's not even properly in her Waiting Place. Her balance is off. She needs help." Charlie felt Maryanne's words shower over her just as the glass had showered on her the night before.

"This is a lot to process…" Charlie trailed off.

"I know, which is why this is all I wanted to cover today."

"Wait… Can I ask…how do you *know*? How do you know for sure?"

"It's my purpose, Charlotte," Maryanne replied. "I've helped guides find their way for more than thirty years. You may only be the second Keeper I've met in this life, but there's no doubt in my mind. From the first moment I met you, I knew. I *know*." Maryanne stared at Charlie for a while longer as they both sat in silence. "I'll see you on Tuesday at 10:00 a.m., Charlotte. You'll be okay." The line disconnected.

# 32

# Gluten Free, Dairy Free, Egg Free, Life Free

Charlie took a big mouthful of cake — which was also gluten, dairy, and egg free, but soaked in delicious citrus syrup. "This is amazing!" she told Dot, who had stayed to watch her take her first mouthfuls. "You can count me a regular for sure."

"Already do, darl." Dot smiled back. "And it's been a hit with the other locals too. Who'd have thought something missing so many ingredients could be so gosh darn tasty." She patted Charlie on the shoulder as she turned to head back inside. "God bless you, darl."

"Dot's pretty religious," Trent explained after she'd walked back inside. "She doesn't judge me and Brent, though. Doesn't judge anyone, that one. Leaves all the judging to Jesus, she says."

"She's lovely," Charlie said, before taking a long sip of warm coffee.

"She'd have to be in this business. So…how are you, honey?" Trent asked cautiously, sympathy seeping into the soft lines of his face. "I can't imagine what it's like losing a parent. I'm lucky so far — both are still alive and kicking."

Charlie smiled at his awkward small talk. "I'm doing good actually. My mum was ready to go in the end. And I had the best conversation I'd had with her in years. Since the dementia took hold, it was like I'd already lost her.

194

But when she was passing, I got her back. Just for a little bit. I actually got to say goodbye. I thought that would be the hardest part of losing someone with dementia: feeling like I never had the chance to tell her what she meant to me. But I did. And it turns out, she already knew."

"That's beautiful," Trent said.

"Yeah, it is, isn't it?" Charlie finished her cake, wiping the syrup from the corners of her mouth with her napkin. "I am ready for a distraction, though. Your message said you have a good one!"

"You bet!" Trent said, clearing aside his polished-off plate of chocolate cake to make room for his satchel. He pulled out his familiar binder, now thicker than ever. "I've got a copy for you too, honey," he said, patting his satchel. "Now you can really fill up that notebook of yours. I have Henry Thomson's full service records – including where he died, where he's buried, even where you can find his name in the Australian War Memorial. He was with the infantry."

"Next time I'm near Canberra, I'll be sure to leave him a poppy at the War Memorial," Charlie said.

"But he's not your man," Trent continued confidently. "Even if his ghost somehow could come back from Africa and haunt the place, I don't think he's the type. In 1901, he received the Victoria Cross service medal for valour. I don't know what the story is there, but it usually involves self-sacrifice."

"I agree — we can cross him off the list," Charlie said. "I'm pretty sure it was one of the stockmen or the overseer."

"Spooky stuff?" Trent asked.

"Spooky stuff," she said affirmatively.

"I did some digging with the dates you gave me. Bill had three full time stockmen from 1935 to 1937: Kapiri, Jacob Smith, and Sidney Noel Scott. If you're sure there was a fourth, he must have been temporary. That makes it harder, I know. But don't worry, honey, we'll keep looking."

"Did any of them die on the property?" Charlie asked, leaning closer to look over Trent's papers.

"No," he answered. "Not that I've been able to find. And after the late thirties, it looked like Bill had trouble keeping stockmen on his farm full-time. Jacob and Sidney left in 1937, and Kapiri left in 1941. Kapiri would have been pretty old by then, but still, there was a lot of turnover of the new stockmen too. The records get a little messy."

"So we could be missing something?"

Trent nodded. "Yep, for sure. History is full of holes. I did find something that'll interest you, though. I was looking through the local newspapers from 1936, and there was a swagman found dead on the road not far from your property."

"Thomas?" Charlie gasped.

"I don't know — he wasn't named. But that's not to say it wasn't him. He was never identified. Several swagmen died or went missing in the Great Depression. It was a tough gig. And lonely."

"Do you think you could find out more about him?" Charlie asked.

"The coroner's records are my next step," Trent said around a mouthful of coffee. "I've got an appointment there next Wednesday. Earliest I could arrange, with work and everything."

"I do really appreciate it," Charlie said. "I always thought I was good with research, but you're a real wizard."

"I'm having the time of my life!" Trent said, packing most of his papers away. He left one folded piece sitting on the table. "I'm even considering writing a book. And if it means free, regular access to the ruins at your place, you'll never be rid of me."

"Is that all this is?" Charlie teased.

Trent pushed her shoulder in friendly response. "It's Brent you need to worry about anyway, not me. He's complaining I'm not spending enough time with him."

"Well, he's very welcome next time you come out to explore the ruins. Make it a picnic. It'll be romantic." Trent laughed. Charlie motioned to the last piece of paper on the table. "What's this?" she asked.

"That's one of the most exciting things I've found." Trent smiled excitedly. "I found Kapiri's great-grandson."

"What?" Charlie said, equally as excited, grabbing Trent's hand. "Really? Oh my God, that's amazing!"

"Like you said, I'm a wizard. I've contacted him already, told him a friend of mine lives at the property where his great-grandfather used to work, and asked if he'd mind answering a few of our questions. His name is Kerry Bell — he lives in Newcastle and he's happy to see us on Sunday morning."

Charlie squeezed Trent's hand harder. "That's amazing. Hopefully he actually knows something. I don't know anything about my great-grandparents."

"He seemed eager," Trent answered. "It's only a ninety-minute drive. Totally worth it." Charlie agreed. If nothing else, seeing Kapiri's living flesh and blood would be a marvel.

\* \* \*

Charlie spent the rest of Friday shopping for light bulbs and hinges. She spent Saturday morning repairing her house and was pleased with her handiwork. One kitchen cupboard hung slightly askew, but other than that, she didn't think anyone would be able to tell what had happened only days before. Saturday afternoon she sat at her dining table arranging her notebook, including Trent's latest research. She came to the newspaper clipping about the dead swagman. Strangled, the article said. Obviously, the rules around what could be printed were looser back then, as there was a photo of the body. The photo wasn't very clear, but it was possible it was Thomas.

She toyed with the idea of entering the Dream to try to find more answers. Although she was afraid, the questions burnt inside her. Physical discomfort had alerted her to her overstay last time. Perhaps it could alert her again this time… She put an alarm on her phone for three hours' time, setting the vibration as high as it would go, as well as the volume. She then messaged Trent, saying if she didn't meet him in Greenfields on time on Sunday, he should come to her house and let himself in. After putting the phone on 'do-not-disturb' (so no random messages would interrupt her), she secured the phone over her right ear with a headband and a beanie. It was the only thing she could think of to ensure there'd be enough pain and discomfort to alert her if she did succeed in getting into the Dream.

Charlie lay in bed, wanting to maximise her chances of full relaxation. This time she was also determined not to rely on Marie to bring her into the Dream, not wanting the girl to put herself in further danger. She thought back to how she'd felt when she'd first entered the Dream, what Maryanne had told her, along with her own instinct. *No emotions. No feelings. No thoughts. Just intent. How did Thomas die? How did Thomas die?*

She lay in bed for an hour, clearing her thoughts, relaxing herself, and repeating this question over and over. Several times she felt on the cusp of entering the Dream but never quite teetered over the edge. *How did Thomas die? I need to know... Only this matters...* Finally she felt herself surge into the Dream. She was suddenly seeing, and tried to get her bearings. It was dark; rain was falling heavily; and the Dream wasn't as crisp as it usually was. It was blurred, muffled, as though she were trying to see through fog and hear underwater. There was thunder booming overhead, and lightning cracked through the sky. The rain fell like sheets, further confusing her.

Charlie spun, trying to find something that might help her connect to her location. She felt like she did the first time she was in the Waiting Place. Everything was rolling like she was drunk, spinning. Finally her eyes locked on to something she recognised, illuminated by a sudden burst of lightning. The gum tree, by the creek, where Marie had buried Mr Buttons's glass eye. Hearing yelling to her right — anguished, angry, broken — she tried to surge forward, to see who was crying out, but she felt as though something were holding her back. The cry rang out again, in deep wracking sobs. *Who...?* Finally she felt herself jerk forward and saw who it was. Through the sheets of rain, kneeling in the mud by the creek, was Bill.

She now stood behind another dark silhouette. *Thomas?* she thought. The shape of him was right, and there was a swag across his back.

"Please, sir!" Thomas yelled desperately, fear tinging his tone. "It wasn't me! It wasn't!"

"You *stole* from me!" Bill hollered, his words finally clear amongst his bellows. "My *most precious...*" His words trailed off, blurred by his anger and anguish and by the thunder and rain pouring down.

"I swear, sir. I swear. I didn't, I didn't! There's nothing here. See? Nothing!" Bill lurched to his feet — lurched at Thomas — his hands closing tightly around Thomas's throat.

"Why?!" Bill screamed, squeezing tighter. Charlie, so close and connected to this moment, felt as though Bill's rough hands had closed around her own throat. The pain was both sharp and crushing, forcing the air from her. "You all keeping taking till I've nothing left!"

Charlie collapsed to the ground at the same time as Thomas, with Bill above her, crazed anger in his eyes. The blurring of the Dream deepened, darkening around the edges. *Out*, Charlie thought desperately, not wanting to experience Thomas's death after all. *'Out...out! Out!'*

# 33

# Oral Histories

Charlie had made it out of the Dream before her alarm had gone off. In fact, it was as if she'd barely closed her eyes then opened them again. She removed her phone, headband, and beanie from her ear and gently rubbed her neck as she sat up. Her throat was perfectly fine. But the memory of how it had *crushed* beneath Bill's hands was still prominent in her mind.

She thought back to Thursday night, when Marie had pleaded with her father from beneath the dining table…saying sorry… *Were you* actually *talking to your father?* Charlie wondered. *Is Bill the Grey?* She jumped out of bed and paced the length of her room. Bill had been in her Dream when she'd asked about the Grey after all, even if only from a distance. Charlie hated the thought of Marie's dad being the source of his daughter's torment. However, being on the receiving end of Bill's enormous anger was almost enough to sway her. She shuddered as she pictured it; she couldn't rule him out now.

\* \* \*

"What did you get up to yesterday?" Trent asked conversationally as they travelled down the highway in Charlie's RAV4.

"Oh…" she answered, remembering again the heavy hands pushing down on her. Then she thought about how she'd fixed the house in the morning after a terrifying creature and a terrified ghost had trashed it. "Well, I went for a walk in the afternoon." That part was true. With her theories running through her head, she'd decided a stroll in her hills had been much overdue. And if not relaxing, it had been at least enough of an exertion to distract her. "How about you?"

"We visited Brent's folks in the next town over," Trent answered. "And he's worried I don't love him," he joked.

The rest of the journey to Newcastle passed pleasantly enough, with the same sort of chatter, and Trent navigating for the last ten minutes of the drive. "Next left," he said. "House should be just up here on the right, number ten." An unassuming Aussie brick house with a concrete driveway and yellowing lawn — mostly weed, if Charlie was honest — stood at number ten. "Don't worry. I told him about the peanut allergy," Trent said for the third time.

The front door opened as they got out of the car. A slightly overweight older man stood in the doorway in denim shorts and a white singlet. His thinning hair was white, his tan skin rough and wrinkled all over. He'd obviously tried to shave but missed large parts of stubble.

"Hi," Charlie said in a friendly voice, as she closed her car door. "I'm Charlie. This is Trent. We're here to see Kerry Bell. He knows we're coming."

"I'm Kerry Bell," he said in a voice as deep and soft as Kapiri's had been. "And of course I knew you were coming — I opened the door, didn't I?" Charlie had to consciously keep her mouth from dropping open. When Trent had said they were seeing Kapiri's great-grandchild, she'd pictured a young man. Kerry looked older than Kapiri had the last time she'd seen him.

Trent walked up the driveway and shook Kerry's hand. "Thanks for seeing us. It must be a bit of a weird request for you."

Kerry shrugged, motioning for them to head into the house. "Yeah," he said. "I suppose. But why not? It's been more than fifty years since I was at that farm. I thought it'd be nice to hear how it's going."

Charlie and Trent followed Kerry down a hallway floored with ugly linoleum and into a sitting room with dark purple carpets. Kerry's house was like stepping thirty years back in time. Charlie bet the kitchens were a horrid peach colour. "You've actually been up to the property?" she asked eagerly. "I thought Kapiri stopped working there in the forties."

Kerry sat in an old floral armchair, motioning for the other two to sit on the worn sofa. "You've done your homework then. Yeah, he did, only a few years before he passed away. He spent his whole life on that property, making it the success it was. My dad also worked there on and off over the years, especially after I was born. The work was hard and his boss was an arse, but the pay was okay."

"Did you li—"

"Who was your da—"

Charlie and Trent tried to ask questions at the same time. Trent motioned for Charlie to go first. "Did you live there too?" she asked.

"Nah, we were in town so I could walk to school. No one but the Evans family lived there after Papa Kapiri and the others left. But when Dad was working there, we'd sometimes pop in on the weekend, and my sisters and I would muck around in the old stockmen's quarters." He nodded to Trent. "What were you saying?"

"Who was your dad, if you don't mind me asking? I've been researching who worked at the station."

"Rupert Bell," Kerry replied. "My Ma was Kapiri's granddaughter. Dad married into the family. Great-grandma got him the job, if I remember what he told me correctly." He leaned back in his chair, looking up as if flicking through a catalogue of memories.

"The stockmen's quarters are still there," Charlie smiled, bringing Kerry's attention back down. "But in ruins now — I needed Trent to tell me what the buildings even were. And the wool shed is pretty much completely gone."

"It would be," Kerry said. "It burnt down not long after I was born. When I was kid, I'd muck about in the tin and wood, but Ma always got so cross when she found out what we'd been up to. And she *always* knew." He laughed to himself. "That's a shame about the stockmen's quarters, but I'm not surprised. The Evans family never went down there after the shed burnt down."

"Do you know how it burnt down?" Charlie asked curiously.

"No one ever told me." Kerry shrugged. "I suppose it was an accident. Ma and Gran said it was like the family was cursed. You heard what happened to the kids, right? First their boy dies of polio because the doctor was too stupid to diagnose it early. Then their girl falls in the creek one winter, gets the flu, and dies. After that, everything seemed to go arse up. The Evans family lost all their money, the sheep got sick, the shed burnt down… They still had folk like my dad go up to look after the sheep until they could be taken to neighbouring farms to be shorn or butchered. But after Mrs Evans died, Mr Evans stopped caring about any of it. I was about ten the last time I went to the farm, when Mr Evans was selling up the last of his sheep. Do you have sheep there now?"

"No." Charlie shook her head. "Unfortunately not. I wouldn't know the first thing about how to look after them."

"Well," Kerry grunted, "I suppose not, no."

"Did you know any of the other stockmen?" Trent asked. "Anything else unfortunate happen to any of them on the station?"

Kerry raised an eyebrow at him. "What kind of research are you two even doing?" he asked gruffly. As Trent shrugged and colour flushed his cheeks, Kerry answered his question. "No, not that I know of. Just your typical stuff: splinters, cuts, heatstroke."

"I'm curious about the people who built the house I'm living in," Charlie jumped in before Trent could raise Kerry's suspicions any higher. "Trent's a librarian, so he has an interest in local history." Kerry shrugged in response. "I'm interested in the Evans family. What were they like? What do you remember about them?"

Kerry rubbed at his stubble patch before answering. "Herrmm…not too much to write home about, really. I never really knew Mrs Evans — she was always holed up in that cottage. Most of the girls had moved out by then too. And I avoided Mr Evans, of course."

"Oh?" Charlie asked.

"Had a temper, that one," Kerry said. "But so did a lot of the old folk who worked through the Depression. Earnt the right, they did. I just stayed out of his way."

"I heard he was a nice man," Charlie probed, hoping Kerry wouldn't question where she'd sourced this information.

Kerry thought a bit before answering. "Gran did say once Mr Evans had changed after everything that happened. Fair enough too, right? She said Papa Kapiri should have left years earlier, as soon as the secrets started."

"Secrets?" Charlie probed. "What kind?"

Kerry shrugged. "I dunno. They never told me. I always assumed it was something to do with all that money Mr Evans lost. But I was just a kid, and I'm just guessing."

After several more questions — and offering to show Kerry photos of what the property looked like now — Trent and Charlie thanked the man for his time and headed back to the car.

"It's a shame he didn't know more," Trent said, waving at Kerry, who stood in the doorway.

"He filled in a couple of gaps for me," Charlie said as she buckled her seatbelt and gave Kerry a wave as well. "And it was fascinating talking to someone who actually *knew* Bill Evans."

"Yeah," Trent said. "More interviews would help, I reckon. I wonder how Marie fell into the creek?"

"Yeah…I wonder too."

# 34

# State of Mind

Trent had invited Charlie over for dinner with him and Brent on the way home. She'd tried to politely decline, absolutely exhausted, and knowing she had another half hour's drive ahead of her. But when she'd stopped to properly introduce herself to Brent, he'd convinced her to stay "just for a bite" so she wouldn't have to cook when she got home. Brent had promptly opened a bottle of white wine and served a delicious chicken with white sauce and salad. Charlie had worried the social interaction would drain her further, but instead it reinvigorated her for the drive home. Brent had a wicked sense of humour. She decided she liked Trent's taste in men.

The conversation over dinner had been like watching a tennis match between the two of them, each sprinting to hit the other with a wittier riposte or jibe. They were infectious company for each other, and for Charlie. And their love for each other expanded big enough to envelop her as well, rather than push her out as the third wheel.

All Sunday night and through Monday, Charlie's house had been quiet. She'd tried sewing but was too distracted to finish even one top. She'd tried calling Tess, and while it was wonderful to talk through everything, there were no miraculous revelations this time. She'd tried going into the Dream, with the same phone trick, but after lying in bed almost two hours, she'd given up.

When 10:00 a.m. on Tuesday rolled around, Charlie was incredibly impatient. So impatient that she spoke before Maryanne could give her obligatory greeting. "Hi, Maryanne," she said before the call had even properly connected.

"Hello, Charlotte. How—"

"I can't connect to the Dream," Charlie said, desperate for Maryanne's matter-of-fact reassurances. "It's been getting harder for a while now, but the last couple of days, I can't connect at all. I'm trying everything that worked before — except using Marie of course — and I *know* it's there, but it's always just out of reach." She stared expectantly at Maryanne, willing her to have the answer.

The psychologist took a deep breath before answering. "This isn't entirely unexpected. It happened with the last Keeper I assisted as well. It's important that you fully disconnect to be able to access the Dream. Focus only on the intent."

"I'm doing that," Charlie replied, pulling at one of her thumb nails. "At least, I think I am. I try emptying my mind, relaxing every part of my body — the things that worked before — but nothing. The last time I succeeded, it was like every time I got close, it pulled away. When I finally connected, everything was dark and blurry and I couldn't see clearly."

"What you've described — clearing your mind and relaxing — are important first steps, but you must disconnect on a deeper level. Fully release yourself from anything that's holding you back. Not just physically. Next time you're trying to connect, don't just relax your body — make a conscious effort to disconnect from it."

"That sounds dangerous," Charlie said. "Is it safe?"

"Charlotte, I think by now you've realised it's not entirely safe to connect to the Dream in any scenario."

Charlie nodded, remembering the thirst when she'd been in there too long and recalling the crushing sensation when Bill had his hands around her throat. "But…what happens in the Dream doesn't affect my physical body, does it? The last time I was there, I experienced someone dying. I *felt* it, but when I was back, I was fine."

"As I've said before, I don't know exactly how it works. I don't believe you can be physically harmed within the Dream, but…" A little colour drained from Maryanne's face.

"But?"

"Just remember, Charlotte…" Maryanne avoided answering her. "You have control. Don't ever forget that. Remember your intent and remember your voice. As a Keeper, you can exert some authority. Especially over the Greys and other lesser spirits."

"Do I have control over time, though?" Charlie asked. "How do I make sure I come back around the same time as I enter the Dream? That I don't enter one day and come back three days later, dead from thirst?"

"If your physical body died while you were in the Dream, you wouldn't return to it." Maryanne said matter-of-factly.

"So how do I stop that?"

"Don't lose your focus. Don't lose your control. *Remember* your intent. Keep it foremost in your mind. I can't promise it'll work every time but try not to let the Dream control you — *you* control it."

"How do I do that?" Charlie asked again, frustration creeping in.

"Remember, Charlotte, I haven't been to the Dream. At least not the way you have. You have to trust your instinct. My lessons to you are all theoretical."

Charlie considered the way Maryanne had worded her response. "But… you have been to the Dream then?"

Maryanne sighed, rubbing her face — a habit she seemed to exhibit when frustrated or worried. "I believe so… A couple of sessions back, you asked me why all this isn't common knowledge. Why more people don't know about it."

"Yes…" Charlie said, intrigued.

"Well, let me answer that for you. Spirits aside — which many people *do* share accounts of, by the way — humans *have* been delving into the Dream for thousands of years. Without necessarily knowing that's what they were doing. And certain people have become obsessed with it — even not knowing exactly what it was they were obsessed with. They've tried to grasp and comprehend even a glimpse of it. It never ends well. Have you heard of the drug DMT?"

"No…"

"It's actually something that's found naturally in the human body and in animals. It's similar — chemically speaking — to magic mushrooms and has been used by different cultures for thousands of years for ritualistic purposes. It's described as a psychedelic that causes hallucinations. The interesting thing is that different people describe similar experiences. Particularly, they describe seeing similar entities…*coloured* entities. And a world that revolves like a kaleidoscope."

"That…that sounds like the Dream…" Charlie said.

"Yes, but with *none* of the control. It is dangerous. Incredibly dangerous. And superficial access at best."

"So why don't more people know about this?" Charlie asked.

"I believe it's because someone, or something, is keeping it that way. Maintaining that balance we discussed. And I believe it's because most people struggle to comprehend what they experience. How many times, before now, did you see something from the corner of your eye? And when you turned to look, it was gone, so you just dismissed it as nothing? When most of us have experiences — even a glimpse of the Dream — it overwhelms us. It's easier to ignore it or dismiss it as something else. Even when we recognise it as something special, something different, it overwhelms us. For example, look at that occultist, Alistair Crowley. He had a *brief* encounter with the Grey, with Lam, and he and his followers created an entire religion about it! One of the most *common* entities!" Maryanne's disdain for the "common" Greys was clear. Charlie felt less apathetic, having seen it in her house several times…

"So…you tried DMT…" Charlie said, a slight smile creeping into the corners of her mouth. She had seen the crack in Maryanne's mask this time, and found herself longing for another peek at the woman behind it.

"Yes, and it didn't go well!" Maryanne said, flustered. After looking at Charlie with big, bewildered eyes for a moment, she burst into laughter. "Please, I don't recommend it… *You* don't need it in any case. And I'd be worried you'd lose control, which is so important to have."

"Okay, I'll try what you suggested instead. The disconnecting. And I'll stay away from illicit drugs!"

"Yes, please!" Maryanne smiled. The mask hadn't been fully replaced yet. She took a deep breath before continuing. "Charlotte..."

"Yes," Charlie said after the pause between them lengthened.

"I found something. Some information I wanted to share with you... It's about the Keeper you described to me, the one with the top hat."

Charlie's eyes widened. "You did? What? How?"

"I'm a Seeker, Charlotte. It's my job. I found out who he is and where he is."

"*Is?*" Charlie parroted back at her. "He's alive? Please, tell me everything."

"His name is Alexander Cooper. And he lives in Sydney... I suppose 'lives' is open to interpretation... I'm going to send you the information I have on him via email, and I'll leave it to you to decide what you do with it."

"Yes, please," Charlie said, desperate to pin him down, to ask him all the questions Maryanne didn't seem to have the answers to. "How did you find him?!"

Maryanne raised a single eyebrow, her dark eyes deepening. "I'm a seeker." Charlie's head was whirling. "I'd like to leave our session there for today. I'll see—"

"You'll see me at 10:00 a.m. on Friday, right?" Charlie smiled. "You got it."

"Goodbye, Charlotte."

\* \* \*

The following day, Charlie was on her way to Sydney. In the last few weeks, she'd racked up more kilometres on her little RAV4 than she'd expected. The information Maryanne had sent her wasn't as detailed as she'd hoped, but it was a good starting point. Alexander Cooper had been a prominent philanthropist in the 1950s — a socialite, harking from a family with *significant* generational wealth. From what Charlie could find online, Alexander had become estranged from his family in the early 1950s before pursuing his philanthropic endeavours. He'd never married, never had children, and in the late 1950s he had just dropped off the map. He'd stopped hosting functions. Stopped appearing in the newspaper. It was almost as if he'd vanished.

Alexander Cooper hadn't physically disappeared, though. Maryanne had provided his current address. No phone number, no email — but at least a residential address in Vaucluse, Dover Heights, East of Sydney, near Bondi Beach. Charlie pulled to the side of the road in front of Tess's house and beeped twice. She was so grateful Tess had agreed to come with her, out of the blue, to a stranger's house in one of Sydney's ritziest suburbs. Not for the first time that day, she thought how lucky she was to have Tess in her life.

Tess opened the front door, then ran down the steps while yelling over her shoulder (probably at Leon). Charlie smiled as she noticed Tess was wearing one of the oversized dresses she'd made her, in pale pastel patterns, above an old pair of leggings and dark moss green boots. *"Je vais y aller maintenant! Le dîner est dans le frigo — des lasagnes. Essayez de ne pas salir la cuisine. Au revoir!"* Charlie thought how lucky Leon was to have Tess in his life as well. "Ah, *bonjour*," Tess said as she jumped into the front seat, leaning over to give Charlie a kiss on both cheeks. "It's so good to see you, *ma chère*. How are you?"

"I'm good, really," Charlie smiled. "Despite my random phone call and crazy request! I promise, I'm doing well." Tess raised an eyebrow at Charlie before tossing her bag into the backseat and buckling in.

"*Allons-y* then. Let's go get on with your crazy request."

# 35

# Don't Forget to Live

Tess and Charlie pulled up out the front of the address Maryanne had provided. The street felt old, established, with narrow concrete paths covered in greenery and stone walls stretching up the street and the hills. Everything was green. The narrow street had limited parking, so Charlie pulled into the driveway. Another car was parked farther in — an old Ford Fiesta. It wasn't what Charlie had pictured for an incredibly rich ex-philanthropist. Although the house was in one of the most expensive suburbs in the country, it wasn't quite what she'd imagined. Houses all around it were being refurbished, even torn down and rebuilt, but this one looked like a snapshot from the 1950s.

"What are you thinking, *ma chère?*" Tess asked, also examining the house closely. "Are we going in?"

"Too late to turn back now," Charlie said, opening the driver's-side door.

Tess followed her as she made her way to the entry. She knocked tentatively, waiting patiently for an answer that didn't come. She knocked again, louder. "I hear someone in there, do you?" Charlie asked Tess, who nodded. Charlie tried to look through the window to the right of the door, but it was too dark to see. She lifted her hand to knock again, and the door handle twisted.

"Hello?" said a quiet woman's voice from inside, heavily accented — probably South or Central American, Charlie thought.

"Hi," Charlie said, trying to peer around the door. "My name's Charlie, and this is my friend, Tess. We were hoping to see Alexander Cooper."

The woman was silent for a long time, shuffling behind the door. "Mr Cooper?" she asked, finally. "You know him?"

"Yes… Well, no. He's a friend of a friend of ours. She asked us to come see him." Charlie and Tess heard the woman mutter behind the door. The uncertainty Charlie had felt since seeing the house grew. "We won't be long, I promise. His friend was quite insistent we see him."

The door slowly opened fully, revealing a tiny woman in a pale-blue polo shirt and chinos. The woman looked them up and down curiously then stood to the side, nodding, and motioning them to come inside. "This way," she motioned over her shoulder, leading the way inside the house. The entryway was clean and well maintained, but like the rest of the house, looked like something from a 1950s design magazine. Wood panelling graced every wall, flowing up to a deep-green painted ceiling. White and black tiles glistened cleanly underfoot, and each piece of furniture — also immaculate — was antique. "Mr Cooper's in the last room, on the right."

"We won't be long," Charlie promised again as they passed her and made their way to the room.

She shrugged back at them.

Charlie and Tess stared into each other's eyes searchingly. *Do we go in?* Charlie thought. Tess gently nudged her shoulder, encouraging her towards the door. Charlie knocked, which caused the small woman behind them to raise her eyebrows in surprise. She motioned them forward again. Charlie pushed the door open and couldn't help the gasp that followed.

Alexander Cooper lay in a large bed in the middle of the room, intubation tubes running from his mouth to a large medical display. The room had been redesigned to resemble a hospital room. The smell was much the same as that of a hospital as well. And on a day bed by the window was the all-too-familiar top hat. Charlie turned her back on Alexander in shock, staring directly at the small woman who'd let them into his house.

For the first time, Charlie read the logo on her polo shirt. She was from a home nursing service. "He's been like this nearly twenty-five years this time," the woman said.

"Twenty-five years?" she heard Tess whisper behind her, at the same time as Charlie said, "This time?"

The woman looked them up and down suspiciously. "I thought you'd know…" she said, trailing off.

"Our friend didn't say…" Charlie also trailed off, turning back to look over her shoulder.

Tess, thinking on her feet, interjected perfectly. "Our friend said he was sick. Had been sick a long time. But she didn't tell us…" She motioned her head. "Didn't tell us the full extent. And…and…she asked us to deliver a message to him. A private message. So we assumed…"

The nurse, who obviously liked Tess, nodded after a moment. "This is the longest episode. When the seizures first started, he'd come in and out. The comas were only weeks at first, then months. Now…" She shrugged.

"Why?" Charlie asked, meaning many questions at once. *Why is this happening? Why do you let this continue? Why won't he wake up? Why doesn't everyone know?*

"We don't know for sure. At first, we thought it was his diabetes. Then an infection. Then epilepsy. Then the diagnosis didn't matter, just the treatment."

"Why keep him like this?" Tess asked, appalled. "He's a vegetable now, *non?*"

"Advanced care directive." The nurse shrugged. "Lots of lawyers, lots of money, and a family who cares a little but not enough."

"Can we have some time alone with him?" Charlie asked. "To…to relay our friend's message?"

The nurse put her hands up in consent, backing out of the room. It wasn't like they could do much worse to him. "But be quick please," she said. "I have to do his exercises in half an hour." Charlie nodded enthusiastically as Tess's mouth fell open.

After the nurse left and Charlie closed the door, Tess blurted out, "How could they leave him like this? *Putain de merde!*"

"Fuck…" Charlie said, disgust and terror warring with her in equal measure. *Will this happen to me?* she wondered. She walked to the bedside, examining the old man. He'd clearly been well looked after, but his skin was pale and stretched, signs of bedsores and old catheter sites marring every visible part of him. As she got closer, she felt the air around her tingle — it was like he was a charged battery. "Can you feel that?" she asked Tess as she moved closer, the hairs on her arms standing straight. She lifted her arm to show Tess.

"*Non…* Nothing…" Tess whispered, keeping a wide berth from Alexander anyway, as though he might sit up and grab her at any moment. "*Nom de dieu de putain de bordel de merde de saloperie de connard d'enculé de ta mère…* What the fuck was that crazy shrink thinking, sending us here? What is this?"

As Charlie got even closer to Alexander, she *felt* the energy coming off him. It felt similar to the sensation she always got whenever she was pulled into the Dream. "I think I might be able to talk to him…" she whispered to Tess, pulling a nearby chair to the bedside and sitting on its edge. She looked up at Tess, who was staring back at Charlie, terrified. "This is going to be a bit weird… Do you remember me explaining to you how I had dreams when I was awake?"

"Is this a good idea?" Tess asked, keeping her distance.

"I need some answers," Charlie replied. "Alexander has something to do with the Dream. Something to do with *me*. This might be my only chance…"

Tess nodded briskly but didn't come any closer. "What do you need me to do?" she asked hesitantly.

"Just stand watch. It might look a bit weird — like I'm actually asleep as well — but I'll be okay, okay? I promise. Just give me a shake if I don't wake up after ten minutes." Tess nodded again, wrapping her arms around her chest.

"Just be careful. *Putain de merde… Je ne peux pas croire ça…*"

Charlie took a deep breath, trying to relax herself and banish her fear before reaching her hand out and placing it on Alexander's cold, soft arm.

She lost her breath as she was sucked into the Dream more fiercely than ever. It was like she'd been dropped off the edge of a cliff, wind rushing across her body, making it hard to breathe, leaving her stomach far behind her. She felt as though she were floundering, trying to find her way, when just as suddenly she stood in a room she didn't recognise. If she'd had a physical body, she wasn't sure whether she should be panting, vomiting, shaking or crying. She tried to take everything in as quickly as she could.

An old woman lay in a bed by a window, breathing so shallowly it was as though she were already dead. Light filtered through her thin curtains, dancing across the sheets draped over her small body. As Charlie focussed, she heard trickling and bubbling from outside the window...a fountain — a familiar fountain. *My mum's nursing home,* she thought. *It's Mum's fountain...* As she looked around the room again, she saw familiarities with her own mother's old room.

She willed herself to the woman's bedside, and looking down realised she knew this woman as well. It was the woman she'd seen the day she visited with Tess — the one she thought was glowing purple. Although she looked much older now it was definitely the same woman. Charlie reached out towards her, laying her hand on top of hers. With that contact she instantly knew this woman. Knew her life. Knew she'd been a feisty and independent woman who had travelled Europe with her girlfriends in the 1950s, before bowing to social pressures in her early thirties and marrying a man much older than her. Not because she loved him, but because society demanded it. Over time, she did grow to love him, but not romantically. Despite his gruffness, she grew to depend on him. And when he died, she lost a huge part of herself — what she thought had made her who she was.

*But that's not who you are,* Charlie thought to her.

The purple glowed brighter around the woman, and Charlie again saw that younger side of her. The feminine side, the adventurer, the independence. She felt what had been buried for so long start to come to the fore again.

Aware it wasn't just the two of them in the room, Charlie turned and saw him. Alexander Cooper — but as she'd first known him. The white man, glowing brightly, his top hat perched on his head. Once again, Charlie found it hard to see his facial features, and once again he stood silently. But she knew he was looking at her with more than curiosity. It was eagerness and purpose.

*Alexander Cooper*, she thought to him, unable to physically form the words. *Charlotte White*, he mentally replied.

Charlie tried to form all the questions she wanted to ask but struggled. It was difficult to express it all the way she wanted to. Instead she reached out desperately. *What? Why?*

Alexander moved past her to take her place besides the old woman, holding the woman's hand as well. *The balance*, he answered simply. As he answered, the woman breathed her last breath, her spirit bursting brightly in a beautiful purple glow. It was the most magnificent thing Charlie had ever seen. Had ever felt. So much so it took her own breath away. As both the woman and Alexander began to fade away, he sent her another message, *My duty will be yours. The balance.*

Charlie took a deep breath as she was suddenly back in Dover Heights, Sydney. Tess had her hands on her shoulders and was shaking her violently. The nurse stood behind Tess, eyes wide, frozen by the door. "Charlotte!" Tess yelled desperately.

"Tess, Tess, it's okay," Charlie answered, lifting her hands to hold on to Tess's, to stop her from shaking her. "I'm okay, Tess." Tess let out a loud whimper then wrapped Charlie in a tight hug.

"What...what was that?" the nurse asked. "What happened?"

Charlie looked between them, trying to figure out what had happened while she was in the Dream with Alexander. "I-I'm sorry..." Charlie said. "I'm okay, really. I-I think we should go." She stood, wobbling slightly as Tess released her. Tess grabbed Charlie's arm and held it tightly as they walked to the other side of the room, squeezing through the door together. "I'm sorry," Charlie said again, the nurse staring after them in shock.

# 36

# Secrets Revealed

As Charlie sat on Tess's bed, a hot cup of Russian Caravan tea in her hands, Leon holed up in his bedroom with Ella, Tess finally asked Charlie what had happened. On the drive home, it had still been too fresh for them. "You were just sitting there, staring at nothing. I waited ten minutes and still nothing. So I shook you, and still nothing. I waited some more… You sat like that for twenty minutes, *ma chère*! And then the nurse came in, and I didn't know what to do."

"I'm so sorry," Charlie answered, holding on to the edge of her friend's hand. "I'm still learning how to control it. I keep thinking I *will* control it, that I'll keep the intent firm in my mind, but every time I enter the Dream, I get swept up in what's happening."

"What was happening?" Tess asked curiously, but hesitantly, as if she didn't really want to know.

Charlie put her empty mug on the bedside table and recounted everything, including what Maryanne had told her the day before.

"What do you think it all means?" Tess asked her, scooching closer to Charlie, their legs touching.

"I'm still trying to figure it all out." Charlie rubbed her temples. "This Waiting Place, these spirits, the balance. It's all so fantastical. But when I was in the Dream, and I helped that woman realise what she needed to process before she could move on, to reconnect with that part of herself that she needed to rediscover and experience fully before she moved on…I think I understood the purpose of it all then. Helping her accept and find the harmony she needed within herself. That was beautiful…"

"I feel like I'm starting to lose you," Tess said quietly and unexpectedly. "I want to be there for you, but I'm struggling to understand. You're leaving me behind."

Charlie leant her head on Tess's shoulder. "I'll never leave you behind," she answered quietly.

Charlie's phone, which was charging on the bedside, pinged — Trent's name popped up on the screen. "It's Trent," Charlie said, unlocking the phone and reading the message. "He said he's discovered something about Marie. He wants to meet for lunch tomorrow."

"Let's do it," Tess said.

"Us?" Charlie asked.

"*Oui*, darling."

"I love you forever, ma Thérèse."

"*Je t'aimerai pour toujours*, my Charlotte."

\* \* \*

It was wonderful having both Tess and Trent join her at Dot's the next day. It felt like she had her own tribe — and happiness swelled in her, despite the oddities of what they were dealing with. Tess and Trent had instantly connected, enjoying the wit and dryness of each other's humour. Trent's keenness and drive to help Charlie had endeared him to Tess. Tess's appreciation of fine food and wine, in turn, landed well with him.

Trent pulled his familiar satchel out while they were waiting for their orders to be prepared. "Get ready to have your minds blown," he said. "As you know, I went through the coroner's records yesterday. There was nothing terribly interesting — nothing new — until I got to Marie. The obituary we found said she'd died of pneumonia, right?"

"Right." Charlie nodded. "And Kapiri's great-grandson said she'd fallen into the creek and caught a chill."

"But the coroner's report found water in her lungs." Trent paused for dramatic effect.

"As in fluid from the pneumonia?" Tess asked, before taking a sip of Diet Coke.

"No. I asked a friend to check for me and he agreed. Marie didn't die from pneumonia. She *drowned*. And she had bruises on her body and a dislocated shoulder too."

"What?" Charlie asked, leaning forward to look at the report like it would make sense to her. "Why would the coroner cover that up?"

"Why indeed," Trent answered. "She must have been murdered. Why else would you cover up the cause of death?"

"Oh, *pauvre ange…*" Tess said.

"Huh?" Trent asked.

"Poor angel," Tess translated.

"She does this a lot — you get used to it." Charlie smiled, Tess shooting her a lively grin in return.

Things were starting to make more sense to Charlie. If Marie *was* murdered, she would have been terribly afraid — and likely in pain — at the time of her death. Which explained why she was at risk of becoming a Grey.

"But who would do this?" Tess asked, looking between them for answers.

Trent shrugged. "I looked through the newspaper records again, from around the time of Marie's death, but found nothing. I have no clues." He looked expectantly at Charlie. "Anything spooky to put us on the right path, honey?"

Charlie thought back to everything she'd experienced in the Dream, trying to piece it all together. "Okay…" she put her hands on the table as she attempted to order her thoughts. "The first time I saw Marie, she was playing by the creek with her sister, Alice."

"She drowned in the creek!" Trent slapped his hand on the table in an aha moment, only to be met by disapproving stares from both women for interrupting. "Sorry," he said. "That was obvious, wasn't it? What else?"

"The first time I entered the Dream on purpose, with intent, I wanted to know how this all started. And I saw Bill and Emma talking about their concerns with money, and Bill wanting to take all their savings out of the bank. That's why I asked you all those questions about the Great Depression, Trent." He nodded as Charlie continued. "It must be something to do with that? Or..."

Charlie paused as she remembered her most recent experience at her property: Bill's hands crushing her throat.

"Or?" Tess asked encouragingly.

"That night, when Marie was terrified when I came home and all the lights burst, she was talking to her dad. Telling him she was sorry. And the Grey was there, in the house. I wondered if she might have been talking *to* her dad. I wonder if Bill is the Grey. I saw him strangling that swagman," Charlie said, turning to fill Trent in. "He was so *angry*. I've never seen anyone so *angry*. He strangled Thomas. What if he also killed his daughter?"

"But why, *ma chère?*" Tess asked. "Why would he do that to his own daughter?"

"I don't know..." Charlie said. "But I have to find out."

\* \* \*

Trent and Tess had both accompanied Charlie home to her property. She'd been worried she might come home to a similar situation as the last time she'd left, but the house was dark and quiet as they approached. Only the kitchen light was shining — which Charlie had left on for Marie.

After a delicious cook-up by Trent — fried fish and golden baby potatoes this time — accompanied by much white wine, they sat in Charlie's living room. They continued to brainstorm for hours, pondering how they might find the answers they needed. Wondering if Bill might have any descendants who could shed light on this. It was Tess who remembered what Kapiri's great-grandson had said, about the Evans family having secrets, and that had got them talking excitedly as the clock snuck closer to midnight.

"Should we, you know, do a séance or something?" Trent finally asked, having enjoyed more than his fair share of wine.

"No," Tess and Charlie both said firmly at the same time, all three of them laughing — spurred on by the wine.

"I guess bed is calling me then," Trent said. "I'm supposed to be working tomorrow. You two are a bad influence on me!" He jiggled his empty glass at them.

"You needed no encouragement." Charlie laughed. "You take the spare room. Tess and I can share my bed." Trent nodded and tottered off towards the bathroom. "There is one thing I could try tonight..." Charlie added, when it was just her and Tess. "I could try to enter the Dream again."

"*Ma chère...*" Tess said worriedly, not thrilled with the idea.

"This time I'll keep my focus. And you'll be with me."

"But I was with you last time and shaking you didn't work. What if you end up like *him* — like Alexander. I couldn't stand it."

Charlie tried to stop the shudder that went through her at the possibility. She thought for a moment before responding. "The thing that worked last time I got stuck was physical pain and discomfort. I was so thirsty it was like I felt my body tugging at me to bring me back. You could pinch me. Or slap me. Or... Hang on..." She ran down to her sewing room and returned with a pin. "Stick my leg with this! That'll work."

Tess sighed. "Okay, *ma chère*. I don't think I can stop you. So...give me the pin."

\* \* \*

Just as it had the last few times, it took Charlie several tries to enter the Dream. The room tilted ever so slightly and she wasn't sure if it was from the wine or her repeated failed attempts. She thought about what Maryanne had told her — about control, intent, and disconnecting fully. The image of Alexander lying in bed, stuffed with tubes, popped into her head, and she dispelled the thought as strongly as she could. *Only this matters*, she thought. *I have to help Marie. Only this matters...* Charlie slipped into the Dream slowly, in stark juxtaposition to how Alexander had drawn her in.

Once again, everything was black around the edges and grey in front of her, as though she were looking through a thick fog. Trying not to let frustration at the lack of clarity get to her, she instead focused sharply on her intent. *How did you die, Marie?* Charlie thought strongly into the mist. She was determined not to lose control this time, focussed on what she needed to know. A giggling to her left captured her attention. *Marie*, she thought, drawn towards the sound.

The fog cleared slightly as she saw Marie at her cottage, on the veranda, talking with someone. It was hard to see who. She tried to focus, but the harder she tried, the more his image and voice blurred. "I have a good story too," Marie said confidently. "About buried treasure!"

"Oh really?" the man replied playfully, but with a dangerous edge to his voice.

"Yeah, I can be an adventurer, just like a swagman." Marie's innocence was painful to watch, knowing as Charlie did that this moment must have occurred days — perhaps even hours — before the girl's death.

"And do you know where the treasure is buried?" the man asked, the eagerness in his tone evident only to Charlie — not to Marie.

"Yeah! I do! It's a secret, though."

"Of course…" the man said. "A secret…"

Charlie pulled herself out of the Dream when it became apparent she wouldn't be able to see who the man was. As she willed herself back, she caught a glimpse of the Keeper — Alexander — from the corner of her eye. *Did he follow me?* she thought as she opened her eyes and sat up straight in her bed.

"What's wrong?" Tess asked. "Having trouble connecting?"

"No," Charlie said. "I did connect."

"But you only just closed your eyes…Oh, *la vache*, this is so weird." Charlie grabbed her notebook from the bedside and began scribbling in it furiously. "What happened? What did you see?"

"Marie told a man about some buried treasure," Charlie said. "I think she must have told someone where her dad hid his savings. It makes sense, right?"

Tess gasped, moving to the edge of the bed. "*Oui!* The misfortune the Evans family suffered. The financial ruin. Maybe someone stole it?"

"Yes, maybe," Charlie said, finishing her notes. "And Bill got mad. He felt like he was ruined. He was desperate."

"My God, you think…?"

"Yes," Charlie replied. "I think Bill killed Thomas for stealing his savings. Then, in anger, he might have killed Marie. I think that's why the death was covered up and why the stolen money was never reported. Why it just became a story of financial ruin and secrets. Bill killed his own daughter."

# 37

# When Need Comes, One Knows One's Friends

Charlie barely registered when Trent entered her bedroom the next morning, two steaming cups of coffee in his hands, and put them on the bedside tables. It was after nine before she properly roused herself, by then the coffee cool in its mug. *I'm more of a tea person anyway*, she thought, swinging her legs out of bed. Tess was already up, her coffee cup gone. When Charlie stumbled to the shower she realised Trent would have left for work long ago.

By the time Charlie was washed and dressed, and in the living room, Tess had made her a fresh cup of tea, and it was nearly time for her appointment with Maryanne. "'Morning," Charlie yawned as she sat at the kitchen island bench. "Thanks for the cuppa."

"Good morning, *ma chère*," Tess said, smiling at her over the rim of what was at least her second cup of coffee for the day. "How'd you sleep?"

"Great actually. I was completely out of it."

"No doubt helped along by the wine," Tess laughed. "I hope Trent doesn't have too bad of a headache at work today." Charlie chuckled too, taking another refreshing sip of tea. "Have you thought about what you want to ask the crazy psych today?"

"Where to start…" Charlie sighed, images of Alexander hooked up to all those tubes at the front of her mind again.

*"Ma chère…"* Tess said, her tone serious, then paused. "What happened to Mr Cooper…it won't happen to you, will it, darling?" Charlie shuddered, and Tess came around and gave her a long hug. "If it will, is it really worth it? Don't leave me, darling. I couldn't stand it. You're my closest friend in this whole damn world — you're my family."

Charlie kissed Tess's hand, which was still wrapped around her shoulders in a loose hug. "I won't leave you, I promise." The clock ticked over to ten and Charlie's computer alerted her to an incoming call. "Always prompt!" Charlie sighed.

"I'll go have my shower…" Tess said, squeezing Charlie one last time.

Cup of tea in hand, Charlie walked to the computer and sat at the desk. She took a long breath before answering.

"Hello, Charlotte," Maryanne said. She wore a bright blue headscarf today and a beige linen tunic. Charlie focussed on every detail, delaying asking the inevitable question that burned inside her. Maryanne let the pause between them grow for a moment. "I take it you met Mr Cooper."

"Why didn't you warn me?" Charlie finally asked. "Why didn't you tell me he would be…like *that*."

"Would you still have gone?" Maryanne asked, letting the question sink in. Charlie thought for a moment then shook her head slightly and shrugged. "Sometimes words can't prepare us. Sometimes the best way to learn is to experience things — to see things — for ourselves."

"Will I end up like that?" Charlie whispered, unable to speak louder; she was barely able to speak the words at all. Maryanne shook her head, and Charlie felt all the tension that had built inside her since that visit release, like a taut rubber band. The relief was instant but snapped sharply.

"I can't say for sure what will happen in your case," Maryanne responded. "I never can. But…" She drew a deep breath and leant back in her chair. If Charlie didn't know better, she would have thought Maryanne was fighting back tears. "Gargh…" she said, rubbing her hands together and leaning forward to the monitor. "Not long after we first met, I told you that accepting what I was telling you as truth would be the hardest part." She paused for a moment. "I lied. That's not the hardest part. *This* will be." Charlie felt as though the rubber band inside her was being pulled taut again. "Keepers only exist in the Waiting Place. They only exist in the Dream." She paused, letting her words sink in.

"I-I don't understand what you mean…" Charlie said, a million possibilities running through her head. Maryanne had told her this before, so why was she bringing it up again? *Am I not a Keeper then? Does Alexander only exist in the Dream? What does it mean to only exist in the Dream?* Then a question Charlie had asked Maryanne long ago came back to her. "Am I dead when I enter the Dream? Time doesn't matter after death…and time doesn't matter in the Dream…"

"I told you I'd found two Keepers in my life," Maryanne said. "You're the second. Another woman was the first. This was many, many years ago, when I first started out as a Seeker. I talked to her for months before she realised what needed to happen. It was a learning experience for us both."

"What happened?" Charlie asked, desperate to know now, *needing* to know.

"She died, Charlotte," Maryanne replied, a tear falling down her cheek. "Just like you, she started to struggle to enter the Dream. Just like you, we figured out — together — that in order to enter the Dream, she needed to disconnect. The more she could disconnect, the clearer the Dream would be. I didn't realise…" She sighed deeply. "I didn't realise just how full that disconnection needed to be. The last time I spoke to her, she told me she knew what she had to do." Maryanne looked up, her dark eyes distant as she remembered. "Somehow I figured it out too, before I saw it reported in the news. I knew she'd gone. It wasn't because she'd missed four of our appointments — I knew before. I kept dialling in, hoping she'd answer, but she never did. I knew she never would again."

"How did she die?" Charlie asked, an emptiness opening inside her.

"She was epileptic. It was a seizure, the biggest she'd ever had. She was in the newspaper because two weeks passed before anyone found her body. She was alone at the end."

"You were disappointed when you realised I had Tess in my life…" Charlie said, recollecting how distant Maryanne had been when they first met. "You

226

seemed not to care when I told you my mum was dying — you *knew* I needed to be disconnected. You wanted me to have as few connections to this life as possible."

"I don't mean to be cold," Maryanne said, her eyes now dry. "But I've been doing this such a long time…and it's not only Keepers who can only exist in the Dream."

"Are you absolutely sure, though?" Charlie begged.

"I'm never sure, Charlotte, not about anything, not anymore." She smiled at her sadly. "But you will be sure. You will know when it's time. My friend knew well before I did. She had the instinct in her. You do too. You'll know, better than I ever could. Better than I ever will."

"I-I can't leave Tess…" Charlie whispered. "I promised —"

"I'm sorry, Charlotte," Maryanne said softly. "I will always be available to you, every Tuesday and Friday at 10:00 a.m. I will *always* keep that time free — whether through video call or however you want to reach out. Just like I'm never available to anyone else at 2:00 p.m. on Mondays and Thursdays…" Charlie felt her heart tighten. To think she hadn't liked Maryanne when they first met. Maryanne, who would always keep a slot open to her, even after she was *gone*. Just like she always kept a slot open for the first Keeper she'd met. "Goodbye, Charlotte."

Charlie sat staring at the screen long after the call had disconnected.

"Finished already, *ma chère?*" Tess asked softly, appearing from the hallway. Her hair was still wet from her shower. "Are you okay?"

Charlie nodded as she stood, turning to look at her friend. *I can't leave,* she thought. "Can we go for a walk?"

\* \* \*

Charlie and Tess sat by the creek, which, as summer approached in earnest, was now barely flowing. The water crept by so slowly it was almost still. Charlie hadn't wanted to go to her hills. The *douloureux* — the melancholy — of the creek felt appropriate. "You've barely said anything," Tess said after a while. "What did Maryanne say? About Alexander? About…you?"

Charlie looked up at her friend, at the anguish in her eyes, and couldn't bear to tell her the truth. Instead she told her a half version of it. "I asked if I'd end up like Alexander, and Maryanne said no."

"Thank God," Tess breathed. "That's wonderful. So why so sad?"

"I guess I'm thinking about Marie," Charlie answered, another half-truth. "I feel like I'm failing her. All this time we've spent researching, all the answers we've found, all the effort — it hasn't changed anything. She's still dead. Worse, she was murdered. By someone she loved and trusted. And she's *tormented* by the fear and the pain of the Grey. She might become a Grey herself. Nothing has changed for her. I've achieved *nothing*. What's the point?"

"Don't be so hard on yourself." Tess placed a hand on Charlie's knee. "You found her. You *remembered* her when no one else did. You made sure people knew her story. And you're trying, *ma chère*. We're here, aren't we?" She motioned around her. "This is where she died, *non*? Do you want to try to connect? I'm here. I'll help you, darling."

Charlie looked up at her friend, thinking how lucky she was to have her in her life. If becoming a Keeper meant disconnecting from Tess, she didn't want it. She'd *never* want it. And here Tess was, offering to help Charlie do that very thing — to enter the Dream, to disconnect — not knowing what she was actually offering. "Come on," Tess said, squeezing her knee. "I'm a *great* slapper. If pain is what it takes to bring you back to me, you'd better brace yourself!"

Charlie chuckled. "Okay, let's try it." She took a deep breath, closing her eyes. She breathed deeply, relaxing every part of her body. *Intent — enter the Dream... Help Marie...* She felt the Dream just out of reach. Like her body was rising to it but falling just before she could release. *Nothing else matters... But Tess matters...* Her thoughts warred with each other, Maryanne's voice echoing above it all: *Keepers can only exist in the Dream...*

Finally Charlie opened her eyes in exasperation, ready to give up. She looked up to Tess, who smiled at her encouragingly, reassuringly. She reached out a hand to Tess then paused as she glimpsed something from the corner of her eye, standing behind Tess, on the edge of the water. *Alexander,*

228

she realised, seeing his top hat. *Stop following me... I'm not ready... I can't leave her yet...*

*The balance...* Alexander's thought hit her strongly. *My duty will be yours.*

# 38

# Life Is a Battle

As Charlie and Tess approached the cottage, they saw that every light in the house had been turned on again. The air around the cottage was so charged that even Tess felt it. Tess stopped a stone's throw from the house, Charlie pausing with her. "Is that what happened last time?" Tess asked through gritted teeth. "Is the Grey inside?"

Charlie grasped Tess's hand and nodded. "Marie turns on all the lights when she's scared. I think if the Grey isn't already inside, it means he's coming." She felt Tess tense besides her.

"But you can tell him to fuck off, *non?*"

Charlie squeezed Tess's hands. "Yep, he's not welcome here." As they walked closer to the house, the light at the front porch burned brighter. "I should have bought more light globes…" Charlie tried to joke. It was normally the type of comment that would elicit laughter from Tess, but in this moment, they were too on edge. Tess clung to Charlie's arm and she clung back.

"This type of shit isn't supposed to happen during the day," Tess complained as they stepped onto the porch. "In the horror movies, it always happens at night! It's not even cloudy…" Again, the attempt to make light brought no laughter. It was like they'd carried the feeling of *douloureux* back from the creek with them. Charlie reached for the door handle and pulled, but it resisted.

"What the…?" Charlie rattled the door handle again. "It's locked!"

"You have your key, *non*?" Tess asked a little desperately, squeezing Charlie's arm, but Charlie hadn't even thought to bring it. They heard a giggle to their right and saw a flash of dark movement. Both turned quickly to see an empty porch. "You saw that too?" Tess breathed. "Open the door, *ma chère*."

Charlie turned back to the door and rattled it again, uselessly. "We'll have to break in…" she said, looking at the windows and side door, considering her options.

"Or we leave…" Tess said, tugging slightly at Charlie's arm. Hearing the giggling again, they turned to their right. The side door creaked as it swung open slowly.

"It's not going to stop," Charlie said. "No matter where we go…at least not for me." She looked at Tess, seeing the fear in her eyes, feeling the clamminess of her hands. "But you can go. You *should* go. Take my car — I'm sure Trent will let you stay with him until I can figure this out." The keys were, of course, inside the cottage.

"No, *ma chère*," Tess replied, pulling at her arm again. "Come with me." They heard feet running inside the house. Small feet. "Please."

"I can't," Charlie repeated, thinking about everything Maryanne had said. "I wish I could, but this won't stop if I leave. It'll just follow me everywhere I go. I have to learn what they need me to do and how to control it." A thump came from inside the house, causing Tess to jump near out of her skin. "Go. It's okay."

"No, *ma chère*," Tess answered, shaking. "I won't leave you. Let's get in there, get this over with." They walked to the side door and peered inside. The hallway stretched past the spare room and to a T-bend, where it led off to the other bedrooms and the living room.

They stepped forward slowly and awkwardly, like running a three-legged race connected at the arms. "Marie?" Charlie called as they entered the house, walking past the spare room. "Marie?" The side door swung shut violently behind them, rattling in its frame and shaking plaster loose from the ceiling. "Marie, don't!" Charlie said a little too forcefully. Although she

231

felt bad for the young girl, she was getting tired.

"Was it Marie?" Tess asked. "Or...or the Grey..."

Charlie considered for a moment, feeling the energy in the air. *Trust your instinct*, she thought. "No...I don't think it's the Grey. I think it's Marie."

"Why is she doing this?"

They spoke as they walked to the end of the corridor, looking left and right but seeing only the empty hallway. "I think she wants us to stay here with her, to help her. But she's afraid. She's struggling with whether she'll become a Grey herself or if she can become something else. She's out of balance. And she's a child..."

"*Un enfant de l'enfer*," Tess muttered.

They turned towards the living room and the kitchen, walking slowly, looking in every corner for signs of the Grey. The kitchen cupboards were all open as they approached. While no longer such a disturbing sight for Charlie, it was a new and unsettling encounter for Tess. "It's all right," Charlie reassured as her friend muttered furiously in French.

"Is this Marie too?" Tess asked as they entered the kitchen.

Charlie considered, trying to trust her gut. "I-I don't know." They stood behind the island bench, looking about them. "Before, I thought it might be the Grey, but maybe it is Marie. Maybe this is that mischievousness Maryanne warned me about."

A rapid grating and clacking sound rang out loudly behind them, causing Tess to scream as they swung around towards the sound. Every dining room chair had been rearranged, stacked on top of the table in delicate precision. Too fast for a human to have arranged in minutes, let alone in a flash of time.

Tess was breathing quickly, tears threatening at the edge of her eyes. "*Notre Père qui est aux cieux*," Tess whispered frantically under her breath. "*...que ton Nom soit sanctifié, que ton règne vienne, que ta volonté sit soit faite sur la terre comme au ciel...*"

While Charlie knew Tess was raised Catholic, this was the first time she'd ever heard her pray. It felt right, and she tried to find calm in her mind, to lean into it. "Marie, we're going to help you," Charlie said as confidently as she could, while Tess continued to pray. "Keep going, Tess," Charlie whispered. A cupboard slammed shut then opened again. Tess screamed again, clutching closer to Charlie. Despite her obvious fear, she kept praying. "I know I haven't been able to connect fully lately," Charlie admitted to Marie, feeling the girl's fear and frustration build. "But I promise I'll help you."

Another flash from the corner of her eye caused Charlie to spin back towards the kitchen. Tess pulled with her, her eyes shut tightly as she continued to pray. Marie stood in the kitchen, where the dining room table would have been. Swirls of blue and grey battled around her. When the blue became prominent, Marie was smiling, laughing, and free. When the greyness took over, Marie's face contorted, her mouth stretched unnaturally wide, open in a soundless scream. Her eyes black, her skin grey, her dress ripped, water dripping from her. Charlie breathed heavily, almost falling backwards as the vision threatened to overwhelm her. "Marie, please," she whispered. "I'm trying…"

Suddenly Marie was no longer standing in the kitchen but was right next to Charlie. So close she would have felt her breath on her skin had she been alive. Even though Marie barely came up to Charlie's hips, Charlie felt like she was the small one. She anxiously wanted to step back, but as with the Grey, she was paralysed this close to Marie. The young girl's face, flicking between innocence and happiness and contorted terror, was even more threatening so close. Charlie felt acid rise in her throat, like she might vomit at any moment. *Help me*, Marie projected, reaching out her small hand and placing it on Charlie's chest.

It didn't feel like the hand of a small child had touched her. It felt like someone had pegged a baseball as hard as they could at her sternum. The breath was pushed out of her lungs as she was pulled more violently into the Dream than ever before. Instantly, she knew where she was. Where she and Marie were. The creek. Marie was crouched under the white gum tree, an excited smile on her face as she dug quickly. The Grey was here in the Dream with her, its entire focus on Marie. Its inhuman form towered over the girl, its chest heaving. Marie continued to smile as she dug, obviously not seeing the Grey as Charlie did. Charlie tried to squeeze her own eyes closed but couldn't — she was completely helpless.

"See?" Marie said, pulling the dirty handkerchief from the dirt. She giggled as she unwrapped it happily. "It's the buried treasure." She looked up at the Grey, the grin falling from her face as the Grey grew in size, beginning to bellow at the small child. She shrank back. "But…but it's just a story," Marie whimpered as the Grey stomped towards her, swiping Mr Buttons's eye out of her hand and into the creek. Whatever the Grey was saying to Marie, Charlie couldn't understand it. All she heard were its horrifying bellows, which pounded through her stomach. "Why would you take that from Daddy? No, no, he'll be mad! No!" Marie jumped to her feet defiantly. She stood stubbornly for a moment as the Grey loomed over her but screamed as the Grey picked her up, squeezing her arms so tightly Charlie heard a snap.

The Grey threw Marie against her tree, more loud snapping making Charlie feel she might actually vomit. She tried to rush forward, to yell, but was paralysed, watching the trauma unfold before her. One of Marie's arms hung unnaturally from a dislocated shoulder, her brown eyes dazed. As her focus reconnected on the Grey, she began to whimper, fear flowing from her in waves. "I-I won't tell," she choked out weakly. "I…w-won't…t-tell…" The Grey strode to her, picking up her limp body with one hand. It walked to the creek, viciously holding her head beneath the water. The pain and fear flowing from Marie was brutal.

Finally, Charlie found her voice in the Dream, screaming as Marie's writhing body went limp. The Grey dropped Marie, turning in shock to stare directly at Charlie. It stood quickly, now shrinking itself. Charlie drew another deep breath, yelling in pain and anguish, the Dream shattering, leaving her standing in her cottage again. Tess was holding on to Charlie's arm, panic in her eyes. Charlie fell to her knees, ripping herself from Tess's grip as she did. She slumped on the ground, her hands in her lap, as the moment of Marie's death replayed in her head. "Oh, Marie…" Charlie whispered.

"Charlotte!" Tess screamed, pointing back to the living room. The Grey was still with them, standing as it had by the creek, its hands dripping water. "Oh my God!" Tess automatically put her arms back to shield Charlie as the

Grey took two long strides towards them, pulling its hand back and swiping Tess. She flung through the air, as limply as Marie had at the end, smashing into the wall, then soundlessly slid to the floor.

"Tess!" Charlie leapt to her feet. "Tess!" The Grey bellowed and Charlie swivelled to face it. *"Get out!"* she screamed at it. *"Get away!"* The Grey shuddered as it gradually disappeared. "Tess!" Charlie ran to her side. She was so still that for a moment all hope — all concern for anything else — fled her. "Tess..." she sobbed, reaching out to put a hand on her friend's motionless shoulder. Tess's shoulder moved ever so slightly as she breathed. "Oh, thank God... Tess..."

Charlie was aware another presence had joined them. She knew who it was, even before she saw his brightly glowing loafers. *The balance...* Alexander sent to her. *My duty will be yours...*

"Can't you just leave us alone?" Charlie sobbed, her hand remaining on Tess's shoulder as she looked up to face Alexander Cooper. "Please...I can't leave her. I just can't. I'm trying, but it's too much to ask."

Charlie hoped to feel some compassion from the Keeper, some empathy. But there was nothing. *The balance...* Alexander mentally projected. He bent over, a white hand reaching towards Tess. In that moment, Charlie knew he was trying to take Tess from her. If she couldn't leave Tess, he would take Tess away.

"No!" Charlie screamed. "No! Get out!"

Just as the Grey had, Alexander shuddered as he paused just before reaching Tess, fading away. The ferocious tension and energy in the house finally dissipated, and the glow of the bulbs returned to normal. Charlie's hairs lay flat on her arms. It was over, for now.

# 39

# This Is Love, Giving Everything

Tess groaned as she rolled onto her back, a hand coming up to her forehead. "Tess?" Charlie asked hopefully, too afraid to move her. "Tess, please, are you okay?"

"*Rien à foutre de ma vie…*"

Charlie burst into tears of relief as her friend sat up. "Oh my God, I thought it killed you." She pulled Tess into a hug, shaking as she cried.

"Is it over?" Tess mumbled, pulling back from Charlie and looking around her. "It feels different in here…"

Charlie wiped the tears from her eyes with a fist. "For now," she said. "Are you okay? Let me see you." Gently she took Tess's face in her hands, turning her head softly so she could look into her light hazel eyes at every angle. Tess's pupils looked the same size, and there was no glassiness. Charlie wasn't sure exactly what a concussion looked like, but Tess seemed okay to her.

"I'm fine, *ma chère*," Tess said, taking Charlie's hands in hers and gently pulling them down. "I was just winded, I think. What was that thing? It was the Grey, wasn't it?"

"Yes," Charlie said, standing as Tess did, watching for any sign of a wobble. "What did it look like to you?" she asked curiously, holding a hand out cautiously in case Tess should need it, but she was steady.

"It was like a flash, just a blur of grey. I didn't really see anything. One

236

minute I was looking at this dark *something* as I yelled for you. Then it zipped towards us, and the next thing I knew I was flying through the air. Then you were sitting over me. This is dangerous, darling." She said it seriously, but they both burst into nervous laughter.

"No shit," Charlie said. "I told you to leave!"

"Never, *ma chère*," Tess squeezed her hand. "Especially when you need me. Come, I'll make us some tea and you'll tell me what the fuck just happened."

They were soon sitting in Charlie's living room like normal, sipping tea. It was almost more surreal than the haunting itself. "I'm sorry you had to see Marie die, *ma chère*," Tess said. "I know you said you just saw the Grey, but do you think…was it her dad?"

Charlie shook her head slowly. "No, I don't think so anymore. It was looking for the buried treasure — for the savings Bill had taken from the bank. But Marie took him to where she'd buried her teddy's glass eye instead. He lashed out in anger when she stood up to him. He hurt her badly. I felt the fear emanating from both of them. He couldn't just leave her after he'd hurt her. Even if she didn't go to the police, there'd be questions. So he drowned her. Just like that.

"You tried your best," Tess said consolingly. "Marie must know that. You didn't do this to her. You're trying to *help* her." Tess really did know Charlie well — how her mind worked and what she'd be thinking. But in this instance, Tess failed to reassure her.

"I'm running out of time. I know time isn't supposed to matter after death, but things are building to a head. Marie's on the precipice of becoming a Grey herself. If I don't help her soon, she might become one. And I can *feel* that's not how it's supposed to be. I need to help her find her balance and become the Blue she's meant to be. So she can play. So she can explore. So she can do all the things she never got to experience in life. Only then will she be ready to move on. I don't know if she'll ever be able to move on if she does become a Grey."

Tess took Charlie's hand again. They'd held hands so many times that day, but it didn't lessen the warmth that flooded through her at Tess's touch. No matter how many times she held her hand, it would always fill her with a tender glow. "I know you'll help her, darling."

Charlie couldn't bear to tell Tess the last thing that had happened…what had transpired between Alexander and her. Charlie knew now — if she was to disconnect fully, to become a Keeper, to be able to help Marie, then she had to disconnect from Tess. She had to let her go. And Tess had to let Charlie go too. It almost felt impossible. She sighed loudly.

"Why can't that fucker Mr Cooper help her anyway?" Tess asked, as if reading Charlie's mind.

"Because Marie's connected to *me*," Charlie said, knowing deeply this was the truth. "He can't. Only I can."

"Don't worry, *ma chère*," Tess reassured her. "I'm here. I'm not going anywhere."

* * *

Charlie lay awake in bed long after Tess had fallen asleep, thinking everything through. Trying to find a way around what needed to happen. Or at the very least, a way to delay. Tess breathed softly in her sleep, her mouth parted slightly, her face beautiful despite its slackness. A deep contentment and sadness wrapped around Charlie like a blanket as she lay there watching Tess.

She sat up as she felt Alexander arrive in the room. He stood by their bedside, a hand held out towards Tess. "You don't have to take her," Charlie whispered, not wanting to rouse her friend. "I know what I have to do. I know how to do it. You don't have to take her." A tear fell from Charlie's eye as Alexander's gleaming hand fell to his side. "Please…just let me have one last night with her."

Alexander stood still for a moment. They both understood each other completely in that instant. This was his way of helping. His humanity was so far behind him that to him, what he was offering was empathy. While in the real world he may have only been asleep for twenty-five years, time didn't matter in the Dream. He had served a *very* long time. It was time for him to move on and for Charlie to accept her duty. In that moment,

Alexander also knew that Charlie would do as she'd promised. She would make this sacrifice, and stop running, in order to protect Tess. And in order to stop the much worse possibility of what might happen if Marie never found peace.

Alexander tipped his top hat to Charlie and slowly faded, his glow twinkling as he dissipated. Charlie lay back in the bed, putting an arm around Tess and crying softly.

* * *

That night, Charlie dipped in and out of a restless slumber. She woke well before Tess, as the dawn light filtered into the room. She heard the familiar sounds of the birds outside her window, chittering with no care. She envied them. Tess slowly blinked as she woke. She sat, staring at Charlie questioningly as Charlie sat upright as well. "Good morning, *ma chère*," Tess mumbled, rubbing the side of her face. "What is it? Are you okay?"

"Tess…"

"What is it?" Tess asked, now fully awake. "What happened? You're scaring me. Don't you dare ask me to leave again."

Charlie shook her head. "No, but there's something I have to tell you. Something I've wanted to tell you for *such* a long time." Her shoulders shook, but no tears fell yet. She paused, looking into Tess's eyes one last time — one last time before she changed everything between them. "I love you."

"I love you too, *ma chère*," Tess said, not comprehending what Charlie was confessing.

"No, Tess… I *love* you. More than a friend. More than just family. As *everything*."

"*Non, non, non…*" Tess said, scooting back from Charlie. "You love me as a *friend*, darling. We are good friends. We are family."

Charlie sobbed, struggling to breathe deeply. Her heart weighing her down as it fell fiercely from her chest to her stomach. It was too late to stop. She had to keep going. "Tess…" she said, as she saw realisation blink into her friend's face. Realisation, along with denial and…disgust?

"You're a *lesbian*?!" Tess said loudly, pained. The tone in her voice tore at Charlie, ripping apart not just her heart but her very soul. The worst part was the *betrayal* that Tess's tone implied. Like Charlie was letting Tess down, unravelling Tess's world at the same time as she was unravelling her own.

"I-I'm sorry…" Charlie whispered, hanging her head. Not sorry for who she was, or how she felt, but sorry for the pain she was causing the one she loved so much.

Tess stood from the bed, backing away from Charlie. "*Non, non, non*," she said frantically.

"Tess…"

"No!" Tess yelled, putting a hand up to silence her. "No! Stop talking. Just stop talking!" She collected her clothes from the floor and fled the room. Charlie's chest heaved — it was so hard to breathe. She heard her front door slam and then Tess's car's engine roared to life. She fell onto the bed, her body heaving as the pain burst from her.

"I'll love you forever, my Thérèse," Charlie sobbed, as she heard Tess drive away.

# 40

# The Keeper

It was evening before Charlie could rouse herself from bed. She'd finally cried as many tears as she could. She had mourned not just the loss of her dearest friend — the closest person she had in this world — but also everything that could have been. She mourned the future they might have had together.

Charlie felt numb as she swung her legs across the edge of her bed. She was still wearing her pyjamas, but she didn't care. It didn't matter. Nothing mattered anymore. She'd disconnected as completely as Maryanne, as Alexander, or as anyone else could have ever hoped. The anaphylaxis had nearly ended her life so many times before this. But *this* — this feeling — was what it truly must feel like to die.

She slipped her sneakers onto her feet, without socks, as she got to her entryway. She opened the door, the warm night air caressing her skin. Crickets sang, hidden in the night. It felt right that things should end in the dark. She stepped outside, not bothering to close the door behind her. That, too, didn't matter. She knew where she was heading — it was where it was always supposed to end.

Despite the depth of the night, Charlie found her way. The moon was high in the sky, highlighting everything in a shimmering silver glow. Clouds occasionally obscured the light but never for long enough to hinder her way. More than anything, she felt the creek pulling her. She could have walked there blindfolded. Charlie didn't stop when she reached the creek's edge; she continued forward. The water rushed into her shoes as she entered the bank, soaking and weighing down her feet. Despite the approaching heat of summer, the water felt like ice. As it flowed up her legs, approaching her stomach, it was as though the chill were stealing the breath from her lungs.

Charlie stopped in the centre of the creek; the cold flowing water slowly passed her chest at its highest point. Her shoes sank into the muddy bottom, dirt creeping in and rubbing against her skin. The irritation didn't matter. Nothing mattered. Charlie closed her eyes and entered the Dream fully, with ease, for the first time. The intent was clear in her mind: *find the truth, bring the balance, do my duty.*

As she hovered in the creek, Charlie knew she hadn't just entered the Dream this time. She'd entered the moment in time Marie would lose her life. Marie approached the creek happily, skipping at intervals, looking over her shoulder and chattering excitedly with the man who followed behind her. Thomas. He smiled back as they came to the creek. Charlie felt Thomas's excitement at the prospect of taking even a small amount of Bill's money, of easing his burden, of perhaps sleeping in a proper bed for the first time in weeks. These thoughts filled him with such trepidatious joy he almost couldn't stand to feel it.

Marie ran ahead of Thomas, reaching her tree and digging into the soil. "See?" she said giggling, as she unwrapped her handkerchief. "It's the buried treasure." Charlie was at Marie's side as Marie looked up at Thomas and saw the disappointment on his face. The frustration and anger as he realised there would be no relief, no warm bed, no end to the drudgery and uncertainty and pain.

"You told me you had the buried treasure," Thomas said hoarsely, hopelessly. "This was supposed to change everything." He took a stumbling step towards Marie.

"But-but…it's just a story…" Marie whimpered, not understanding the source of Thomas's pain and frustration, but still very much aware of it. He swiped the button from her hand, so light it barely made a sound as it hit the creek and sank from view.

"No!" Thomas yelled angrily, gruffly, throwing his swag to the ground. "Your father's savings! Where is it?! I *need* it. Just a little bit."

"Why would you take that from Daddy? No, no, he'll be mad! No!" Defiantly, Marie jumped to her feet. In a sudden rage, Thomas surged forward, picking her up, holding her so tightly Charlie heard — felt — a familiar snap.

"I'm the one who's mad!" Thomas yelled. "Mad from hunger, mad from thirst, mad from walking so bloody far every week!" Marie whimpered at him and he threw her away from him in anger and disgust. Disgust at himself, at how his life had turned out. He shuddered and cowered as he heard the snap when Marie's little body struck the tree.

"Oh, no…" Thomas cursed himself as he walked over to her, looking down at her broken shoulder. "You've ruined everything," he sobbed, fear building in him so strongly Charlie could tell he felt he was about to lose his mind. "What will I do?!"

"I-I won't tell," Marie choked out weakly. "I…w-won't…t-tell." Thomas closed the distance between them, picking Marie up gently. She groaned in pain as he did.

"I can't risk it," Thomas whimpered, carrying Marie to the creek and kneeling beside it. Charlie felt the intense emotions flowing from him — understood in that moment the difficulty and agony his life had been. How afraid he'd been, from the moment he first picked up his swag, to the moment he'd tossed it to the ground. He held Marie's head under the water. She struggled weakly, splashing as she did. Thomas started crying. "I'm sorry. I'm sorry. I'm sorry," he whispered.

As Marie died, thunder echoed in the skies. It was as if the whole world mourned her death, the heavens opening and rain pouring down in sheets. Thomas spun around as he heard footsteps running behind him, pounding as they approached the creek. His fear swelled higher. He stumbled upright, trying to run, stopping only to grab his pack.

"Thomas!" Kapiri thundered at him. The fear was so strong in Thomas that he lost control of his bladder, warm liquid trickling down the front of his thigh.

"I-I…" Thomas said as Bill ran up behind Kapiri. Bill looked from Thomas to Kapiri, to the creek. His eyes fell on his daughter.

"Noooo!" Bill yelled. Charlie's whole being tingled. *"Noooo!"* he cried, running to his child, falling beside her, and cradling her lifeless body in his arms. He rocked her back and forth, throwing his head back and roaring with the same anguish he'd felt when Jack had passed — but deeper, rawer, madder.

Thomas tried to back away, his fear now overtaking every rational thought. Kapiri held him firm by the shoulder, not allowing him to leave. "No, you don't," Kapiri said firmly, his voice deep with anger and sadness.

Alerted by Kapiri's warning to Thomas, Bill gently laid his daughter down, then surged to his feet, running full speed at Thomas. Kapiri let Thomas go as Bill barrelled into him, pushing him so firmly he fell to the ground. Thomas scooted back, away from Bill, and to his feet. His whole body shook. He pulled his swag — which he hadn't let go of — across his back.

"Please, sir!" Thomas yelled desperately. "It wasn't me! It wasn't me!" he denied foolishly, too afraid to think. His hands still dripped with water from the creek as he refuted what he'd done.

"You *stole* from me!" Bill yelled. "My *most precious…*" His words trailed off, blurred by anger and anguish and by the thunder and rain pouring around him.

"I swear, sir. I swear. I didn't, I didn't! There's nothing here. See? Nothing!" Bill lurched at Thomas again, his hands closing tightly around the man's throat.

"Why?!" Bill yelled, squeezing tighter. "You'll all keep taking till I've nothing left!!"

Thomas collapsed, Bill above him, crazed anger in his eyes. Kapiri approached Bill, tried to pull him back, but Bill's anger was too great. And then it was too late.

Charlie turned away from the scene and willed herself back to Marie's body. She reached out a hand towards her, unsurprised to see her arm glowing just as Alexander's had when he'd reached for Jack. *It's all right,* Charlie willed to Marie. *You don't have to be afraid. You've been afraid enough for this lifetime.*

As Charlie's hand touched Marie's body, she felt a wonderful jolt. All the curiosity, all the joy, all the adventure and playfulness that had made Marie who she was flowed strongly through them both as they connected. She felt everything Marie had never been able to experience but that had been meant for her. And as she released Marie's blue spirit, she felt such a sense of completion herself that Bill, Kapiri and the now-lifeless — and grey — Thomas faded away.

Marie stood there, a small, brightly glowing blue spirit. From one hand hung Mr Buttons, her precious teddy. *Come play with me*, Marie sent to her.

*That's your purpose, not mine*, Charlie sent back. The balance was finally set right.

***

After Charlie released Marie, she pulled herself further into the Dream — into the Waiting Place with its greyish white archways. It felt realer to her than ever before — more alive with activity. She could have taken herself anywhere in that moment, but still feeling the loss of Tess keenly, she knew there was only one place she wanted to go. Only one person she wanted to talk to.

Charlie took a step and found herself by an archway, looking down onto a familiar scene. Elsa lay in her bed, covered in a white blanket up to her chest, hooked to monitors checking her vitals. Charlie — a Charlie from the past — sat beside her on the edge of her seat.

"Ah, I'm not ready to leave you and your brother," Elsa said, closing her eyes.

"We'll never be ready to leave you either," Charlie replied. "But you know what? You know what I think? I think the moment we pass away, time is meaningless. It doesn't exist anymore. I think that when you pass over, we'll be together again. Straight away, no waiting. And I'll have lived a full life, and so will Robert, and all your grandchildren. But we'll all be together. No pain, no weak bodies giving out on us."

Elsa breathed out long and slow, as her breaths became shallowed. "That's nice." Elsa smiled. Charlie the Keeper entered through the archway and into the moment as well. "Oh!" Elsa blinked as she looked at the Keeper. "It's back...the glowing man..."

Charlie let go of her mother's hand, spinning around, standing as she did so to glare behind her. "Fuck off!" Charlie yelled. "Get out of here! Leave her alone!"

"Charlie..." Elsa said softly. "Charlie, it's okay." The Keeper willed herself to her mother's bedside. "I'm not afraid anymore," Elsa said. "I'm ready. Thank you, Charlie." Her mother smiled as she looked up at the Keeper. *I'm ready Charlie,* Elsa thought to her. The Keeper reached out her hand, touching her mother's shoulder and releasing her spirit.

\* \* \*

Charlie gasped as she came to, shivering violently. The sky was breaking into dawn, and the heavens had opened spectacularly — just as they had at the moment of Marie's death. Now driven by her body's base instinct to survive, Charlie stumbled her way out of the creek, her shoes left behind her in the mud. She fell onto her hands and knees on the bank, coughing, shaking, but blissfully free of the water. *Thank God it's nearly summer,* she mused, the normality of the thought shocking.

She stumbled to her feet and looked around her. *Why?* she thought. *Why am I here?* She'd thought that as soon as she'd fully committed herself to her duty, as soon as she'd become the Keeper, that would be the end of it. Like Alexander — and like Maryanne's Keeper before her — she would completely lose her connection to this life. She'd be gone.

Despite her confusion, Charlie made her way back to her cottage, fuelled by a need to get out of her wet clothes, to find her phone, to check in with Tess. *I don't care if she doesn't want me,* she thought defiantly. *I need to know she's okay.*

Charlie ran the last of the way to her cottage and entered through the door she'd left open, not caring about the mud she tracked into the house. She raced to her bedroom and grabbed her phone from the bedside table. There were twenty-four missed calls from Tess, starting from the evening

Charlie had left the house and going all through the night until morning. Charlie unlocked her phone, opening a message from Tess. *Please, Charlie,* the last message said. *I made a mistake. Please answer me.*

Charlie looked up suddenly as a beautiful thought hit her. Marie had her teddy bear with her at the end. The Grey — Thomas — had been dripping with water. And Alexander Cooper had his top hat. Maryanne's voice replayed in her head: *It happens sometimes. Some Blues have objects that defined them in life. A ball, a doll... Some Greys bear physical scars... For this Keeper you're seeing, there's a connection to that hat from his human days...*

"They're a tether…" Charlie breathed, suddenly realising what it meant. "And why only an object? Why not…?" She looked back to her phone and tapped to open all of Tess's messages. *If a hat can tether Alexander. If water can tether Thomas. If a bear can tether Marie, why can't I have my own tether?* she thought keenly.

Charlie scrolled to a message that made her broken heart rise from her stomach on wings and glow as it pulled itself together back in her chest. *Please, Charlotte,* the message read. *Je t'aimerai pour toujours.*

# About the Author

JJ Carpenter has been writing books since she was six years old — a collection of kooky tales she would staple together and hide in a shoebox under her bed. She penned her first novel at the age of twelve; since then her love of all things creepy, supernatural and wild has never left her. Join JJ as she journeys through haunted places and chilling mysteries across the beautiful country, and rich history, of Australia.

JJ was born in Canberra, Australia. She spent her childhood in various locations, including the Barossa Valley, South Australia, and Hampshire, England. As an adult, she's spent much of her career living and working in the South Pacific: Solomon Islands (twice), Vanuatu, Fiji and beyond.

**You can connect with me on:**
- https://www.jjcarpenterauthor.com
- https://twitter.com/jjcarpenterbook
- https://www.facebook.com/profile.php?id=61554566154490
- https://www.instagram.com/jjcarpenterauthor

Printed in Australia
Ingram Content Group Australia Pty Ltd
AUHW012158170424
393168AU00005B/7